Spring In

2019 Edit

With Stories from:

Joanna Maciejewska

James Pyles

Terry Sanville

J.G. Follansbee

Kevin Stadt

Elizabeth Hosang

Margaret Karmazin

Andrew Sweetapple

Stephen McQuiggan

Alex Minns

Anthony Engebretson

Tony Conaway

Sam Fletcher

Foreword by Ian Hugh McAllister

Cover Design by:

Steger Productions

https://stegerproduction.wixsite.com/design

Published by:

Cloaked Press, LLC

PO Box 341

Suring, WI 54174

ISBN: (Paperback) 978-0-9991690-6-3

Library of Congress Control Number: 2019943109

Table of Contents

Foreword

In theory there is a clear distinction between science fiction and fantasy. In its strictest terms, sci-fi covers postulated, future, or probable science. Fantasy deals with magic and the many alternative sciences of the imagination. Both these definitions are open to interpretation and question of course, and the vast array of published work needs to be considered as a complete spectrum of sub-genres.

My parents met at England's Liverpool University in 1952. They were part of a group of modern young people who smoked and drank too much, enjoyed both classical and jazz music, and traded their pulp sci-fi magazines. I was born in 1960, and grew up in a house full of books of many genres. There was a huge bookcase crammed full of heavily thumbed Astounding, Analog, and Galaxy editions, and that was where my imagination was stoked, a trend that would last a lifetime.

Dad would find me sitting on the floor surrounded by the pulps, as they were known, trying to locate a June 1955 edition so I could follow a serial. My head became filled with rockets, alien invasions, hero spacemen and their girlfriends, and strange unlikely planets. My parents stayed friends with that university group all their lives. When we visited Uncle Gordon or Uncle Richard, I would find time to stop playing with their kids so I could scour their bookcases for that June 1955 copy, or some other missing link. Sometimes they turned up.

Many of the serial and short story writers from that time came back and compiled their works at a later date. Several of the pulp owners and editors were happy to allow the stories to be retrieved and developed, and so was born the 'fix-up' novel. Many of the most respected sci-fi works of all time came into being in this fashion, novelized from earlier short story sequences, or expanded pulp serials. Isaac Asimov's Foundation is a prime example of how successful that approach could be.

I gradually settled into hard sci-fi, and it was many years before I became a keen fantasy reader. My favorite of the hard sci-fi authors was Hal Clement, in real life a Massachusetts science teacher called Harold Clement Stubbs. Whereas Asimov developed his famous Three Laws of Robotics, Clement worked to define his chosen genre. The following is a précis of several of his statements on the subject:

"Writing a science fiction story is fun, not work. I treat the whole thing as a game with simple rules. The reader has to find as many statements or implications which conflict with the facts as science currently understands them. For the author, the rule is to make as few such slips as he possibly can. Personally I make certain exceptions, such as faster than light travel, but fair play demands that this be mentioned as early as possible in the story. Once the story is published, my work is done. The game then turns on the ability of the readership to catch me out if they can."

Clement used his Harvard Astronomy degree to write a scientific paper on the subject of his planet Mesklin. In fact that piece, 'Whirlygig World', is included in 'Heavy Planet', a collection of connected works about the Mesklinites. Many years later scientists decided that his calculations on gravity were off, but he was content to let them win on that occasion, reminding them that he was depending on the relevant science as known at the time.

Fast forward over forty years, and in 2018 Drew Ferrell's Cloaked Press published my first hard sci-fi novel. I am still on a high after making good on a forty year old threat to write my own piece in the genre.

In many ways the Cloaked Press compilation series 'Spring Into Sci-fi/Fall Into Fantasy' harks back to those 1950s era pulp magazines I grew up with. Ferrell is encouraging some of the brightest new writers in exactly the same way that Editors such as John W. Campbell did with Clement in Astounding, publishing an early version of his first Mesklin book 'Mission of Gravity' as a serial in 'Astounding' during 1953.

In this new edition you will find a robotic grandparent, a breakthrough in DNA research, and some difficulty programming driverless cars, among other more outlandish concepts. There is something here for every science fiction fan. Happy reading.

- **Ian Hugh McAllister, Dorset, England, May 2019.**
Author, "To Visit Earth"

Black Eyes, Luminous Monsters
by Joanna Maciejewska

The bunker trembled, and Kyara gave it a worried glance as she knelt by the wounded soldier. His vitals were stable, but his bloodshot eyes, wider than his voiceless mouth, made it clear he needed more advanced treatment than the psycho-balancers Kyara kept pumping into his bloodstream. If he screamed, at least she'd know he was still fighting, but his horror-frozen face gave her little hope as did the black, burn-like mark that had cut deep through all his protective gear, skin, muscles, and even some of his organs.

"I need a medevac." Her voice was drowned out in another rumble. She fought off a sudden shiver; the bunker had to hold. It always did.

Just a few meters away, soldiers fired plasma rounds through the narrow firing slots, and slower, steady thumps of the sonic repulsor punctuated their guns' rattle.

"We need a medevac for the whole friggin' planet." The communications specialist squatted down beside her with one hand pressed to his earpiece as if it could isolate the incoming messages from the noise. "I don't think any pilot will risk landing nearby, but I'll see what I can do. HQ is considering retreat."

She bit her lip. Retreat meant they were giving up on containing the Anomaly at present positions, just like they did many times before.

The Anomaly, a spontaneous outburst of alien biomass no one expected on a fully terraformed and colonized planet, altered everything it touched: plants, animals, and humans alike. It didn't seem sentient and

4

resisted everything except for plasma and sonic waves, spreading faster than gas from a ruptured cylinder and just as volatile.

Kyara had seen it up close only once: a hellish tangle of tentacles, tendrils, and strings, spreading and grabbing everything within its reach. The trees blackened upon its touch, and the animals shrieked in pain when the Anomaly proved faster than them.

Of course, the jagged line of small, hastily-built bunkers couldn't hold it off forever, and was only meant to slow its expansion while the military prepared better defense systems further away. Only once they managed to contain the biomass, or found a more efficient way to eradicate it, could they think of retaking the lost land.

Her gaze sought her surroundings again and found the soldiers at their shooting posts. At least the last supply drone made it to the bunker, so they had enough rounds, but with only one sonic cannon, they couldn't even dream of driving the Anomaly back.

The comms specialist stiffened, and his face changed as he scribbled down a series of numbers. He didn't even look at Kyara before heading straight for the squad's captain.

"Retreat confirmed," he called out. "Leaving in ten. Coordinates are here." He paused as the new message caught his attention. "No need to set up the plasma charges. They're sending a Stab."

He spoke during the sonic repulsor's pause, and the last word hung in the sudden quietness of the bunker. Then the cannon fired another shot and broke the spell, but it couldn't erase the uneasiness weighing on Kyara's shoulders. She looked at the unconscious soldier. Along with the others from his team, he risked his life to ensure they hadn't gotten cut off, setting up plasma charges along their escape route, and death was to be his reward.

5

A Stabilizer—or a Stab as the soldiers had nicknamed the agents specially trained for handling the Anomaly—meant that they'd be retreating in a hurry… leaving behind anyone unable to walk on their own. The comms specialist threw her a glance over his shoulder and gently shook his head. Nobody would be coming for one wounded man who likely wouldn't even make it to the healing ward.

The bunker trembled once more, and this time the rumble rose instead of dying out in a series of fading echoes. A fissure crept along the powerfield-enhanced concrete wall, and the hole in the bunker widened faster than Kyara's eyes.

The soldiers at the shooting gallery leapt backwards, but they couldn't outrun the oily substance pouring in through the crack. Nobody ever escaped the Anomaly once it broke through the defense lines.

As the sickly-green strings spread, they enveloped everything and everyone in their way, and Kyara could only be thankful that the men's and women's screams died as soon as the Anomaly reached their faces.

A few of the soldiers standing further away dashed for the exit, and Kyara scrambled backwards, mesmerized by the green doom devouring the bunker. With her way out already cut off, she stared at her own death encroaching.

She jerked when the first oily string wrapped around her leg, and its cold touch pushed a scream out of her lungs. She wasted all her breath on it as the feeling of being eaten alive accompanied the Anomaly's steady progress up her body.

Another green tendril wrapped around her throat promising an end to her suffering as she'd drown or suffocate—whatever it was that the Anomaly did to people.

With her last thought, she registered the bunker trembling again, and a violent wave tore through everything inside. It shredded the oily substance, forcing the Anomaly back out through the crack. Kyara collapsed onto the floor, and even though the pain faded, her body refused to move, limp and drained of energy.

A lonely figure stepped into the range of her blurry vision. The black, simple coat her comrades had been joking about in a better, safer past left no doubt the Stabilizer arrived. Even from the distance Kyara felt the man's strange power that kept the Anomaly at bay. It shivered around like hot air on a summer's day, almost as mesmerizing as the oily substance it was fighting.

The Stabilizer turned his head toward Kyara. "Evacuate, if you can." His pure black eyes locked on her. No irises, no whites, just the tar of perfectly smooth eyeballs. "I can give you about thirty seconds."

If she'd had any strength left, she'd have laughed. Thirty seconds wasn't enough to get to a safe distance even if she wasn't so drained.

Regardless of the Stabilizer's efforts, the oily strings sneaked through the crack in the bunker again, and at the memory of their cold touch Kyara forced herself to crawl. The exit was too far, but an abandoned weapon seemed reachable.

Her fingers closing on the grip released a wave of relief. She wouldn't fall prey to the Anomaly again, her medic's oath be damned. With a last effort, she dragged the gun closer, but before she pulled the trigger, the world around her exploded with darkness.

*

The darkness still surrounded her when she woke up, but neither pain nor cold accompanied it. Instead, Kyara felt herself restrained in an eerie silence that contradicted the expected sounds of combat. An image of being trapped within the Anomaly hijacked her thoughts, and she fought the cocoon around her.

"Hush, it's just a bed cover," a gentle female voice said as someone's hands eased back onto the softness of what Kyara now recognized as a pillow. "I'm nurse Lane, and you're in a hospital."

"How——?" she creaked with a sore, dry throat. In the solid darkness around her, she could make out a blurry silhouette of a woman leaning over her.

"The rescue teams found you and one more soldier, sergeant Liam Fergus" the same person replied. "Do you remember what happened?"

"The Anomaly breached the fields." Kyara didn't want to remember, but she replied nevertheless. As a field medic, she'd asked similar questions many times to evaluate cognitive damage. "Then a Stabilizer arrived. Why are the lights off?"

The darkness swirled as if the woman looked away. "They aren't off. Your eyes… they're covered with an oily substance we can't remove," the woman said. "It's not anomalous," she added quickly. "The doctors cleared you."

Kyara breathed out with relief. Those who survived the encounters either with the Anomaly itself or its monstrous manifestations often suffered from physical and mental distortions.

"Except for my eyes," she replied quietly.

The darkness shifted as the woman shrugged in response. Whatever happened to Kyara seemed beyond the doctors' capabilities. They must have been satisfied with confirming she wasn't about to spontaneously burst into a heap of murderous oily tentacles and didn't bother with anything else. Maybe in the times of peace she'd be studied more closely, and they'd have time to discover the reasons for her condition, but during the war they offered only the minimum treatment.

Too many other soldiers waited to be checked against the Anomaly's taint.

"We'll run more tests, and you'll stay with us a little longer," the nurse said as if reading Kyara's mind. "It might be some unknown reaction to the Anomaly, and it might pass on its own too."

Kyara snorted. She'd offered similar comfort many times, so she could read between the lines. She'd be blind. And the fluctuations of the darkness she believed to see were nothing but her mind's renditions, a defense mechanism against the thought that she wouldn't be able to see again.

"You should rest now." Shuffling accompanied the nurse's words as she got off the bed. "I'll be back in a while."

Kyara returned to her pillow, listening to the fading footsteps. Her mind circled around only two truths.

She'd live.

She'd be blind.

*

The sound of steps and the nurse's voice made Kyara sit up. She'd been in the isolation room for a day, and any changes to the darkness and silence around her were welcome.

"All medical scans are in order, and the substance over her eyes seems to be neutral," the woman said in an explanatory tone, and Kyara fished out another rhythm of footsteps accompanying her. "Yet, we can't remove it without damaging the patient's tissues."

"I see."

Only two words, but Kyara wouldn't forget his voice. Back in the bunker, the Stabilizer didn't say much more to her, but the tone identical and devoid of all emotions.

9

She froze on her bed trying to find a reason for his visit. Gossip had it that hardly anyone survived an encounter with a Stabilizer, as if they wanted to ensure nobody could give an account of their actions. With the adrenaline already pumping through her veins, and the sound of footsteps approaching, Kyara searched through her memories for anything she could have seen that would make her a threat to the Stabilizer. As the images filled her mind, another thought struck her.

She'd seen him. She'd seen the Stabilizer. She still had her sight when he arrived, so it wasn't the Anomaly that brought on the darkness.

The sound of footsteps died out in front of her.

"Kyara, this is Daclan Ohara," the nurse said. "He's a—"

"—a Stab," Kyara finished for her. "I know."

She moved her head out of habit and froze when in the surrounding darkness a darker shape stood out, one she believed to be familiar, Daclan's silhouette. She shook her head to chase the strange afterimage away. He was one of the last things she'd seen, so her mind must have substituted her vision with a memory.

"Why have you come?" she masked her confusion with the first question she could think of.

"To check on you of course. It's rare someone survives our work," Daclan replied, and Kyara could swear she caught sarcastic undertones. "Tell the doctors she's fine, nurse. No trace of the anomalous changes. She shouldn't stay here much longer, and she needn't be isolated."

Kyara's anger flared up. She jumped out of the bed and darted forward to where she believed Daclan stood. As she crashed into a chair, the pain from her bruised legs tearing through her rage, the darkness stirred, and the black silhouette moved away.

10

"I'm not fine!" she shouted. "You know I'm not fine!" After all, he was the one who took her sight.

Her own voice drowned in the nurse's calls for help, and someone's strong arms pulled her back onto the bed. The hiss of an injector accompanied male voices asking her to calm down, and as the tranq-shot spread through her veins, Kyara had to submit. Her thoughts and words slowed. "I'm not fine…! I'm not fine…"

"I apologize," nurse Lane said, and her voice faded away. "Some patients have difficulties in coping with their new situation."

"I understand," Daclan replied in his calm, detached voice. "I'm ready to see the other survivor now."

Kyara made one more attempt to lift herself, but her body refused to obey. She seamlessly drifted from one darkness into another, but at least the oncoming void offered an escape from reality.

*

The therapy bracelet was supposed to help Kyara cope, but instead it served as a reminder of what she'd lost. Its navigational system offered an illusion of independence guiding Kyara through the hospital, but its automated voice, as emotionless as the Stabilizer's, carried. Instead of helping her feel normal, it announced to everyone that she was blind. She asked for a headset, but nurse Lane claimed Kyara had to learn to compensate with her other senses, and wearing an earbud would impede her hearing.

Frustrated and disheartened, Kyara switched the bracelet to silent mode. Short impulses were supposed to warn her of any change in her environment, but she still had to learn their meaning.

Night time seemed best for practice. Empty corridors meant no witnesses to her mishaps, and with the silence, she could always activate the bracelet's audio guide on the lowest volume setting if she really needed to without drawing too much attention.

As she walked down the corridor, resisting the urge to trace her hand along the wall, it felt almost like walking through a street back when she could still see, and Kyara allowed herself to daydream. To stroll through the busy market square full of colors and shapes, feeling the sun on her face... her face that almost smashed into the wall when Kyara missed the bracelet's impulse warning.

She refrained from cursing as she gathered herself and felt the wall in front of her. Confused and surrounded by darkness, she had no way of telling where she was.

"It'd be easier if you enabled the voice guide," Daclan said, and she almost jumped. His voice sounded different, almost human.

She searched, and there he was, a solid black form leaning against what had to be the wall she walked into, making the darkness around him seem a bit lighter, though no more transparent.

"Leave me alone," she grumbled. "Isn't it enough that you made me blind?"

"You're not blind," he said with confidence. "I know you can see me." He took a step forward. "A silhouette, blacker than the darkness itself."

"That doesn't make me sighted." She didn't try to deny, and she scampered backwards as he approached with the wall as her guide. "You lied to the nurse. I'm anomalous."

Daclan sighed, and she caught impatience in it. "I don't have time for it."

With one leap, he was by her side, and Kyara lifted her arms in futile defense, but the blow never came. Instead, he grabbed her and pulled her somewhere. Before she got her bearings, the sound of closed

12

doors made it clear they weren't in the corridor anymore. The air was still and carried no sound, lending no clues.

"I can give you your sight back," Daclan said.

"Just like that?" she couldn't resist.

"It's not complicated," he ignored her sarcasm. "But before I do, I want something in return. Until morning you'll do as I say… no questions, no arguments."

Kyara hesitated. He was a Stabilizer, fabricated to fight the Anomaly whose training stripped him of his humanity, and whatever he had in mind, it wasn't her well-being. He needed her for something, and his offer was just a means to get it.

"Maybe this will convince you I'm serious." He pressed a vial into her hand. "Rub this into the shell on your eyes."

Kyara turned the vial in her hands as if the sleek shape could reveal its content.

"If I wanted you dead, I'd have left you in the bunker," he added, and once more impatience rang in his voice.

She could refuse. She could walk away, learn to cope with her new condition, and never think of him again. But that slim chance she would be able to see again, to be independent and complete, made Kyara uncork the vial.

The substance inside was thicker than water and lightly sticky. It had no distinct smell, and Kyara didn't bother guessing its color.

"This stuff is gross," she muttered as she rubbed it into the shell-like substance covering her eyes.

"I believe it'd have been even more gross if I licked your eyes instead of letting you do it," Daclan replied with some amusement.

His words gave Kyara a pause, but she didn't dare to inquire whether he was serious. The mere thought she was rubbing his saliva into

13

her face conjured the depths of how sick the Stabilizer's sense of humor was. But surprise replaced her disgust when the shell over her eyes, the very shell the doctors deemed unremovable budged and separated from her skin as if it was never grown into it.

Its pieces crumbled as Kyara pulled them off her face. She blinked for the first time in days, and the darkness around her brightened. Daclan's silhouette remained as black as before, but everything else turned dark gray. It reminded her of standing in the night, with only starlight to give shape to her surroundings. She recognized metal shelves typical for a storage area, and other, smaller objects that must have been the hospital's stock of cleaning agents and other chemicals. With her heart pounding, Kyara reached where the light switch would be.

"I'm afraid this is as good as it gets." Daclan placed his hand on hers. "At least for now."

"But you can give me my sight back?" She hated herself for sounding so hopeful, so eager, but the change in her vision only intensified the feeling of loss. She could see shapes in the dark, but no colors, and she could forget about reading even a simple label.

"I can. If you agree to my terms."

Only a fool would give in to senseless hope, but Kyara didn't care. "What do you want me to do?"

"Come with me." He headed for the door.

She didn't catch any satisfaction in his voice as if his victory went uncherished.

*

Daclan led her through the hospital's corridors without a word, and his rushed steps made it clear it wasn't the right time to ask questions, so instead, Kyara pondered his motivation. Common people knew little of the Stabilizers, save for the propaganda praising their successes in slowing

14

down the Anomaly's progress on the planet, and the gossip among the soldiers that regardless of their effectiveness, hardly anyone would make it out alive when they arrived. Daclan's promise to give her vision back seemed out of character for what the Stabs were made out to be.

They passed only a few nurses on their way. Their dark silhouettes almost melting into one with the surroundings seemed to step away at a mere glance as if Daclan scared them. Nobody questioned Kyara's presence by his side, and she simply enjoyed that she could tell their shapes apart from the darkness around them. It wasn't clear sight, but it felt blissful in comparison to the abysmal blackness she'd been plunged into before Daclan offered her a way out.

"Here," he stopped by a patients' ward, one of the many along the corridor. "Stay quiet."

The door slid open with a quiet hiss, and as soon as they entered, Daclan pulled her to the side and led her along the wall until they squatted down by one of the empty beds.

Kyara could hardly make out the shapes of people in the ward, but their steady breaths, interrupted only by occasional snoring, told her they were all fast asleep. Yet Daclan seemed determined to stay hidden and quiet, so Kyara waited.

She nearly gasped when a spark of light flashed over one of the beds. After two days of seeing nothing but shades of black floating around, the sudden brightness seemed like a signal flare. As she refrained from shutting her eyes, a luminous figure rose from the bed, sluggish and disfigured, with long bright tentacles swaying in the air. Within it, a darker figure moved. It resembled a human, but its silhouette's details drowned in the surrounding light. The tentacles' flow, like seagrass bending in the waves, reminded Kyara of the Anomaly's oily encroach, and she shivered.

"Watch," Daclan ordered quietly.

15

The being moved swiftly and leaned over another sleeping patient. When the radiant tentacles wrapped around the dark shape in the bed, a moan rose and died in the quiet symphony of steady breaths. Kyara moved, but Daclan's hand held her in place.

It wasn't long before the luminous monster returned to its own bed. Its light faded, but Kyara could still make out the horrid shape around the man who seemed to be falling asleep unaware of what transpired.

Only when the room became serene again, Daclan led her to the monster's bed.

"This is what we really do." His voice hardly disturbed the silence. "Keeping the Anomaly contained in the outbreak area is only part of the task. The other is finding its seeds among the population."

"Anomalous soldiers," Kyara whispered.

Everyone who enlisted knew the risks. The Anomaly swallowed whole bunkers and units, and that was a calculated risk, but sometimes the biomass spat people back out, changed and crazed, attacking everyone in sight. To learn that some of the survivors might have also been warped... Her heart skipped a beat like a wheel bumping on an uneven road.

"There's no rule to it. Some come out of the Anomaly unchanged, some become monsters like poor Liam here. Some..." He turned his head to her. "Some come out like you... and me."

She gaped at the suggestion in his words. The Stabilizers were supposed to be humanity's weapon against the outburst of the alien biomass, not a by-product of its expanse. And now he claimed she'd become one of them.

"What will happen to him?"

"We can't help him." He leaned over the bed, and as his hand brought the control panel to life in a series of quiet beeps, the security belts darted over the patient's body and locked in place with a click that rang with final judgment. Liam woke up, but before the scream rose in his lungs, Daclan put a pillow over his face. "Don't look if you don't want to." His voice returned to its normal disturbing chill.

She didn't see much anyway, just a human-shaped swirl of gray jerking against what had to be the bed, almost equally gray. But unless she put her hands to her ears, she couldn't block the muffled sounds and the trashing body trapped within the security straps as Liam fought for his life.

Her fingers rounded into fists when she pictured Daclan standing over her own bed ready to end her life if she turned out a monster.

Light rose over the bed, and the tentacles grew like sun-soaked plants, but the luminous being couldn't free itself, still bound by the material form of its host. Daclan didn't seem to pay attention to the struggle nor the sudden brightness, as if his task was as mundane as a daily chore... as if he didn't care he was taking life of a soldier who fought the same war he did.

The room brightened, and at first Kyara ignored it, tangled in her feelings. Then, more tentacles rose, and she realized they weren't coming from Liam's body; they were coming from behind Daclan.

She reached for him across the bed, straight through the luminous strands, and the cold of the anomalous touch pressed a shriek out of her mouth, but she managed to push Daclan out of the way.

Other patients stirred in their sleep as Daclan rolled across the floor and rose with the agility of a seasoned fighter.

"Run!" he ordered as he faced the second monster, and Kyara had no doubt the order was meant for her. The subtle change in the tone of his voice suggested Daclan wasn't expecting to get out of the fray alive.

The radiant tentacles swirled in the air and then darted through the dark for Daclan. He dodged skillfully and swatted at the luminous limb with his hand shrouded in blackness. Kyara could swear his palm's edge cut off a piece of the monster, but the speck of light died out as soon as it separated from the shiny body.

Liam was awake, and he didn't thrash in the bed anymore. His bright eyes stared at Daclan, and the tentacles rising from his body stretched out and joined the attack. With so many strings of light, it was no surprise that some reached their target, and Daclan stumbled backwards.

"What the hell...?" One of the patients got out of his bed, and collapsed when a tentacle pierced him. His shrilling voice halted immediately giving Kyara hope that the man didn't suffer much before he died.

She stood in place, torn between the urge to flee and the urge to help. If she ran, the thing that attacked Daclan would have everyone dead as soon as it was done with its opponent, but the memory of the tentacles' touch brought a shiver. She didn't know how to fight these things.

Her eyes fixed on Liam. He was still immobilized in his bed, but the light that enveloped his body kept attacking Daclan. She couldn't fight the monsters, but she could kill a man.

All the principles of a medic, all the oaths of preserving life and health ran through her head as she reached for the IV tube on the nearby stand. As her fingers closed on the rubber, she hushed the concerns about the patient she was robbing, and wrapped the plastic cord around Liam's head.

The tentacles shot for her, and she ducked but didn't let go of the tube. She coiled it around her palm and put her whole bodyweight on it, pulling down. Above her, the light raged in a futile search, and Liam again

18

struggled in his binds, fighting for the air Kyara was taking away from him.

Then the ruckus stopped, and the light faded and died as if leaving with its host's last breath. And only her own heart, drowned in adrenaline, thrashed in her chest just like Liam did in his bed.

Kyara scrambled back to her feet. Other patients cowered in their beds, unsure what was happening and too afraid to try and leave after what happened to the first one. Further down the room, the tentacles surrounded Daclan, closing him in a cocoon, and it seemed he had no clear way out. The light intensified as if in triumph, but then it dimmed when sudden darkness burst around Daclan.

Kyara recognized what he was doing and dropped to the floor, covering her head. With her eyes shut, she could only imagine the blackness devouring everything and everyone around, just like it did in the bunker. She could almost feel it raging above her, as if it was wind or water, but at least this time she didn't lose her consciousness.

In the silence that followed, she heard his footsteps, and then his voice, "Can you get up?"

The darkness around was no darker than before, and Daclan's black silhouette still stood out. The whole hospital seemed serene, as if no one was aware of the death match that just took place.

As she stood up, he reached out and felt her face. "It didn't affect your eyes this time. Good." His hands slipped lower. "No other wounds?"

Kyara froze as his fingers traveled along her body, skimming past her skin and hospital gown. There was nothing sexual in what he did—he was confirming she had no injuries.

"You can't see either," she whispered the sudden realization. It seemed so unreal, with all his confidence and composure. He didn't act as

19

if he was missing something, as if he was incomplete. For the first time since Kyara lost her sight, she pondered her own desperation and feeling of loss. It must have been equally hard for Daclan, but he seemed okay with who he was; with how he was.

His first response was dry laughter. "You seem surprised. The contact with the Anomaly changes us, enabling us to see its offshoots, but we all pay the price for it."

"So when I get my sight back…"

"You won't see the monsters anymore," he replied to her unvoiced question. He took a step back, and looked around. "I should take care of things here." He indicated their surroundings.

The room was quiet, and nothing moved in the darkness. As Kyara recognized the motionless bodies in their beds, she listened to the shuffle of Daclan's coat, and the quiet beep of a phone being activated.

"It's me," he said. "Two in the hospital; it's quite a mess. I'll need a clean-up crew."

"What happens now?" Kyara dared to ask.

"I'm done here, and you have a choice to make." He pressed a vial into her hand. "I just wanted to make sure you see this before you make it. I'll notify the crew to leave you alone, so take your time."

A choice to make… a choice that should be obvious.

"Why?" she asked. "Why would anyone give up their sight and whole life for… this?" She made a frantic gesture trying to encompass the room.

He moved his head around, as if making sure no one else was conscious. "We might lose the battle against the Anomaly," his quiet voice was lined with sadness. "We're already having a hard time containing it, and there aren't enough of us to keep it in check if it spreads more. Discussions of the impossible, of the planetwide evacuation arise more and more often. Whether we'd be able to take all the people off the planet is one thing, but imagine what could happen if some of these things tagged along. Sometimes they just kill to… feed, I guess. But sometimes they pass the sickness."

Kyara gasped. The images that filled her head were those of all the other human planets struggling to survive. Death, panic, maybe even in-fighting if the truth of the hidden beings slipped out.

"We do what we can to help in containing the Anomaly," he said. "But the vital part of our work is away from it."

All Kyara could muster was a nod. She couldn't argue his logic, but putting the innocents' lives on line clashed with her medical training.

"I don't think I'm cut out for this."

Daclan laughed. "You don't say," he didn't soften the blow. "I'm actually surprised you killed Liam instead of running. But I understand," his voice lost its sarcastic edge. "If you can't stomach killing not only people, but also your own compassion, use the vial. Rub the rest into your eyes. But one more thing before you do. Anyone can be trained to be a field medic. Anyone can be trained to shoot a plasma gun. But being what we are… You can't teach that."

She didn't reply, and Daclan left as if there was nothing else to say, not even words of gratitude or farewell. She turned the vial in her hand. A moment of gross application, and she'd have her old life back. She'd enjoy the colors, and the shapes, and she could smile to herself in the mirror every morning again.

Yet, the thought of the luminous monsters lurking in the darkness she'd no longer be able to see, she'd no longer be able to defend from, chased away any happiness Kyara tried to find.

*

Kyara sat in the empty room absentmindedly listening to the newsfeed from the hall. The reporter was recounting an incident in the hospital in so many exalted words describing a patient killing seven people including a nurse in an episode of unexplained violence. Kyara almost snorted at the speculations, none even close to what really happened.

The doctors ran one last check on her, smugly commenting on the substance over her eyes being gone as if they were confident all along it'd dissolve, at the same time ignoring the fact that she was still blind, and then she was discharged as healthy. Of course, they offered contacts to therapists, armed her with the text-to-voice brochures, and reiterated that she should contact them if anything changed. Then they left her alone.

The images of the previous night still haunted her, and the memory of the luminous touch made her fingers clutch the vial Daclan gave her.

She relaxed and checked the navigation bracelet at her wrist. Then, among the dark shapes, she fished out her duffle bag and took a moment to feel the rough, hard strap before she slung it across her back. The vial remained secure in her breast pocket: waiting, luring, calling.

In the daytime, the black before her eyes varied in depth, so she made it through the hospital with relative ease, though only the faint hiss of automatic doors prevented her from walking into them before they slid open. To her surprise, she found enjoyment in relying on her other senses: smelling the faint mix of sweat and perfumes on the people who passed her by, and separating their voices from among the noises of a busy hospital.

As she stepped outside, the sun's blaze hit her face, but the darkness around remained as it was, swirls and vortexes of almost unrecognizable shapes, and Kyara hesitated. Sounds hit her, familiar but too entangled to provide guidance, feeding panic to her thoughts. Her hand darted for the pocketed vial, and Kyara resisted retreating back to the building.

"I thought you weren't cut out for this," Daclan's voice emerged from the noise like an arm offered to a drowning woman. Even the slight sarcasm he lined his words with brought the comfort of familiarity within the darkness.

"I'm not," she said.

"Yet, I can still see you."

Kyara almost smiled. She must have been as black of a silhouette to him as he was to her. "I thought I could at least try." She turned her head to him. "That is, if you think there's a point."

Voices and footsteps made her move to the side before she even recognized the wavering of shadows, but people coming in and out of the hospital seemed to part anyway, as if they paid extra attention around her. Something in how their dark bodies moved made Kyara think of fear or uncertainty.

"You can wear shades if their reaction disturbs you," Daclan said. "Some of us do." He offered his arm. "Come, I'll get you to Bryda. She's going to teach you everything you need to know."

He held her tight when she accepted his help, weaving through the crowd with all the confidence that Kyara envied.

"You know, it's not really a sacrifice," she said. "Knowing you can always go back to what you had. And I'm guessing I don't even really need that vial you gave me, do I? I could use my own saliva."

To her surprise, Daclan stopped, raising grunts of annoyance and protests around them when other pedestrians had to change course at the sudden obstacle. Several insults thrown in passing suggested they didn't notice the black eyes of a Stabilizer.

"No, it isn't," he agreed. His voice had an eerie calm about it, like an ancient dam holding fast against a river of rage. "The sacrifice comes later. When you hear how many people had to be carried away in body bags after your work was done. When you try to convince yourself that their deaths weren't pointless while en route to another place where you're needed. When you kill innocent people who happened to be anomalous."

Kyara swallowed, flooded by regret. She shouldn't have pushed him, but after the night spent fighting both her remorse and the returning images of the luminous monsters, she needed to know if being a Stabilizer still meant being human. Daclan seemed so composed and detached… she had to unearth his buried emotions to reassure herself she wouldn't become the being she saw in him, the being she wanted to see back in the bunker: cruel and unconcerned.

Now, faced with Daclan's emotions boiling under his shell of confidence, she wouldn't be able to find a fitting apology. But she could tell him she understood.

"The sacrifice comes when, regardless of all those thoughts and feelings and doubts, you decide to carry on," she whispered.

At first, silence hung between them, unstirred by the noises of a busy street. Then Daclan nodded. "You'll do well enough," he muttered as he led her through the crowd again.

The darkness around, without a single luminous string in sight, brought comfort.

Joanna Maciejewska is a Polish-born resident of the United States who writes fantasy, science-fiction and anything in-between, never shying away from a dash of romance. Her fiction appeared in Polish and English magazines and anthologies. You can find the list of her publications at her website, http://melfka.com. Besides reading and writing, she enjoys arts&crafts and video games, and she doesn't start her day without a cup of tea.

Sea Change

by Terry Sanville

1.

Don woke to the sound of whines and yips He groaned and rubbed sleep from his eyes. "Now what?" he muttered and rolled out of bed.

Pulling on a pair of ratty jeans, he stumbled into the sunlit kitchen and checked his watch. *Christ, it's still early.* He stared out the window over the sink. In the yard, his German Shepherd, Caesar, stood with front paws on the top rail of the fence that separated Don's lot from the one next door. Caesar's tail wagged furiously.

The ruckus grew louder. A frantic barking coming from the other side accompanied Caesar's audio antics. Donald pushed through the back screen and crossed the brown grass, his bare feet recoiling from treading on a patch of burclover.

He called, "Come here, Caesar. Come here, boy," and paused to pick burs from his toes.

The dog looked over its shoulder before resuming his whines and yips. But the barking from the other side stopped. Don hobbled to where Caesar stood and peered over the fence into a yard choked with dead weeds, the dried remains of a vegetable garden, and a rusted swing set. Near the house, a Golden Retriever climbed the steps and slipped through the screen door held open by a woman of indeterminate age with a nice profile but her face obscured. She turned inside and the door clicked shut behind her.

Quiet returned to the shoreline neighborhood, broken only by the low rumble of the surf sliding up the strand. Damn, I bet that dog's a female. Caesar will go crazy. I wonder when they moved in? Didn't see a car in the drive…nobody's been around that place for months…probably just a fall rental.

Don clicked a leash onto Caesar's collar and tugged. But the dog resisted. He pulled harder and the Shepherd followed him inside. Smoothing the bed covers, he lay on the sheets and slid a pillow over his face. Caesar flopped onto the bed next to him and shoved his rump against Don's hip, something that used to piss off Anita. But two years back, he'd kept the dog but divorced his software engineer wife. *Yeah, I got the better end of that deal…except she smelled better.*

2.

Colleen waited until early morning to let her dog out. The run-in with the neighbor's German Shepherd a few days before had almost screwed things. *I might have to get rid of Lola if she keeps it up. But I love her…she's my only friend.*

Colleen chose that particular house to rent after learning from her boss that the guy next door owned a trawler out of Morro Bay, fished for West Coast salmon and albacore, and would likely be gone most days. She wondered how a fisherman could afford a shoreline home in California.

Two hours before dawn, she snapped a leash onto the Golden Retriever, grabbed her knapsack, and left the house. She trudged along a path that wound through the chest-high dunes carpeted with red sand verbena and salt grass, the beach and the foaming Pacific beyond. With a full moon and no fog, she gazed across Estero Bay at the twinkling lights of Los Osos.

After walking for over a mile and leaving the neighborhood behind, she tied Lola to a sign warning swimmers of rip tides and filled the dog's water bowl from an old canteen. Scanning the beach for early morning strollers and finding none, she stripped off her jeans, sweatshirt, and underclothes and stuffed them into her knapsack. A strong on-shore wind chilled her naked body. She gritted her teeth and waited for the shuddering to stop. The longer she stayed ashore, the longer it took to become her other self.

After several minutes, she strapped a small carrier to her front and waded into the sea. When the water reached her shoulders, the changes began: clear membranes slid over her eyes, her arms flattened into broad appendages, her legs fused together and her feet extended and broadened to become clawed flippers. Her skin toughened into a sleek hide that held in the warmth. She tested her nose and found that it automatically closed off underwater.

Colleen fell forward and slid through the waves, swimming quickly just below the surface. Her jawline and face had stretched into a snout with whiskers and rows of pointed teeth. At the nearest offshore buoy, she paused and let the cresting waves break over her, felt the strength surge through her glistening body.

She turned north and swam toward the flashing beam coming from the Piedras Blancas Lighthouse. The distant bark of sea lions called to her. Colleen moved toward the sound, following the course transmitted to the sensors embedded in her neck. *At least they could have told me how long I'd have to swim…I'm already getting hungry and those black perch look tempting.*

3.

Don's life felt like nothing but failures. His marriage had gone bust and his fishing business could be next. Competition from China and South America and limits placed on the size of the catch meant less money and pressure to raise prices. But working anyplace but the sea seemed sacrilegious to him. He often told his bar mates that he had saltwater in his veins, like his father and grandfather before him.

To add to his misery, his dog kept waking him before dawn, as if every day was a fishing day. *Maybe I should leave the dog outside overnight until breakfast. Nah, he'd be howling from the cold and wake me anyway.*

With the first rays of golden light turning the sea from gray to cerulean blue, he set out to walk Caesar on the beach and clear his head of bad late-night TV and booze. A bitter autumn wind whipped his stringy hair. He pulled his knit cap down over his ears, ducked his head and walked at the sea's edge, moving north. The strand and dunes gave way to a boulder-strewn beach backed by sea bluffs. *Damn dog...maybe I should get a cat. At least they can use a litter box. But Anita liked cats...so that's no good.*

Caesar began to pull hard at the end of his leash. Don disconnected it and the dog shot ahead. Far down the oceanfront a lump of something moved slowly onshore across the wet sand. He could just pick out the neighbor's Golden Retriever jumping up and down, tied to a signpost. Cursing under his breath, Don started to run, his legs stiff from the cold, his joints aching. Halfway there, he pulled up and leaned forward with hands on knees, chest heaving. The lump continued to struggle across the glassy surface, looking like a seal or sea lion from a distance.

What the hell am I killing myself for? That critter will turn and be gone by the time I get there. But where's that dog's owner?

4.

At a point in the tumbling sea no different than any other, Colleen felt the embedded sensor vibrate. She turned shoreward and dipped below the waves. In a flash, a pod of sea lions emerged from the blue-green deep and broke the surface. They barked loudly and headed toward land. The sensor vibrated again, turning off the transformation response to her leaving the water.

She followed the sea lions into the shallows, to a narrow deserted beach where they joined their larger colony. It took awhile for them to arrange themselves and settle down. Colleen waited impatiently, knowing she had at least two more colonies to visit and get back to the house before dawn.

With the swipe of a flipper, she opened the watertight carrier strapped to her chest and approached small groups of two or three sea lions while avoiding the dominant males and their harems. The young lions paid her little attention until she shook her torso and several clear spheres doused in fish oil dropped onto the sand.

The youngsters touched the clear balls with their flippers or noses. Some took them into their mouths to lick off the oil. Colleen smiled to herself while listening to the chatter of the sea people, their complaints about lack of fish, and their stories about marauding Great Whites, or the Orcas passing through. When she finished serving the prime candidates, she closed the carrier, lumbered back into the sea, and continued north, bucking a strong current the entire way.

After recruiting two more colonies, she turned homeward, exhausted, craving food and the warmth of her own kitchen. The sun rose and turned the sea's surface golden. Colleen cursed herself for taking so long and tried swimming faster.

With energy failing, she pulled up offshore. Lola stood barking on the beach, the dog's water bowl upended. The sensor in her neck once more vibrated, activating the transformation process. With her last strength, she pushed and pulled with her flippers and hauled herself out of the water, her body changing as she struggled. Off to her right, the neighbor's German Shepherd charged toward Lola, then the man ran toward her. She collapsed onto the wet sand, rolled onto her back and stared upward at the blue-gold sky with skittering clouds, waiting for the final changes and hoping they'd come quickly.

5.

After a brief rest, Don continued his dash toward the animal that crawled from the surf. The wind in his face made him tear up and he tried to focus on the creature's details. As he got nearer he picked up speed. *Jesus, that thing looks human…and it's not moving.*

Black spots fringed in yellow formed in his eyes; his heart hammered. He stared at the figure laying before him, a woman, naked, mature, and beautiful. Reaching forward, he unbuckled the container strapped to her front. His gaze shifted to her face and he jumped back. Thick lenses slid upward to reveal piercing green eyes below a tangle of red hair. *What the bejesus was that?* He wiped his watering eyes on his jacket sleeve before advancing again. Freckles dusted her pale body. A natural redhead, he noted.

Grasping the woman under her arms, Don dragged her beyond the reach of the sea and onto the dry sand near where her dog yipped loudly, being circled by an equally enthusiastic Caesar. The woman moaned and stared at him, then immediately tried to cover herself with her arms and hands.

"I'm sorry. Ya must think I'm a pervert."

The woman shook her head, sat up, and looked around.

"Ya want your knapsack?" Don asked.

"Yes…yes please. I'm so embarrassed. I'm usually out of the water and dressed before anyone comes along."

"No need to be embarrassed. I've seen pretty women naked before."

"Yes, but you haven't seen me...and I don't normally expose myself on a first meeting." She frowned and turned from him. The silence grew. Don retrieved her pack.

"Please give me a little privacy so I can dress?"

Don turned his back to her.

In a few minutes she called, "All right, you can look."

Don gazed at the woman. "So, how do your...your eyes feel?"

The woman's mouth dropped open. "Why...why do you ask?"

"When I found ya, your face was kinda like, I don' know, meltin'. And some kinda thick lenses covered your eyes."

"Huh. You haven't been tilting the whiskey bottle this morning, have you?"

Don stared at his feet. "No, I usually wait till noon to do that. It's one of my rules."

"Ah, a gentleman with rules. Well, one of my rules is to get warm after my morning swim." She shuddered and grabbed her knapsack and reached for the watertight carrier that lay on the sand beside her. Its top had flopped open with a half-dozen spheres exposed.

"How did this come off me?" she demanded. "I had it strapped tightly to my chest."

Don grinned. "Well, ya looked like ya might need CPR, so I took it off…"

"Yes, I'm sure to get a better look."

"No, nothin' like that."

"Did you touch any of what was inside?"

"Well, yeah, but I didn't hurt nothin'. What are those ball thingies anyway?"

The women's cheeks turned even paler and she clasped her hands over her face.

"Are ya all right? Ya want me to take ya to the health center?"

"No, no. But I'll need to talk with you."

"Sure, I'm not workin' today or tomorrow…can use some company."

Their dogs had completed their introductory butt sniffing and sat on their haunches, tails sweeping the sand, watching their owners.

"Come on, let's get some coffee," Don said.

"My name's Colleen, and you're…."

"Don. Colleen, that's Irish ain't it?"

"Yes…my family originally lived near Galway. It's on the West Coast of the Emerald Isle. But we've been in the States for many generations."

"My family's been fishin' the Central Coast for generations. But I've only been out here five years…was born 'n' raised in Texas, but fished all over the South, includin' the Outer Banks. I inherited ma boat from ma Uncle Skip, God rest his soul."

"You still have the accent."

"And you speak flawless English."

Colleen laughed, displaying perfect teeth. The couple wandered down the beach with their dogs ranging out front, chasing seagulls and sandpipers. By the time they reached her house, he knew her vitals: 41, single, a marine scientist working for a large corporation doing some kind of research, rented the place for two months, avid swimmer, liked men, loved the sea.

"Look, I must rest for a few hours," she said. "But come over this afternoon. I make a mean margarita."

"Why thank ya, ma'am. That's mighty neighborly."

"Tell me, are you really a good ole southern boy, or are you just laying it on thick?"

Don grinned. "Pretty impressive, huh? Us Texans talk slow 'cause it gives our brains time to catch up."

She smiled, turned landward and disappeared into the dunes.

Don watched her go. She's all right...for a West Coaster...and sexy too. But that thing with her eyes was...was real. Something's going on...

6.

Colleen hustled inside, poured herself a double shot of brandy and tossed it off. Her body shuddered, partly from the cold and partly from her encounter with Don. She sat in front of the fireplace and watched the blue-green gas flame flicker, warming her, causing more shudders. Finally, after a second brandy, she sucked in a deep breath, retrieved her cell phone and thumbed a number.

"Seven Seas Scientific, can I help you." The operator's voice sounded smooth and professional.

"This is Field Agent 82. Please connect me with Control 45."

"One moment, please."

The familiar voice sounded tired. "Yes, Colleen. How was your day of recruiting? I trust that you received the course headings clearly."

"Yes, Aidan. I was able to make contact with three colonies and dosed probably two dozen recruits."

"Good, good. Any problems with the locals? You mentioned something about your neighbor's dog."

"Well...that's why I called."

"What's the problem?" Aidan's voice sounded all business.

"The neighbor, a fisherman, caught me coming out of transformation."

"Shit."

"Yes, that was my response. I think he only saw the very last sequence, and I'm not sure he believed what he saw. He was too busy staring at my privates."

"You may want to stay out of the water for a few days. We don't want him snooping around. We'll have other field agents counsel the recruits when they come ashore after transformation."

Colleen sucked in a deep breath. "Well, that's not the worst of it."

"What, there's more? Tell me."

"The fisherman handled some of the transfusers."

"What the hell, Colleen. Shit, shit, shit."

"Is it really that bad?" She bit her lip and listened to Aiden's breathing.

"Yes, it's bad. The enzymes from the spheres flow trans-dermally into the blood stream. They trigger a chimeric response within 24 hours. For sea lions, they develop different populations of genetically distinct human cells."

Colleen tisked. "Yes, yes, I know all that. I don't need the lecture. But I've heard rumors from other field agents about…"

"They're more than rumors." Aiden sighed. "In about 60-percent of the cases that have been observed, the enzymes also trigger a similar response in humans. They can transform into sea lions or seals."

"Is the change triggered in the same way?"

"Yes, entering any saltwater body will cause the change. So as long as your fisherman stays out of the ocean, he'll be okay."

"But can you imagine the shock if it happens? He could blow our whole program. What should we do?"

A few long seconds clicked by before Aiden answered. "I'll talk to corporate here in San Francisco and call you before nine tonight."

"Right. But I'll tell you, Aiden. This fisherman seems like a good man, not some dumb redneck. I'm not going to be part of anything violent."

"Don't get your whiskers in a knot. This isn't the first time this has happened. And I wouldn't feel too sorry for him. You know what fishermen do when they snag seals in their nets."

Colleen shuddered. "Don't remind me."

"Look, I'll talk with you tonight. Just try and relax."

"Right, tonight before nine." She hung up.

After a four-hour nap, Colleen rose and ate three tins full of sardines in oil, half a loaf of French bread, gulped a glass of wine, showered, changed into a skirt and blouse and ensconced herself on the outdoor deck overlooking the beach. Her entire body still ached from that morning's long swim. *I'm too old for this crap. Let the twenty-year-olds handle the fieldwork. I'm ready for a shore job. I'm better at orienting the new recruits anyway.*

7.

Don spent the rest of the morning and early afternoon sleeping and then daydreaming about Colleen. Her wet naked body lying there on the beach had been a real turn on. But he couldn't stop thinking about that thing with her face and eyes. For a split second she'd looked almost like the sea lions he'd sometimes snag in his fishing nets.

In mid-afternoon he showered, trimmed his gray-streaked beard and slicked back his hair. He donned the only clean pants and shirt left in his closet, grabbed the new bottle of Patron from his liquor cabinet, and stepped outside.

Colleen waved to him from her deck and he moved along the narrow side yard between their houses and joined her. *She looks GREAT. I'm not going to get much fishing done while she's lounging about next door.*

"How are ya feelin'?" he asked.

"Much better. But I'm still exhausted from my morning swim. Must have been the rip currents. I had a hard time getting ashore."

"Yeah, they can be bad this time of year…even worse when we get a blow up from Baja or the Pineapple Express."

Colleen disappeared inside the house and returned with a bowl of ice, tall glasses, coarse salt, limes, and margarita mix. She watched Don expertly handle the ingredients and deliver an ice-cold tart drink. They lay on chaise lounges and stared at the rolling sea, exchanging life histories, at least the parts people disclose on first dates.

Something's strange, Don thought. All she talks about is her job and how she got here…no details about her family or past.

The sun dropped slowly toward the Pacific. The beach and dunes with their crop of salt grass turned golden. She invited him inside while she cooked dinner: huge T-bones, baked potatoes, Swiss chard for a vegetable, and hot corn muffins with chilies in the mix.

"You look like a meat eating man and are probably tired of looking at fish."

"Yeah, but a good albacore or halibut steak is hard to beat."

"We have similar tastes in protein."

He fixed her another drink and they watched the sunlight fade on the sea and the moon and stars come out. Flocks of gulls lay in formation on the dry sand, heads resting on their backs with their beaks nuzzled into their feathers. The couple ate dinner slowly. She peppered him with questions about fishing, about weather conditions during fall and winter months, about his boat and whether he worked alone or with a crew.

Over digestifs of twenty-year-old port, Don finally asked the question that had bugged him all day. "Remember this mornin', you said you needed ta talk with me. Sounded important. What did ya wanna talk about?"

The far away look disappeared from Colleen's eyes and she sat up on the sofa. "I...I'm not sure I remember."

"It was right after I told ya I'd messed with those things in your...your chest pack. What are those, anyway?"

"They're...they're part of the marine research our firm is conducting. I can't tell you anything more because it's a trade secret. But it's legal and we have all the permits."

"Huh. Ya seemed frightened when I told ya I touched your stuff. Those things aren't bad news, are they?"

The buzz from Colleen's cell phone startled both of them. She stood and retrieved it from the mantel above the fireplace. "Look, I'm expecting a call from corporate headquarters. I'll need to take this. Shouldn't be more than a few minutes."

Before he could say anything, she moved out of sight down a hallway. He heard a door open and click shut, then muffled conversation that he couldn't make out. *I've got this strange feeling I get sometimes on the sea at night, when the moon is down and I can hear the whales breathe. She was about to blow off my question...wouldn't look at me. But holy moly, she's gorgeous...and she can cook.*

8.

Colleen entered the bedroom swiftly and shut the door. She keyed the phone and could hear Aiden calling her name.

"Not so loud. The fisherman is here with me."

"Where are you? Can you talk? And what the devil is *he* doing there?"

"I'm at home. Yes, it's okay to talk. We've just finished dinner. I was trying to show him that I'm a normal person...but I think he's still suspicious."

"Damn, that's all we need. But we've figured out a plan."

"Great, I think. After talking with this guy for a couple of hours, his good ole boy demeanor is all an act."

"What do you mean?"

"He's smart, knows the sea, understands the environmental issues, and is more open to change than other fishermen I've met."

"I suppose he's also handsome."

Colleen felt her face flush. "Well, yes, in a grizzled salt-of-the-sea way. He's only five years older than me."

"Ah, I see you've got all his vital statistics."

"Most of them. Just tell me your plan…and it better be good."

"Okay, okay. I've talked with our Head of Security and others and we have a two-pronged approach."

"Am I gonna like it?"

"Probably not."

"Tell me."

"By tomorrow morning your fisherman will be ready for transformation."

"Yes, so…"

"We want you to make a date with him to go swimming."

"Are you nuts? He'll see me fully transform. How are we going to keep *that* a secret?"

"Let me finish, PLEASE."

"Sorry, go ahead."

"You both should go into the water at the same time. Hold his hand. Tell him you're scared. When you start to transform, if the enzymes work, so should he."

"But he's going to totally freak out."

"Remember, there's only a 60 percent chance that he'll change. If he does, then you'll need to show him the ropes, sort of the reverse of what you show our normal sea-based recruits. Show him how to swim and dive, to avoid predators."

"Yes, but why?"

"We've checked up on this guy. He's an ex-Navy Seal, divorced, no kids, and few friends. We can use a smart fisherman in our program, a land-baser who can experience our world first hand. And you say he has a boat, a perfect vehicle for our recruitment activities."

"Well, being stuck teaching this guy could have its benefits," Colleen murmured, feeling her body grow warm.

"What was that? I didn't quite hear you."

"Nothing, nothing. But what if he doesn't transform?"

"That would…would be a worse problem, because he'll have seen you change — and there's no explaining that away."

"So what should I do if he stays land-based?"

"You do nothing. Just swim out to the buoy and stay offshore. Other field agents will take care of…of the problem."

"Wait a minute, what are you going to do?"

"It's better that you don't know. Just concentrate on how you're going to help him. If he transforms properly, your fisherman should understand our sea language."

The silence grew between the two of them. Finally Aiden asked, "Colleen, are you still there?"

"Yes. I…I understand the plan. We'll be there on the beach tomorrow morning before dawn."

"Good. I knew I could count on you. Now get some sleep."

"Not likely." She rang off, sat on her bed and shook, her mind racing. Finally, a soft tapping sounded on her door.

"Colleen, you okay in there?"

"Yes…yes. Come in…and bring that bottle of port with you." If this guy is headed for Davy Jones' Locker, he at least deserves a memorable sendoff.

9.

He awoke with Colleen warming his body while some stupid alarm clock buzzed. She struggled to reach it. Don didn't want to let her go. Her touch aroused him in the darkness. But she again showed her strength and broke free. The quiet returned along with Colleen to his arms.

"Do you take your coffee black or with cream?" she asked.

"Black's good. Ya really want to go swimmin' at 0-dark-thirty?"

She snuggled closer. "Lola needs to be walked and a good dip in the sea feels so refreshing. What, are you chicken to join me? You've got nothing to be ashamed about."

"Ya know I've dived in colder waters than off these shores."

"Let's not think about the cold just yet." She pulled him on top of her and they continued their hot love making from the previous evening.

During their brisk walk down the beach with their dogs ranging far and wide, she seemed nervous and confused. Several times he asked her questions and she stared ahead and didn't answer. By the time they reached the stretch of isolated beach, hidden from the coast road by the bluffs, his muscles had warmed and he felt better about swimming in the dark sea.

Under a charcoal gray sky, they tied their dogs to the warning sign and stripped off their clothes. They stood at water's edge and watched the faint glow of light build to the east. The undersides of clouds turned silver then gold.

"Are you ready?" she asked.

"Are you? You're still shakin'."

"It must be the cold…and I'm a little scared from the last time."

She slid her hand into his and they walked across the glassy wet sand. They stayed silent until the water reached their waist.

"Why don't we swim out to that buoy?" She pointed to the bobbing light offshore.

"That's a pretty far reach. Ya gonna be okay?"

"If you're with me, we should be fine. Stay close."

Colleen moved forward, still clasping his hand. He followed. When the water reached his upper arms he felt a tightening of his shoulders and legs. *Damn it…cramps are coming on…I'll just work through them.*

Colleen stopped. "You feeling all right?" She stared at him strangely.

"Just a little tight. I'll loosen up when I start swimmin'."

They moved slowly outward. The cold disappeared even though the waves lapped at his shoulders. He turned toward her and shrieked. The head of a sea lion bobbed next to him. He raised his arms and twisted in the water to flee. But he had no arms, just thick flippers, and his legs wouldn't work. Something closed over his eyes. He fell forward into the sea. Just before going under he sucked in a deep breath. But once below the shore break it felt strangely serene. His nose had closed off and he didn't strain to hold his breath.

A sleek female sea lion circled him. He floated just below the tumbling waves, the rocky bottom strewn with broken shells. He inspected his body, a muscular sea lion's, and shuddered. *This has got to be a dream. I'm going to wake up in Colleen's arms. She'll make me black coffee with a little cinnamon and coco added and we'll have a good laugh.*

The dream persisted. The sea lion continued to circle, making strange moans and humming sounds. It approached and pulled up to his side. The sounds increased and…and he understood them.

"Don't be afraid. You're safe with me. You are one of us now."

He tried speaking and similar sounds came from his vocal cords.

"Who are you? What's happened to me?"

"I'm Colleen. And you have transformed into a sea lion, into a sea person."

"This is one wild-ass dream I've got goin' here."

"It's not a dream. This is real. You saw me transform before, and now you have done the same thing."

"But how…and why?"

"That will take some explaining. But let's continue our swim and I'll show you how to be a seal."

"I'm gonna change back, aren't I?"

"For certain, just like me. We are kindred spirits."

They rose to the surface and skimmed along the sea. Don watched Colleen as she used her front flippers for propulsion and her rear ones to steer. In short bursts they could race as fast as a human sprinter. And the turns and leaps she could make seemed incredible, vaulting through the wave tops into the air and landing without a splash.

Once off shore, they dove into the blue-green darkness. "How deep can we go?" Don hummed.

"Up to 300 meters or about 980 feet."

"No kiddin.' Do we get the bends if we go deep and come up too fast?"

"No. Our lungs are different than humans and prevent the absorption of too much nitrogen into the blood stream."

"Son of a bitch…that's so cool. I can dive deep without havin' to buy special gear. How long can we stay down?"

"About six minutes, maybe a little longer. But we can dive all day long if we want."

The two played in the water as the sea slowly grew lighter with the rising sun. From out of the depths came a slate-gray shape, a streamlined torso with a huge dorsal fin.

"Shark," Colleen barked. "Follow me."

She tore off like a porpoise across the sea, heading toward the blinking buoy. Don's flippers ached as he struggled to match her speed. At a certain point she turned abruptly and flew out of the water. Don did the same. The head of a Great White shot between them, its mouth gaping, razor teeth ready to shred their hides.

"Head for the buoy and climb up," Colleen ordered.

"What about you?"

"Don't worry."

Don raced toward the buoy, dove below the surface then vaulted upward, landing hard on its metal decking. He pulled and pushed with his flippers to haul himself away from the edge. The morning wind howled and he shuddered. In a few moments, his body transformed into that of a naked man. He stood on the tilting platform and studied the sea around him. The shark circled, its fin cutting the water. Colleen had disappeared, but with no signs of blood.

The shark turned and swam away, but turned again and charged, pushing the sea before it. With a crash, it rammed its side against the buoy, its black eyes staring angrily at Don, as if blaming him for surviving. Don grasped a tower strut with a death grip as his refuge tilted wildly, almost dunking him in the sea. But it righted itself. He gasped with relief.

The shark continued circling. The minutes ticked by slowly. Don remembered the time he had run into a raft of sea lions beyond the mouth of Estero Bay. They had circled his boat, barking and carrying on until one or two of them got yanked below. Bloody body parts floated to the surface. Some of the younger sea lions jumped over the gunnel and slammed onto the deck, frantic to get away from their nemesis – a pod of Orcas moving south.

The shark finally quit its circling and slid beneath the waves, surfacing farther north on a course toward the Piedras Blancas Lighthouse and the barking sea lion colony. *Come on, Colleen, come back to me,* he pleaded. *If you do, I'll never hurt another seal again.* Don began to lose feelings in his legs. And his left forearm had gone numb where he had banged it against the buoy's metal superstructure. He stared at the deserted shoreline and wondered what it would take to swim ashore as a human and how quickly he had covered that distance as his transformed self.

Without a sound, the head of a sea lion appeared next to the buoy. He wasn't sure it was Colleen. He lowered himself into the water anyway and once again became a sea person.

"It's me, Colleen," she hummed.

"What happened?" He wanted to hug her, to comfort her, but didn't know how.

"If you play them right, you can out-maneuver the sharks. The trick is not to let them surprise you from below. They can go deeper than we can. But they can't maneuver quite as well. That brute finally got tired of our cat and mouse game and came looking for you. I'm glad he didn't snag you from your refuge."

"Yeah, now I know what it feels like to be the one bein' hunted."

They dove beneath the waves and headed for shore. Don's mind filled with a hundred-and-one questions that he'd ask Colleen…in front

45

of a warming fire with a snifter of good brandy. As they swam nearer to shore, two SUV's pulled away along the frontage road and he wondered who would be out that early – another question for Colleen.

While in the water Don felt warm and alive. But struggling on hands and knees from the ocean caused pain in every joint. He watched closely as Colleen transformed. The curves, angles, and features of her seal body seemed to melt and rematerialize into their beautiful human form. Once onshore, naked and exposed to the bitter wind, they struggled to dry off and dress quickly, calm their yapping dogs, and head back at a brisk pace.

10.

They walked in silence. Don pondered their narrow escape from the Great White and his altered life, mulling over its advantages and challenges. Arriving at her house, Colleen took his hand, led him inside and lit the gas fire. They sat on the sofa and drank brandy.

He tried to make sense of what had happened. "Ya sure this ain't some kind of wakin' dream?"

She smiled. "It's no dream. Look at your left forearm. How did you get those scrapes and bruises? You know the answer, don't you?"

He nodded and gulped his brandy.

"Where do you want to start?" Colleen asked. "I know what to do when I'm interviewing new recruits that have just come out of the sea as humans. But this whole thing is new to me."

"Why don' ya start right there? What recruits…and whose doin' the recruitin'?"

She sucked in a deep breath. "I belong to an organization called 'Seven Seas.' Our mission is to find young and healthy sea lions and seals from around the world and recruit them to our cause."

"What's this recruitment thing? I remember signin' up to be a Navy Seal but…"

"Yes, it gets complicated fast. Those clear spheres you found and handled in my chest pack contain enzymes that allows any sea lion that touches them to change from a seal to a human, once it leaves the ocean."

"Is that what happened to me, only the other way around?" Don asked, eyes wide.

"Yes."

"Is the change permanent?"

"Yes."

Don chugged the rest of his brandy and Colleen splashed more into his snifter.

"But why do ya need recruits? Is this some sort of 'Planet of the Apes' revolution where y'all take over the earth?"

Colleen snorted. "Hardly. As a fisherman, you probably know about the Irish and Scottish legends of the sea people called Selkies."

"Yeah, I was thinkin' about that. The story goes that they live as seals in the sea but shed their skin to become human on land."

"Well, the legend is real…except we obviously don't shed our skins, and the transformation process is much more complex. Seven Seas has figured out a way to make it happen."

"So how many of you Selkies are there?"

"Ah…remember Don, you're one of us now."

"Oh, yeah."

"There are about 2,500 Selkies worldwide."

"Why are ya recruitin' more? What ya doin', anyway?"

"You've heard of global warming, haven't you?"

"Ah, jeez. Not another rant about…"

"It's no rant. Our numbers have been declining. As the polar ice melts, the water temperature increases and the ocean levels rise. Nursery areas for our pups are being flooded."

"Can't y'all just move?"

"In warm climates we compete for space with the land-basers. And as the seas warm, the ocean currents are changing. Storms are tearing up our traditional breeding grounds and more predators are moving into our waters. Because of changes to our food chain and habitat, our young aren't as strong as before and are easier prey for the sharks and orcas."

"But why change seals into humans? You tryin' ta move 'em ashore? We got enough problems with too many folks."

"No, we don't want to move on land. But we've found that the land-basers have failed to deal with the problem of global warming, overfishing, and pollution of the oceans with chemicals and trash."

"Yeah, I've heard about that Great Pacific Garbage Patch."

"Well, we want our recruits to work in industries and governments that can change things to protect our seas."

"So, you want the recruits to become…what's the word, *advocates*?"

"Yes, yes. You understand. Land-basers will listen to other humans sometimes…much more than they can empathize with creatures they can't communicate with."

"So, y'all want to influence change, not take over?"

"Yes."

"Huh. But does that mean you're gonna take away my fishin' rights?"

"No. But things have to change so that there are fish left to be caught. I think both land-basers and the sea people want that."

"Are there other sea people?"

"God, yes. Whales, walrus, penguins, manatees, sea otters, and dolphins are sentient…but they can't transform like us."

"Yeah, can ya imagine the size of a transformed blue whale?" Don grinned and Colleen giggled, breaking the tension.

He stretched out on the couch and she came into his arms. Her kisses tasted salty.

"So what does all this have to do with me?" Don asked.

"Well, you can help in advocating our interests in the fishing industry."

"Ya gotta be kiddin'. I'm just a good ole boy from Texas."

"Don't give me that 'ah shucks ma'am' crap. You can help by showing others how to fish properly, to release seals trapped in your nets, to argue for sustainable fishing."

"That's all well and good for the cause. But what's in it for me?"

"Does your boat have sonar to find the fish schools?"

"Hell, I can't afford that gear."

"Well, I could be your seal sonar. I can dive deep and find the fish. And you can spell me when I get tired." Colleen became more and more animated. "And we can travel together, along the coast north and south of here…you fishing and me finding new recruits. If I work from your boat, it'll save me a lot of time and swimming. And maybe later, we can cruise the Caribbean for sunken ships and Spanish treasure."

"So…so ya want to come fish with me…come be with me?" Don asked.

"Listen, it's the female sea lion that makes all the provocative moves."

"Good thing I like strong women."

The couple tossed off their brandies and kissed passionately.

With wagging tails, Lola and Caesar sat on their haunches on the deck, staring in through the sliding glass doors.

"What do ya wanna bet they do it right there on the couch," Lola whined.

Caesar snorted. "Yeah, and Don complains when *I* take up too much of the bed. Humans, can't live with 'em, can't eat 'em.'"

Terry Sanville lives in San Luis Obispo, California with his artist-poet wife (his in-house editor) and two plump cats (his in-house critics). He writes full time, producing short stories, essays, poems, and novels. Since 2005, his short stories have been accepted more than 340 times by commercial and academic journals, magazines, and anthologies including The Potomac Review, The Bitter Oleander, and Shenandoah. He was nominated twice for *Pushcart Prizes* and once for inclusion in *Best of the Net* anthology. His stories have been listed as "The Most Popular Contemporary Fiction of 2017" by the Saturday Evening Post. Terry is a retired urban planner and an accomplished jazz and blues guitarist – who once played with a symphony orchestra backing up jazz legend George Shearing.

Fear Regulation Chip
by Kevin Stadt

Corporal West's heart rate held steady in the low 70's as the three men reached the doors to the cryopod bay, even though he could hear the creatures scuttling in the air ducts, and he'd seen what they did to people. Sarge never used his Fear Regulation Chip, so sweat dripped from the big man's dark skin as he clutched his rifle. Meyer, the skinny maintenance tech in red coveralls, was no soldier and had no chip and had not uttered a single word since they'd stumbled on him hiding under a desk in engineering. Posting up next to the doors, West pet Rocky's head. The 150-pound, genetically-engineered battle K-10 watched West intently, waiting for a command.

Squatting on the other side of the doors, Sarge spoke, keeping his deep voice at a whisper. "West, send the dog in."

Sarge tapped the control panel and the doors slid apart. West flashed a hand signal to Rocky, instructing him to go in and sweep the cryopod bay. Although the ship's AI had told them that sensors showed no intruders in this area, they didn't want to take any chances. The aliens had proven adept at avoiding detection.

West peeked around the corner to watch Rocky. The Doberman-like animal worked methodically through the cavernous room, his nose sniffing high and low, his nails clicking on the metal floors. The colossal cyropod bay housed several thousand sleeping colonists and took up nearly twenty percent of the SS Terigon, but Rocky's bioengineered senses quickly confirmed that the bay was clear, which he indicated by returning to sit quietly in front of West. So far, it remained free of the organisms that had invaded the ship and killed most of the crew unlucky enough to be awake for this particular seven-year shift of the 84-year journey to Gamma Argosi.

Each of the three men raced off to check on their families. White pods with softly glowing blue interactive windows lay on racks in hundreds of rows from floor to ceiling. As often as West had come to see Nikki and Jason in the four years since he'd been awakened for his shift, he effortlessly navigated the maze of pods.

The second he reached them, he touched Jason's screenwindow, checking his son's vitals and pod integrity, and then Nikki's. Both were healthy and undisturbed, for now.

West knew he should be scared. He recognized on an abstract level that terror in this situation would be perfectly normal. And although part of him realized that the lack of fear was unnatural, another part of him thanked God for the FRC. How could he do the job without it?

He studied his son's face, touched the cool, smooth surface of the pod. The boy seemed peaceful. West noticed his own reflection in the glass. They looked so much alike with the same pale complexion, delicate features and blond hair. And not only did Jason resemble him physically, he was introverted and anxious, too, just like West had always been.

Or just like West had always been until the FRC implant.

He turned to Rocky. The dog had dutifully kept watch over all of them while West checked Jason and Nikki. West slung his rifle onto his back, squatted next to Rocky and pet the dog with both hands. Although Rocky had the bite force of a crocodile, with tenth-generation ProTek muscle fiber and ultra-dense OrtegaCorp bone mass, plus splices from half a dozen apex predator species, he was still West's puppy.

West scratched him behind an ear and the dog wagged his tail. "Who's my boy? That's right. You're my buddy, aren't you?" Rocky had become his constant companion in the four years West had been awake on the Terigon without his family to keep him company. West couldn't talk to his wife or son, would never see his hometown or parents or the ocean again, ate nothing but printed food. But Rocky's friendship had kept him sane. The dog gave his days a purposeful routine with the feeding and bathing and training, made him laugh with the way he tried to curl up on West's lap on the couch and kept him from feeling alone at night by crawling under the covers and pushing West to the edge of the bed.

"West, Meyer. On me."

West trotted over to Sarge, Rocky on his heels. Meyer came from the other direction. Sarge addressed them both. "Your families good?"

West answered, "Yes, sir." Meyer nodded, his huge eyes skittishly probing the corners and shadows.

"All right." Sarge's gaze went unfocused, the look of someone accessing his mindscreen. Also commonly called the mental desktop or skullHUD, it allowed Marines to internally link to shipwide systems, weapons and coms.

"This is the plan." As soon as Sarge said it, an image of the long, muscular SS Terigon sprang up on West's mental desktop. "We're here." The image zoomed in and expanded, a flashing red marker appearing on their location. "And we need to get to the armory, here." Another marker appeared far on the starboard side of the ship, and then a dotted red line connected them, mapping the way.

West glanced back toward his family's pods. The idea of leaving them made him ache down to the bone. But he'd have no chance of saving them if he didn't make it to the armory.

As Sarge continued, casualty readings and last known intruder locations popped up on West's skullHUD. "Here's the situation, gentlemen. As soon as we entered orbit around Dysis Prime for research

53

and resupply, seven small vessels approached the Terigon. Automated defenses took out five of them, but two reached the hull. They attached themselves, cut through and handed us our asses. Most of the Marines who were on shift went down in the initial onslaught."

"How many, sir?"

"Over 96%." They fell silent for a moment, each man looking at the floor. "We have to be double careful to not let them touch us to use their biological EMP capability, which can fry our personal weapons systems. There's a tech waiting for us in the armory. He's working on recalibrating the sensors to keep better track of these hostiles, and he's got anti-EMP nodes and lots of shiny gear. West, run a systems diagnostic, then we leave in three."

"Yes, sir."

Meyer stood off to the side, hugging himself. The maintenance tech seemed so young, so terrified, that West wished he could do something to reassure the kid.

"Hey, Meyer. Don't worry. Sarge is the best. He's not going to let anything happen to you. We'll get through this."

Meyer stared at him, mouth closed tight and unblinking eyes open wide. After a moment, he nodded almost imperceptibly.

West mentally clicked on various systems icons on his mental desktop and initiated diagnostics, petting Rocky at the same time. When he turned his attention to the dronelink icon in the upper right of his mental desktop—a stylized image of five attacking wasps—an infobubble popped out of it to tell him the drones in his exoskeleton armor were still almost fully charged. But his rifle had just 38 shots left. Once that was gone, he'd be down to his sidearm and knife.

A few moments later they gathered at the door, ready to head out, and just at that instant the lights blinked on and off a couple times, then died altogether. Sarge swore under his breath and Meyer whimpered. West rationally recognized the development as a challenge, but had no emotional response. Dim, red backup lights flicked on. West linked into the shipwide net by turning his attention to a cartoon-like ship icon in the upper left of his mindscreen, and an infobubble popped up to report that the lights had gone out due to unknown electrical malfunctions, likely related to invader activity.

It was going to be dark. In the faint red glow, he saw Meyer had begun sobbing soundlessly.

Sarge's voice broke the silence. "Let's move. Meyer, stay between us. Don't worry, son. Everybody keep your head on a swivel and we'll be fine."

They crept out into the long, metallic hallway, crouching and advancing slowly, fingers hovering over triggers, trying to make a minimum of noise. Rocky led the pack, his nose and ears twitching.

Who could guess what senses the alien creatures had? Did they see, hear and smell? Or were efforts to remain quiet a waste of energy? For all West knew, the things were deaf but could see their electromagnetic signatures through walls.

No one spoke. Watching others gripped by fear is odd when you feel nothing, like being the only sober one at a party full of drunk people. Why didn't Sarge switch on his chip? Escape from the horror was just a click away.

They made it along the hallway, around a corner and down another passage before they reached the mess hall. Like the cryopod bay, the mess hall had a lot of places for the organisms to hide, so they followed the same procedure and posted up at the door, sending the dog in to sweep.

Rocky went in enthusiastically, inspecting the room in quadrants, weaving between the tables, checking behind the counters and in the attached kitchen. Finally, he came back to them and sat quietly in front of West, giving the all clear.

They filed into the room and headed for the doors on the other side. West's mind wandered, an unwanted side effect sometimes associated with a lack of fear. He wondered if they were intelligent, or just operated on instinct. He wondered where they came from, and if other colony ships would encounter anything similar.

Rocky halted, snapping his attention up toward one of the air ducts, growling, barking viciously, his hackles raised. All three men froze. West and Sarge raised their weapons, while Meyer disappeared under a table.

A creature squeezed out of an air vent slot above the kitchen door, a dark gray ball of slimy, groping, thin tentacles extending out from a vague central mass, the whole thing not much bigger than a hand. It rolled along the outside of the metal duct, released its sticky hold and fell onto a table near Sarge. Rather than rolling now, it stepped toward him with its flagella-like limbs undulating in waves, making a faint slurping noise as it progressed. It moved slowly, cautiously, as if sizing the soldiers up.

Sarge said, "I got it." He aimed his plasma rifle and squeezed off one perfect shot of crackling blue energy. The round hit squarely, leaving nothing on the table except a gooey smear.

Fresh growls burst from Rocky. Another creature squeezed through the vent, and another. Within seconds dozens of them had emerged.

Sarge fired again and the things scattered. "West, deploy!"

56

West focused on his skullHUD, activating the wasp icon in the upper right corner. A dozen dime-sized ports on the back of his exorig opened, and a tiny drone buzzed out of each. He tagged Sarge, Meyer and Rocky, marking them with blue "friendly" flags on his mindscreen.

Once the drones knew who not to kill, they whirred around the room firing miniscule darts tipped with a chemical bioweapon West prayed would work on the aliens. Each drone found a target, fired and moved on to the next with automated efficiency. Every time an organism took a dart, it emitted a high-pitched cry, writhed and then burst open with an audible pop.

An infobubble informed him that it had taken 32.6 seconds for the drones to eliminate the enemies. West ordered them back to his rig, standing perfectly still as they returned. Sarge smiled and patted West's shoulder.

"Badass, Corporal. Nice job."

"Thank you, sir."

Was he really a badass? Sarge was, for sure. Sarge had twenty years in the Corps, and had seen action on Ganymede, Titan and Europa. All without an FRC. But the Moon Wars were before West's time, and anyway back then the Marines never would have taken someone with a history of anxiety and panic attacks like him. The FRC made him artificially fearless. The drones were badass, but all he'd done was activate them.

West's drill sergeant in boot camp had looked down on him with unhidden disdain, and had shouted his opinion loud and often. "As far as I'm concerned, you're not a real Marine, and you never will be. You're just a faker, too much of a pussy to even feel your own goddamn fear." The drill sergeant had seen three generations of Marines come through, and held no high opinion of the new batch, so reliant on implants.

57

West never pretended to be a natural-born killer. He'd gone to university to be an elementary school teacher. But he laid aside his dream of teaching when the military, desperate for recruits, began offering soldiers much-coveted spots on ships to the new colony worlds. Increasingly violent and unpredictable coronal mass ejections from the sun were wreaking havoc on Earth, regularly peeling away the planet's magnetic field. The resulting geomagnetic storms not only crippled power grids, communications and satellites, but also left everyone on Earth exposed to life-threatening radioactive proton storms. So, in return for securing passage for his family, West signed up to do a seven-year tour awake on the Terigon's journey.

The drill sergeant's voice still echoed in his skull years later, and deep down West believed the old soldier was right.

As these thoughts pulled at West's attention, it happened.

Rocky raised his nose in the air, flattened his ears and growled. The next thing West knew, something cold and slimy slapped onto his face. He let go of his rifle and reached up to pull it off, struggling to breathe. Before his hands even got there, a sharp zap shot through his skull. His body went rigid, fell over, and his consciousness snapped off like a computer monitor.

*   *   *

West woke with a jump, sitting up suddenly and raising a hand to his face.

"Easy, West. You're all right. We're clear. Can you run a diagnostic?"

West tried to stand, but a wave of dizziness overcame him. The thing had left a rank fishy smell on his skin, and a sickly nausea grew in his gut. Sweat broke out on his hands and forehead, while his heart picked up speed and his breaths came short and shallow.

He didn't need a diagnostic to tell him the creature had shorted out his FRC. Icy panic gripped him for the first time in years. The room spun. He tried to say his head hurt, but the words didn't come out right. His vision stretched into a tunnel, with the center pulling away into the distance and the edges blurring. Sarge called his name, but it sounded muffled as if underwater. His consciousness drifted off, lazily this time, the nothingness settling over him like a soft, heavy blanket.

He woke to Sarge over him again, and immediately felt fear take a back seat to shame. He'd just let the grizzled veteran see him faint like a young woman in a Victorian romance novel.

"You all right, soldier?"

"Yes, sir. FRC is fried...it caught me off guard. Sorry, sir."

"It's okay, son. Run a diagnostic. Let's see what the damage is."

West tried to pull up his mental desktop. Nothing happened.

He concentrated and tried again, with no better luck. He ground the palms of his hands into his eyes. No, no, no! This couldn't be happening. Not now. Please, God, just–

"Corporal West, report."

"I, uh...I don't have a screen. My skullHUD's down." The drone operating system. Weapon and ship links. FRC. All gone. "Sir, that means I won't even be able to deploy drones the next time–"

Sarge cut him off. "All it means is that you get the opportunity to enjoy a time-honored tradition of the Marine Corps. You get to kick ass implant-free, the way God intended." He reached out and helped West up. "Let's move."

As Sarge started toward the door, Meyer spoke for the first time, his voice hardly more than a squeak. "You okay?"

West didn't say no, he absolutely was *not* okay. He didn't say he felt 90% sure he would throw up. He didn't say he felt panic clawing at his chest so intensely that he worried he might have an actual heart attack. And he didn't say that he felt frozen to the spot and wasn't at all clear his feet would move when he ordered them to.

Instead, he tried to put a semblance of confidence into his tone. "Thank you. I'll be fi—" His voice cracked and he cleared his throat, feeling his face get warm. "Fine. I'll be fine. Just stay close to Sarge. I'll take up the rear."

Meyer nodded uncertainly, concern evident in his expression, and fell in. Rocky sat at attention, ears up, whining and nuzzling West's hand. The dog obviously sensed West's emotions and didn't know what to make of the situation. "I'm okay, buddy. Don't worry." Then he flashed a hand signal, telling Rocky to stay alert for further attacks as they moved on. The dog licked his hand and took point ahead of Sarge.

They crossed the mess hall at a glacial pace, knowing another creature could jump out of any crack, any shadow, any corner. West crouched low as he walked, keeping his rifle up. He wiped sweat from his forehead. The sound of something moving in an air duct above him made him yell and squeeze off three rounds upward, each shot missing the duct completely.

"Corporal!" Sarge spoke through gritted teeth. "Save your fire unless you have visual confirmation of a target!"

"Yes, sir. Sorry, sir."

West shook his head and scolded himself. God damn it. Pull yourself together. You're a fucking Marine, for Christ's sake. Just man up and get to the armory. For your family.

They passed through doors into a long hallway, this one with only the barest minimum of red backup lighting. Sarge paused, letting Rocky go ahead a little and check things out. The dog lifted his nose in the air and growled.

All three men tensed. Sarge and West raised their weapons, while Meyer pressed himself against the wall.

West's heart hammered in his chest. He gripped and re-gripped his weapon, squinting into the shadows.

They stood there like that for what felt like hours, but after a while Rocky's hackles lowered and he tested the air again. Finally, he sat and fell quiet.

West let out a breath he hadn't even realized he'd been holding. He relaxed his muscles, heavy and tired from the adrenaline dump. Sarge made eye contact with Meyer and West in turn, then nodded for them to press on.

As they filed step by step down the hallway, hugging the wall, West's mind raced. If more of those things popped out, did they have enough ammo left to have any chance of making it through? How many aliens were between them and the armory? And even if they did make it there, would they be able to save all those sleeping colonists?

They covered thirty feet of the hallway and had as much to go before they'd reach the T where it branched off. Rocky stopped suddenly, letting out a rumbling growl while baring his fangs.

West dropped to one knee and frantically inspected the dark end of the hallway through his rifle sights. Meyer squatted behind Sarge, peering over his shoulder. None of the three men made a sound.

Pointing his weapon into the distance, struggling to keep his breathing as steady as possible, West didn't see anything. Where were they? Could Rocky be wrong? Maybe the dog had just heard or smelled some of the aliens passing by through the air ducts or in a parallel passageway.

Then it appeared, dramatically bigger than the ones in the mess hall, half the size of a man. It rolled around the corner on the ceiling with its slimy flagella, and suddenly paused as if regarding them. It emitted watery gurgling sounds and rolled forward.

Sarge fired. The creature dodged the blast and took to racing toward them in a zigzag pattern, even as a half-dozen more similarly large aliens rounded the corner behind it.

Sarge fired again, this time obliterating the animal in the lead. West put one of the things in his sights, breathed out and squeezed the trigger.

It exploded, parts of its body making a sickly slapping sound as they hit the walls and floor. But the rest of the pack accelerated in a frighteningly quick zigzag advance, and West struggled to get a bead. Even knowing he had little ammo to work with, he had no choice but to fire haphazardly into the approaching horde.

With both soldiers shooting wildly, the creatures got closer every second. He was dimly aware of backing down the hallway as he fired, though Sarge hadn't ordered a retreat. Out of the corner of his eye, West saw Meyer take off back the way they came.

Expending more ammo than they could afford, they hit one, then another and another. The last one exploded in a goopy mess just ten feet away.

West took a deep breath and lowered his weapon, his legs trembling. He leaned against the wall and closed his eyes, only to hear a shriek from Meyer.

The maintenance tech had almost made it to the mess hall, only to run straight into a mass of smaller organisms. He desperately tried to swat off the first few that had dropped onto his hair and shoulders from the ceiling, but even as he managed to swat one away, three more took its place. Within seconds, dozens crawled onto him, and he spun wildly and fell.

West turned to Sarge. They held each other's gaze for a moment, racing through an unspoken debate. West's first impulse was to help Meyer, yet deep down he knew it was too late. He checked the ammo meter on the rifle. Six rounds left. But even if he had a thousand chances, there was no way to shoot those things without hitting Meyer.

With sadness clouding his face, Sarge shook his head once, and gestured for them to retreat the other way down the hall. Both men stepped backwards, guns trained on the mass overtaking Meyer.

It was the third time West witnessed firsthand what the aliens did with a human. He didn't want to watch, but couldn't look away.

As Meyer screamed, thrashed and shook, they rolled and slithered into any hole they could find. Guttural choking noises replaced Meyer's screams as they slid into his open mouth. Even at this distance, West could see lines of smaller ones streaming into his nostrils and ears. Some squeezed their squishy bodies into the corners of his eyes. Others disappeared into the neck, sleeves and ankles of his coveralls. Meyer scratched at his face so violently, he drew his own blood.

What did the organisms do once in the body? Did they eat you from the inside out? Did they lay eggs?

West shuddered and felt a wave of dread spread through his gut. Luckily, they reached the end of the hallway and rounded a corner. He pushed his back against the wall, scrunching his face up tightly and pressing a hand against his chest.

"You all right, Corporal?"

"Yes, sir."

West peeked around the corner. Meyer had stopped moving, and now dozens of creatures raced along the ceiling and walls toward them. "Sir, they're coming!"

Never in West's life had his heart beat that hard. Blood thudded in his ears. Sarge glanced around and pointed at a maintenance closet. "In there!"

They scrambled to the door and West opened it. The faint backup lighting revealed it to be little bigger than a spacious closet. Several housekeeping bots rested in charging ports on one side, with cleaning equipment and supplies filling shelves all over the rest of the room.

As soon as they were in, Sarge closed the door behind them and touched the lock button, wincing at its audible beep. Both men backed away from the door and listened, guns at the ready. West gave Rocky the hand signal to keep silent, and the dog instantly stopped growling.

For what felt like a long time, West didn't hear anything except his own heart and breathing. But then he detected a vague commotion passing by in the hall. West pointed the rifle at the door, finger trembling over the trigger.

The sound got closer and closer, and just as West thought his heart would explode, it passed by.

Sarge whispered. "Let's wait a few minutes before we head back out there."

Relief washed over West. "Yes, sir." Back against the wall, he slumped to the floor, breathing in slowly through his nose and out through his mouth. When he could tell by the look on Sarge's face that he'd focused on his mindscreen, West lifted his left hand.

It shook uncontrollably. The beads of his bracelet caught his eye, and his thoughts jumped back years to the day his son gave it to him.

Jason sat up in the pod and said, "Daddy, close your eyes and hold out your hand."

"You're the boss." He squeezed his eyes shut, then felt cool metal beads slip onto his wrist. "Can I look now?"

"Yeah."

A dozen little, silver spheres hung from a black cord. Jason said, "Watch this." The boy double-tapped one of them with the tip of his finger, and instantly the bead projected a holographic image of West and Jason on a boat at the lake, a picture Nikki had taken the summer before they left Earth.

"Every bead has a cool picture." The boy tapped different parts of the bracelet, which threw glowing blue scenes of their family into the air. "Do you like it?"

He hugged the boy tightly, holding him a long time. "I love it. Was this your idea?"

"Yeah. I picked the pictures and Mom helped upload them."

"Thank you, buddy. It's my favorite thing in the whole world."

Sarge's whispered voice pulled him back to the present. "How are you holding up, Marine?"

West nodded. "Fine, sir."

"Scared?"

"No, sir." He felt his cheek twitch as the whispered words left his mouth.

Sarge chuckled quietly and shook his head. "You don't have to bullshit me, Corporal. I know you've never been in combat, and that you have a history of panic attacks. And now your FRC is fried." West looked down and Sarge continued. "I've been in battle more times than I want to remember, and I'm scared shitless. So talk to me. Permission to speak freely."

Rocky lay down next to West, and West stroked the dog's fur as he spoke. "Well sir, in that case, I'm fucking terrified."

Sarge smiled and leaned forward a little. "That's all right, soldier. You'd be crazy if you weren't."

"May I ask a personal question, sir?"

"Sure."

"Why don't you use your FRC?"

Sarge waved a hand dismissively. "I don't care what the Corps' official stance on the implant is—I don't trust that shit. The way I see it, thousands of generations of humans have evolved to have fear. All those lives, all those experiences and dangers they faced through millennia, and fear is one of the tools the fittest survived with. Way I see it, if the emotion was a survival disadvantage, we wouldn't even have it in the first place."

"But…" West struggled to find the right words. "But it's so awful. Just a lot easier to turn it off."

"I've seen too many young Marines with implants daydreaming when they should have been laser-focused on the danger right in front of them. Fear makes you sharp. Strong."

"I feel like it just makes me shaky and rubbery."

Sarge pointed at West, punctuating his words with his index finger. "You don't need an FRC. You need to learn to work with your emotions. I knew a captain who practiced Buddhist meditation, and he told me the best thing to do is watch your fear. Step back from it, get some distance to see it clearly as just a passing phenomenon. I tried that for a while."

"Did it work?"

"Hell no. At least not for me. But I'll tell you what does."

West found himself almost holding his breath, hanging on Sarge's words. The older man leaned further forward, his tone conspiratorial. "Don't try not to be scared. That'll never work. Just shift your focus to

66

the stakes. Picture your wife. Your boy. They're asleep in pods and monsters are here to kill them. Think about what those things will do to your family. How does that make you feel?"

"Pissed."

Sarge leaned back. "Good. Use that. Stoke a fire in your belly so you can kill some motherfuckers like the Marine you are."

*   *   *

When they peeked out the door a few minutes later, the coast looked clear. Rocky entered the hallway first, nose probing the air, and then signaled that he detected no immediate threats. As they inched down that hall without incident, and then the next, and the next, West began to think maybe their luck had changed. Maybe those things had moved to another part of the Terigon, or who knows–maybe they even left.

But as they rounded the corner of the very last hallway, the one leading directly to the armory, Rocky barked and an air duct cover above them creaked, popped its screws and fell to the ground with a clang that made West's heart leap into his throat. The biggest creature he'd seen yet dropped out, right on top of Sarge.

The thing had clearly compressed itself to fit into the duct, and as it came out, its flagella expanded, almost filling the narrow hallway. Its limbs stretched toward Sarge, who tried to raise his rifle but couldn't get it up in time.

The beast hit Sarge so hard they slammed to the floor. Grunts and growls and wet squishy sounds echoed off the metal walls. West raised his rifle, but couldn't get a clear shot. He signaled for Rocky to attack and he sprinted toward Sarge, drawing his knife.

Rocky snapped at the tentacles as West stabbed. Their assault had precious little effect, though, as the body of the alien hid safely behind countless groping limbs.

Suddenly, dozens of tinier creatures streamed outward on the tentacles toward Sarge, like baby spiders freshly hatched. The older Marine grappled with the beast, grimacing, his two hands little use against the endless limbs and streams of smaller organisms. West threw himself into slashing at them, but they quickly reached Sarge and flowed into his mouth, nose and ears. Screaming at the top of his lungs, tears blurring his vision now, West swung the blade with all his strength, trying to penetrate to the core of the beast.

It turned its attention to him.

The tentacles released Sarge and extended toward West instead. He took a step back but slipped, falling hard. The organism was on him before he even caught his breath. West tried to sit up, kick it off, raise his arms, but its gooey mass pinned him down.

Rage burned in his blood and he flailed like a madman to get free, pushing with all his strength against the weight pressing on him. He screamed, got an arm loose for a moment and slashed wildly, only for the beast to again tangle him up and press him down.

Suddenly the beast emitted a gurgling cry. Rocky had somehow managed to push through the mass of flagella and fixed his bio-engineered bite onto the body. The dog had an unbreakable lock on the alien, and shook his head violently. Viscous black liquid poured out around the wound.

It went limp, its full weight slouching heavily onto West.

He rolled it to the side with a grunt and sat up, glancing around for smaller organisms. It seemed they'd all disappeared into Sarge, who lay on the floor, not breathing. West hung his head. Rocky stepped closer and nuzzled him, whimpering softly.

West put his arm around the dog's neck and hugged him. "Thanks, buddy. You're a goddamn good dog." He crawled over to

Sarge's motionless body and felt for a pulse with one hand while holding his sidearm at the ready with the other, in case those things decided to pop out.

There was no pulse. West stood and backed away, leaden sadness weighed heavy in his chest.

"GET IN HERE NOW! THEY'RE COMING!" A voice erupted from the hallway's intercom speakers so unexpected and frantic that it made West jump. "Hurry!"

The armory door at the end of the hallway slid open with a whoosh. West scrambled toward it, Rocky following. He heard a commotion behind him, and he glanced back to find not one but three of the big aliens rounding the corner on the ceiling and rolling toward him.

He put all the strength he had into getting to that door, and when he and Rocky passed the threshold, it slammed shut behind him. West bent over, hands on knees, sucking air. When he finally raised his head, he saw a uniformed tech engineer standing at a holoscreen station. No other people were in the long, rectangular room filled with racks and shelves of weapons.

The freckled, red-headed tech didn't look old enough to shave. "We don't have much time. I'm showing that your implants got shorted, right? We need to reboot you and get you back out there. I activated some bots that killed a lot of the intruders, but they all got knocked offline by some of the bigger fuckers. Scans indicate there's a mass of those things moving straight for the cryobay."

"What about the ones that crawled into the bodies? Any idea yet what they're doing?"

"Not yet. I've sent maintenance bots to seal the bodies and space them. All except one, which I quarantined for study."

"Is that a good idea?"

"Captain ordered it. Before he died."

West's mind spun out for a moment, considering all the ways keeping the infested body on board could go south. But there was no time to debate it now.

"How many waking crew are left?"

The tech locked eyes with West and paused before speaking. "Just me and you."

West ran his fingers through his hair. "Holy shit. There's not one other Marine standing on this ship?"

"No. But listen, I can set you up with what you'll need to end this. Those things attack mainly by their EMP capability and by penetrating orifices, right?" He glanced around and spotted a black case on a shelf, then took it down and opened it. The tech lifted a black, full-body skinsuit out and held it up. "No way they can get you through this. It's a high-density, weaponized smartskin weave. It covers you completely, head to toe, so you'll be safe. It'll link into your desktop when you put it on. I'd be wearing one myself, but I don't have the clearance to actually use any of this stuff."

Even if they couldn't get into his body, West felt utterly drained. The hours of fear and fighting had exhausted him, and he knew he'd be useless without a serious boost. "What's your name?"

"James. Jimmy."

"Jimmy, got a combat cocktail around here?"

The tech nodded and opened a drawer. He pulled out a pen-shaped delivery device and held it out. West took it, popped off the cap and pressed the end against his neck. The burning pinch of the needle was followed by a soft hiss.

His lungs sucked in breath and his whole body tensed. Strength surged through his muscles, and a deep reserve of energy radiated from his core. His senses instantly sharpened and his thoughts became clear and precise.

After Jimmy rebooted his implants, West stripped down and put on the smartskin and then the most heavily loaded drone rig in the whole armory. Then he lifted a triple-barrel rifle off the wall, the TX300, a favorite among Marines heading into heavy shit, its deadly heft a comfort. Finally, the armory tech fitted all his equipment with anti-EMP nodes.

For a brief moment he paused and accessed his mental desktop, contemplating the sky blue icon that activated the FRC. He could turn off his fear right now with a simple click. All would be calm in his mind, like a quiet Zen garden.

But he didn't.

He squatted down in front of Rocky and scratched his neck. "Listen, buddy. I'm going to need you to stay here. Hold down the fort, okay?"

The tech broke in, his brow furrowed. "You're not bringing your K-10? Don't you think you'll need him?"

West rose and adjusted the smartskin covering his face as he spoke. "Probably. But he saved my life today, and now I want to save his."

He neared the door, his heartbeat hammering in his ears, his mouth dry, his hands slick with sweat. As the familiar harbingers of panic began to take hold, he remembered Sarge's advice. So he pictured those monsters getting to the cryopod bay, slithering up to Nikki and Jason's pods, flattening themselves and sliding through the air exchange ports or the cracks in the control panels, rolling and oozing into his sleeping family's mouths and noses to do God only knows what…

They want to *kill my family*.

Sarge was right. The fear didn't disappear, but alongside it West felt a burning fire of anger in his gut, a fury that was just enough to break the panic's icy grip. He nodded to the tech and gave a hand signal for Rocky to stay. The dog whined and looked unsure, but West repeated the gesture to make it clear.

Then he took a deep breath and tapped the control panel to open the door.

When it opened, the organisms seemed to be resting on the walls and ceiling as if waiting for him, and suddenly they sprang to life, rolling and oozing forward. Each of them released dozens of smaller creatures as he stepped through the door and let it close behind him.

The TX300 linked into his skullHUD and overlay a targeting reticule system onto his vision so that when he pointed the weapon, it automatically indicated where the projectile would strike. He leveled the gun at the nearest big one and fired a plasma burst that hit the beast exactly in the center. It exploded in a gloopy mess that sizzled on the floor and wall.

The other two big animals appeared unfazed and kept coming. In one breath, he pointed at each in turn and pulled the trigger, frying both the same as the first.

But the dozens of smaller ones streamed toward him on the ceiling and walls. He tapped a button on the rifle to switch to another barrel, then pointed at the swarm on his right and fired, holding the trigger down continuously.

The TX300 shot a steady spray of bluish liquid onto the organisms. He covered the ones up the right wall, then across the ceiling and down the left wall. Seconds after the liquid drenched them, it flash froze and crackled, turning everything it touched into a solid block of ice.

The tech shouted in West's head. "You have to get to the cryopod bay now. I'm seeing five big ones heading for it. Hurry!"

West sprinted, the combat cocktail giving him incredible speed, his legs and lungs and heart pumping with a strength that seemed bottomless. He made the journey in no time, and as he rounded the corner into the hallway that led to the cryopod bay, he spotted them on the ceiling and walls, approaching the bay doors.

He tapped a button to select the third barrel of the TX300, and a primal yell emerged from deep in his chest as he raced toward them. When he got within a dozen paces of the nearest creature, West leveled the gun. It shot an angry red burst of flame, roasting the animal and leaving it bubbling like a slug doused in salt.

The other beasts took the chance to converge on him, releasing hundreds of smaller ones as they did so. He turned the flames toward the closest one, but they overwhelmed him, piling on with all their weight, immobilizing him with sticky appendages.

They zapped with their bio-EMPs, but the anti-EMP nodes kept his systems functioning. Swarms of tinier animals probed all over his body, looking for a place to get in, but the smartskin kept them out. He felt the TX300 yanked from his hand and the weight of the creatures squeezed the breath out of his chest.

They want to kill my family.

West closed his eyes.

He accessed his skullHUD, brought up the smartskin's interface and clicked on an icon that looked like a yellow bolt of lightning. It prompted him to choose between 300 or 800 kilovolts.

West chose the latter.

The hallway filled with the sound of energy crackling and guttural cries as the suit released a burst of electricity over its entire surface, shocking all the animals touching him. Their howls lasted only a brief moment, and then silence settled over the space as thin wisps of smoke drifted up from their corpses. The remaining smaller creatures scattered.

West pushed the dead off and rose to his feet. He accessed the drone controls and clicked the wasp icon.

Small sphincters opened all over the exorig on his back. Fifty tiny drones buzzed out, filling the air, and set to methodically firing bioweapon darts into every remaining intruder, spreading out both ways down the hall in pursuit of their fleeing targets.

West watched the scene unfold around him as if in slow motion. One after another was struck by a miniscule dart, stopping instantly in its tracks, uttering a horrid little cry, doing a spastic death dance and then popping open, its dark blood oozing out.

The last living alien organism on the Terigon, an especially tiny example of its species, rolling pathetically along a corner of the floor, with nowhere to hide and no way to fight back, took a dart and fell.

West backed up to the wall and slid to the floor. He leaned forward and put his face in his hands, resting like that for a long time, his mind as blank as the void outside the ship.

*   *   *

A few days later, West stood between Nikki and Jason's cryopods, Rocky at his side. He ran health checks and pod diagnostics, occasionally reaching down to pet the dog's head. When the scans finished, he kissed the glass over Nikki's face and watched Jason sleep for a while. West lay his hand on the window, the bracelet clicking against it, and wished his son sweet dreams.

He randomly picked a bead on the bracelet and tapped it. A hologram sprouted, showing him and Jason and Nikki together, holding their new puppy up in the air, their faces lit up by laughter.

74

But the moment was shattered by a red alert icon that suddenly flashed in the middle of his skullHUD. He closed his eyes and clicked on it. Jimmy appeared on his mindscreen, his face showing terror and his words coming out in a rush.

"West, get to quarantine right now!"

"Calm down. What's going on?"

"See for yourself." A video feed of the quarantine room replaced Jimmy's face. In the center of the otherwise empty space, a middle-aged man lay on a hospital bed—the one infested body they'd kept for research. West watched for a long moment, and was about to ask Jimmy again what the hell was going on, when the dead man's hand twitched.

The corpse jumped up suddenly and squatted on the bed. It peered slowly around the room, the face it wore empty of any human expression, its eyes void of human light.

Kevin Stadt is an English teacher with a master's degree in teaching writing and a doctorate in American literature. His stories have appeared or are forthcoming in anthologies and magazines such as Enter the Aftermath, Kzine, Lazarus Risen, Phantaxis, Stupefying Stories and many more. He lives in South Korea with his wife and sons, who are interdimensional cyborg pirates wanted in a dozen star systems.

Never Trust A Remittance Man
By Margaret Karmazin

Scowling, Weston Dow entered Le Chat Vert. He didn't remember feeling this mean since early secondary school when Louis-the-Jerk Yetter systematically bullied him. It was with some pleasure that he had learned of Yetter's death in a domed city experiment in Antarctica.

Le Chat Vert was packed. When someone got up from a stool at the bar, Weston grabbed it. Behind the counter was a breathtaking salmon tinged, Cydonian view.

Next to Weston some blond kid monopolized a sleazy-sexy woman wearing a pseudo French look, including a feathered beret.

The bartender appeared in front of him and Weston ordered a double shot of Klempt. "We don't got it," said the bartender.

"Scotch then," barked Weston.

He slugged it.

The blond kid turned and Weston saw he wasn't really a kid, more like thirty-five.

The guy stuck out his hand, which Weston didn't take. "Hey, I'm Har. This is Valenteen. How long have you been here?"

The girl turned away and seemed to be examining the ceiling, totally ignoring the fantastic Martian scene outside.

Weston longed to fester in peace, but he answered. "Five months, two weeks and five days."

"I'm here," laughed Har, "because they're paying me to stay away!" He seemed delighted about it.

"You don't say," said Weston. It took all kinds, especially on Mars.

"What're you here for?" persisted Har.

"Cyber engineer," said Weston.

Just then an extremely shady character arrived, eyed the girl possessively, then fixed Har with a murderous glare.

"Cool down," said Valenteen. She had the classic face of a tough girl - hardly there eyebrows, tiny chin, slit thin lips. "Har here wants some stuff."

The man slid his eyes toward Weston who turned away, pretending not to have heard.

Har, however, seemed oblivious to any need for secrecy. "How much?" he asked, loud and clear. When shady-guy whispered the amount, Har blurted, "Holy shit! I just got here! Haven't checked my account yet. You take a down payment? Maybe just let me have a sample?"

When Shady imperceptibly shook his head, Har turned to Weston. "Hey, dude, could you advance me something? I'm good for it, definitely by the sixteenth. Today's what? The tenth?"

"I don't think so," Weston said primly.

"I'm good for it, you'll see."

"I don't even know you. Why would I trust you? Besides, I don't lend money, even to friends." That would be assuming he had friends here.

Har appeared to fall into deep thought, then suddenly perked up. "I know! How about you buy something from me?" He flashed his wrist datahold. "Eledo, next to latest model! Fast, dependable, gorgeous holo projection."

"Not interested," said Weston.

Har grabbed the lapel on his jacket. "What about this? Smartest piece of clothing I ever owned. Monitors your temp, chemical composition, nutritional needs and even your mood! Warms and cools perfectly, adjusts to any body shape within reason or current comfort need. Whaddya say? Two hundred?"

Weston looked at him with interest. He certainly could use a better jacket. It appeared to be high quality; in fact better than he could normally afford. And covered with pockets, just what he needed in his line of work. "You have a deal."

Har laughed, stripped off the jacket and handed it over. Weston took Har's number, transferred the money to the man's account and slipped on the jacket.

"Looks good, bro. Just one thing. Try not to get it wet."

"Why?" said Weston.

"It just has a little kink in it when it gets wet. Nothing serious. If it does happen, just take it off and hang it up till it dries."

"But what-?"

Har, however, was surreptitiously checking a packet the shady man had slipped him while Valenteen was led off. Har darted off after her.

"Hey!" yelled Weston to nobody left.

There was little chance of getting the jacket wet on Mars anyway. Water was hard enough to come by.

Earlier that day, Weston had awakened to his alarm with a gut clench. Was it an ulcer? The medics in New Paris, Mars were, in Weston's opinion, alcoholic quacks and he hoped to God he wouldn't have to deal with them. Besides, he'd had his body scanned, implanted chip read and updated just one month before.

As he showered his allotted four minutes, Weston grumbled. He hated Mars. His fiancée Mya was eighty-nine million miles away, the distance increasing daily. What had possessed him to take this hideous job?

Well, if he survived, and it was probable that he would since now over three million Earthers lived on Mars, most in the completed cities of New Beijing and New Chicago, he'll have made himself and Mya a fine chunk of capital to begin their lives together, once she finished her doctorate. Though anything could happen. He was working in a slipshod, partly constructed city with a skeleton population of five thousand. Mars underground was still mostly an unknown, and Mya might find someone else during his absence. Two years was a long time.

They also had their differences. Mya was politically progressive and a Buddhist, while he was straight-laced and conventional. He looked the part - tall, well built, sporting a buzz cut. He believed in Reason and Logic. For a cyber engineer, any other way of thinking would be professional suicide.

There was the matter too of his supposed inability to empathize and express emotion. Mya occasionally got on him about this. A couple of those times had ended with sobs and slamming of doors. He didn't understand what the fuss was about.

His wrist-pod signaled. "Dow," he answered.

"We got an issue here." It was Klando, City Manager, pain-in-the-arse.

"What is it?"

"Avenue C is off-line."

Weston sighed. "I'll be right there."

Before locking his door, he looked at the pic montage by his bed. A wave of his hand sent the pics rotating to show Mya in various poses, full breasted and lush, her upper lip arched provocatively. Every time he looked at it, he felt a pang of despair. Men were probably beating down her door, those pseudo-intellectual grad students and ego driven future anthropologists. How he hated their collective guts.

Klando's round little self waited in the intersection of Avenue C and Rue Camus. He was sipping his usual coffee froth. "Lights down, funny buzzing noise," he said. "That building there - see that? Third floor, something flashing in there. That's Eurobank. Can't have the money bin screwed up."

"I'm sure it's nothing," said Weston, his tone barely civil. He'd planned to work on the stadium today, not piddle away on some miniscule issue an assistant could handle.

"Well," said Klando, "gotta please the bigwigs first. And Avenue C is the financial district. Much as we don't like it, they run things, right?"

"I thought the corporations owned our undies," snapped Weston. "I never considered banker slime anything to kowtow to. They can camp out if they're stupid enough to arrive before schedule."

Of course he had no choice and would have to see to it. He stalked off, muttering.

His foreman Pinot was waiting at the arena, looking anxious. "Got a buzz from Lapp's. The Grik generators have a potential malfunction. Since it'd take three months for another batch to arrive...."

Weston's gut clenched harder. "There's no way we can get the arena running by deadline if we wait for new Griks. We'll have to jerry-rig."

The foreman's brown eyes looked blank. "Uh-"

"You have two degrees from Rutgers, right?"

"Yeah, but that wasn't in design and nothing to do with -"

"Your IQ is 142. Figure it out."

"Right, Boss." Pinot saluted good-naturedly.

Weston felt around his old jacket for his heartburn meds, then remembered the useless thing didn't have pockets and the meds were back in his apartment. What kind of idiot designed a jacket without pockets? His better one had been ruined in a minor explosion. By now his head was thumping and his esophagus burning.

"We want you to take your regular R&R!" his company psyche officer had transmitted the week before. "We're not spending millions for you to have a breakdown because you're too cement-headed to take care of yourself! Stop endangering the job! Take a trip to one of the other cities and do some sightseeing."

The woman sounded threatening, but Weston hadn't given her serious thought. He always focused on a job like a laser - they'd hired him knowing that about him. All he wanted was to get this thing done without time extensions. If he had to endure an extension, then they'd indeed see someone explode.

Meanwhile, Harwood Jamison IV, known to cronies as "Har," hiked up his backpack and began the series of airlocks in exiting the ship. To the other arrivals, who knew him pretty well by now (some approving, some not), he appeared as he actually was - a happy-go-lucky ne'er-do-well, lanky and good looking with trusting blue eyes and shaggy blond hair. He brought to mind tennis games in casual whites, gin and tonics, country club dances and debutantes, everything he wasn't anymore.

"Hey," he said to the person behind him, a man in the food preservation business, "can you believe we're actually on Mars? Can you believe it, man?"

"Well, it's true, so get over it," snapped the man.

Har shrugged good-naturedly and announced, "Something must have crawled up his butt!" He laughed and a couple of others joined him.

"Hey," he said, "you guys wanna get something to drink soon as they let us out?"

A young woman ahead of him turned around. "Sounds good to me. I could certainly unwind after being stuck in this tin can. Hey, I like your jacket."

Har shot her a grin. "We're on!" He looked down at his jacket, a well-cut, navy blue, tailored affair with several handy pockets. "You like this? It's very talented, but it's got a few kinks."

She didn't seem interested in the jacket's kinks.

After major red tape, they made good on their plans and located the only bar yet of any consequence in New Paris, "Le Chat Vert." With a vodka martini in front of the girl and a pint of ale in Har's hand, they were ready for conversation.

"Your name?" said Har.

"Valenteen. I'm here to entertain the troops, so to speak."

He nodded. "Are you a singer?"

"Among other things," Valenteen said drily. "What brings you here?"

Har laughed. Pretty much everything made him laugh. He had what his cynical brother-in-law called "good brain chemicals." "I'm a remittance man," he said.

"What's that exactly?" asked Valenteen.

"My relatives pay me to stay away."

"You're kidding! I'd love it if people paid me to do that!"

Har chuckled and glanced down at his drink. "Well...I don't know, honey. I embarrass them. A few months ago, I had another little screw up and this time they all got together, even the cousins, and decided I needed to *really* get out of town. Hong Kong wouldn't do anymore. I've never seen Grandfather so pissed. They figured Mars would be a good way to keep me out of their hair, so here I am in New Paris even if it's not finished."

Valenteen took a slow sip of her martini. "I figured I'd come here to get in on the ground floor. Not much competition yet."

Har smiled. "Wanna refill?"

After the bartender complied, he said to Valenteen. "Wonder where I can pick up some snort."

Across the city, Weston received another transmission, this time from Hoffmeyer Schmidt, a city planner. The highbrow's horsy face filled the screen. "The arena is important, yes, very much so," he said, "but the financial district is top priority. We need it by deadline. Our backers come from all over the globe, Dow, you know that. They'll be watching like hawks on amphetamines, understand?"

What was wrong with him, Weston wondered. Not the city planner, but Weston himself. Why was he growing so contemptuous towards this project? "All right," he replied.

"Good," said bony neck. "Get to it."

Five minutes later, Mya buzzed on. She was dressed up, wearing fancy earrings and a weird, ethnic hat.

"Westie, sweetness?" she said. "How are you?"

"Looks like you're all dressed up," he said, voice neutral.

"Yeah!" Her face glowed with happiness. "Department dinner. This famous cultural anthropologist is speaking. He's the one who analyzed those giant skeletons they found in Kentucky. I am sooooo excited. A few of us might get to have drinks with him later. And for such a reputation, he's only thirty-five!"

Why did she have to get all fancied up for that, he wondered. And this jerk was only thirty-five? He was sullen. "Well, have a good time."

"Westie, what's the matter? You seem so...I don't know..."

"Gotta go," he said briskly. "They're buzzing me."

83

Her face registered disappointment. "Well, okay, but you know I won't be able to call you for three days. I've got that field trip to Mexico and there's very little reception."

"Yeah," he said, "well, enjoy your night out," and clicked off.

Then he felt like a complete jackass. His fingers touched the now blank screen and lingered there.

All systems were down on Avenue C. "I'm running my second diagnostic," said Pinot. "The Grik's doing fine at the Arena. Wasn't any big deal. This problem here is way worse. Temp control, elevators and lights out. Street bounce gone, no gray water getting to the trees. Can't figure it out. I gotta get something to eat or I'll keel."

Weston felt like running amok. He hated this stupid planet, his loneliness, what was going on with Mya, and much of the time, he hated himself.

"Go eat," he said to Pinot. "Then go home and sleep. Come in when you wake up. I don't give a shit. I'm going out and get sloshed. Don't call me."

"But the trees, Boss! They're figs, but they still need *some* moisture!"

"Screw the trees!" snapped Weston.

Which was how he ended up in Le Chat Vert and acquired the new jacket with a few kinks in it Har had failed to describe.

Weston arose next morning in a much better mood. On his way out, he slipped on is new acquisition and tried not to wonder if Mya had come home after the party or gone somewhere else with Mr. World Famous.

He arrived at Avenue C to see Pinot fussing about the fig trees along the street's walkways, the man's forehead creased in worry. Weston felt guilty for having dismissed the trees so glibly.

84

"Relax, Pinot, we'll figure it out. Show me your data from yesterday."

Pinot gave one particularly dry looking tree a motherly pat before whipping out his datahold. Weston pulled out the viewer from his own, hooked it over his ear and opened a screen in front of his face. Pinot transmitted the data. "There does seem to be a glitch in section twenty-six, see?"

"Hmmmm," said Weston. He headed for the underground entrance to the controls with Pinot at his heels.

Once down there, he danced his fingers over the grid controls until he located twenty-six. "There *was* a glitch and now there isn't. Wait. What's this? What turned the pump off?"

Pinot moved in closer. "Yeah, but it's more the energy stream than the pump, right? Some kind of disruption in communication from the main computers."

Both men stood, figuratively scratching their heads. Weston said, "What's the weather been out there?"

"There was a dust storm yesterday," said Pinot. "According to one report, about eight hundred miles wide, but it only lasted three hours. You didn't see the dust devils out there?"

"Missed it," said Weston.

"You think maybe it messed with the sensors? A temporary off-line situation? Then the pump never kicked back on."

"Let's look," said Weston.

When they got to section twenty-six's pump, it was dead silent. "Merde," said Pinot.

"Merde? You're swearing in French now?"

"Keeps me in a New Paris mood," said Pinot. "See here, it should have kicked back on, interruption or no interruption."

85

"Bad part somewhere then," said Weston, crouching.

"Could be a leak somewhere too," said Pinot, pointing. "Let's follow this down the avenue."

Weston dreaded the narrow underground passages, but followed his foreman.

"Look!" cried Pinot. "This wasn't here yesterday."

Weston crowded him. What he saw twisted his already sore gut. "Holy crap, stop it up!" he yelled. "No water to waste here!"

"Well, it's not exactly wasted," said Pinot, infuriatingly calm, "being that it's collected below and pumped back up."

"Not a hundred percent!" yelled Weston. He twirled around, smacked his head into a pipe and slipped on the wet floor, landing on his back in a cool stream heading somewhere down the line. He was half soaked.

Pinot checked what he could see of the pipes. "There's a leak in the main somewhere," he said.

"Get a crew out," barked Weston as he struggled to his feet. "If they have to work all day and night, then they do!"

The drenched jacket seemed to have grown more form fitting and Weston remembered Har's warning.

"Damn," he said. "I'm going to go change and grab something to eat while you get the crew out. Get Patel and Solokov if you can."

He stepped into a tram, planning to head home, but when he saw he was approaching a little sandwich place, hopped off to eat first, wet or not.

By the time he ordered, he felt odd. Haughtily superior, for one thing, something he never normally felt. Then he found himself annoyed with the woman at an adjoining table because her boots clashed with her outfit. Ordinarily, he rarely noticed clothing and should he happen to be glancing at a woman (of course he didn't make a habit of *that* after his engagement to Mya), his main interest would be breasts or rear, certainly not her *outfit*. But here he was, wondering what had possessed her to combine tan boots with that gray and black ensemble. It just didn't work. Not only that, her suit widened her form instead of elongating it.

He shut his eyes and shook himself, but then spotted a waiter carrying a tray and thought, *carries himself well, could work the runway, yes!*

Panicked, Weston jumped to his feet to run from the place, when his own waiter appeared with his food. "Something the matter, sir?" he said.

"Uh...uh, no, no," Weston stuttered as he lowered himself into his chair. He managed to cram down half his sandwich before making his escape.

Back in his apartment, he stripped off his clothes and noticed that the jacket had indeed seemed to shrink. But Har said just to dry it out, right?

Knowing how to trick the water settings, he took longer than his permitted allotment of shower. He found himself mentally running over the clothing hanging in his closet and tsk-tsking in his mind. *What on earth was I thinking? Those hideous baggy olive pants, those god-awful puke brown shoes?*

What on Earth, he meant *Mars*, was wrong with him?

Exhausted, he collapsed onto the bed. Maybe it was being in a city names New Paris? Something about the air and the street names? Parisians were traditionally overly interested in clothing, no? That had to be it. Snore.

A buzz from Pinot woke him. "Boss, we found the leak. The pipe was eroded. Solokov is on it."

"Uh, good, Pinot," Weston murmured, still half asleep. "Listen, I kinda need a day off. Not up to par, so carry on."

Weston Dow *never* took time off. But he fell back to sleep and didn't wake until seven that evening.

Almost dry, the jacket looked spiffy when Weston added it to his ensemble. He leaned into his bathroom mirror and said, "We really must grow out that hair," then jerked back in horror. Why was he caring about his stupid haircut? He wore it short because it was convenient. He bent back to the mirror. Longish might look good on him, maybe sort of hanging in his eyes. Sexy.

At the tram station he studied the city list on the wall, searching for somewhere new to have dinner, somewhere more stylish. There were only five working restaurants open at this date and two were breakfast/lunch joints. The only one remotely posh was Chez Arlene on Rue Morot.

He swept into the place in an oddly cocky manner and demanded a side table so he could "peruse the room." When he ordered a gin and tonic with a twist of lime, the obnoxious waiter laughed. "Sorry, Sir, but I'm not sure you're aware that we're on *Mars?* I'm afraid at this point, we only have wine, vodka and beer."

Weston performed a masterful eye roll. *"Mon Dieu,"* he said. "I'll have to make do with an Evansfeld Chardonnay Reserve '62. Chilled, please."

The waiter laughed so hard he doubled over. "Forgive me," he said, eyes teary, once he'd caught his breath. "Apparently, you're suffering some kind of delusion. I repeat, WE'RE ON MARS. The wines are generic stuff made over in N'Chicago and N'Beijing. There's dry white, dry red and rosé, take your pick."

Weston sniffed and chose the white. "I'll have the disgusting soy chicken," he said, flipping the menu at the waiter.

That night Mya transmitted from Mexico. "Surprise! They have a system in the hotel! We got here yesterday and thank God because I'm so filthy I'd commit a serious crime for a bath. How is my Westie? I so miss you. You'd love this little town, it's sooooo cute."

"My God, Mya," Weston exclaimed, "what *did* you do to your hair? It needs serious conditioning. The ends are all flyaway!"

Mya's face enlarged as she moved closer to her screen. "Weston? Are you feeling all right?"

"Really energetic, actually," he said. "Ready to go dancing!"

"*Dancing?*" Mya looked seriously alarmed. There was a moment of static, then she returned, quite perturbed. "You *hate* to dance. What's the matter with you?"

He felt a wave of emotion roll over him and suddenly found that he was weeping.

"Westie? What's the matter, honey?"

A gigantic sob erupted from his mouth. "It's...it's just too much! I can't *stand* it!" he blubbered. "And people are so stupid! So disloyal, so *despicable!*"

"Weston, I want you to get on the next transport out of there and come home! Who cares if you make a bunch of money? I don't! Don't say you're doing it for me because you're not! You come home now!"

Weston stood up and stared blankly around his room. He gave a quick glance at the screen, then said, "I have to go, Mya." Another sob was building up; such a peculiar crashing back and forth of moods. He raised a hand to his forehead and said in French, *Si je ne dors pas, je vais mourir!* and with a grand gesture, switched off the screen and passed out on his bed.

Next morning Weston showed up for his weekly report to Klando ten minutes late and in a temper.

"What happened to *you*?" said Klando. The man was his usual shiny self, neatly ensconced behind his perfectly arranged desk. "You look like hell."

"Hell, do I?" snapped Weston, arms akimbo. "*Casse-toi!* What do you know of how I feel, stuck in this godforsaken hole, so far from everything that matters that I might as well be *dead!*" Why was he cursing in French? He hardly knew any French. Was he having a complete breakdown?

Klando looked astonished. "Weston, for heaven's sake, sit down, lighten up. Let me get you a cup of tea."

With intense effort, Weston refrained from blurting out the strange array of emotions he was enduring. Unfortunately, Klando snapped this attempt at self-control.

"Katsumi Sasaki and Gabriela Moretti arrived on yesterday's flight. Mr. Sasaki had a bit of stomach trouble so is resting. They'll be ready to start work tomorrow."

Weston drew a blank. "Who?"

"The first financial people from Eurobank. They'll be opening their offices by the end of the week. I assume Avenue C is now topnotch?"

"What?" Weston slammed his fist on Klando's desk. "I didn't expect them till *next* flight!"

"Well, Weston, you knew we have to get things operating. Every flight is bringing more citizens. How do you expect this place to run without a banking system?"

"I-I thought it could run perfectly well using Earth banks! Doesn't New Beijing do that?"

"Well, yeah, but you know the Chinese like to keep control. New Chicago has its own system and so will we."

Weston wailed. "I simply cannot imagine why you're so cruel! You *know* how fragile my nerves are, how unable I am to work when treated with such inconsideration!" He sprang from the desk and dramatically drew his hand across his forehead. "I think you're doing this just for the pleasure of *tormenting* me!"

Klando's cheeks flushed. "I have no idea what you're talking about, and I must say your behavior is quite bizarre! It's *you* who are trying to squelch normal functioning!"

Weston felt another weird shift inside him. "It's always *men* who make a mess of everything they touch!" he yelled. "If women were in charge, things would never reach this state of affairs!"

"*What* state of affairs?" demanded Klando. "And women *are* in charge! What do you call Maria Fenn in Medical and Julia Duval in Street Maintenance?"

Weston hesitated, then distractedly waved an arm. "Oh, you know, everything, just *everything.*" He turned and made for the door.

"Just a minute," said Klando. "I expect Avenue C running by tomorrow, 8:00 am, is that clear? After that, you report to Medical for a complete workup!"

"Yes, *sir*," said Weston, with a smirk and hard military salute as he flounced out.

Heading to Avenue C, he had a crazy urge to buy a brilliant white scarf to dress up the jacket. As there was only one operating clothing store in New Paris and getting to the two other cities half a world away not yet feasible for any kind of quick, personal run, he'd have to make do. But Pinot buzzed him, how annoying, and it was imperative that he get to work.

Next to Pinot stood a severe looking woman, her attention riveted on her datahold. She'd floated a screen in front of her face and was flicking her fingers around in it. For a fleeting second, Weston found her uncommonly attractive, then suddenly repulsive. These moods were disturbing. He wondered briefly if he could have a brain tumor.

"Boss, this is Gabriela Moretti from Eurobank." Pinot gave Weston his little eye scrunch that signaled a sexy female.

Weston jerked. "I thought you people weren't starting till tomorrow?"

Gabriela shut down her screen and looked at Weston for the first time. Her eyes were long and lustrous. "I didn't know I was banned from the office until then. Mr. Klando didn't-"

Weston cut her off. "He *wouldn't*," he said, voice high and sarcastic. "He just doesn't *care* that we aren't finished! The grid is off, we've been at it for hours and hours! And I've got the most *splitting* headache!"

Gabriela gave him a studied look. "Honey," she said, "I know exactly how you feel." She cast a glance at Pinot, then said to Weston, "Why don't you and I go get ourselves a little something to calm our nerves, and let Mr. Pinot here handle this mess."

Weston shot her a look of gratitude. Finally, someone who understood! "Oh yes, let's go *do* that!"

She tucked her arm through his and walked him off down Avenue C, a delightful bounce in her step.

Le Chat Vert was hopping for 10:30 am MT. First thing Weston saw was Valenteen at the bar, looking worse the wear with her arm draped around a huge Nigerian businessman.

"Look, those people are leaving," said Gabriela, making a beeline for a table.

Weston was fascinated, all parts of him, whatever those now were, by the mix of customers and Gabriela herself. She was sexy, he could see that, though he felt nothing in that vein at the moment. He did appreciate her style. She had an understated way about her - quietly dominating, utterly sure of her power.

Once settled, she said, "So, do you have a lover here yet, Weston?"

Was she coming on to him? "Um...I'm engaged," he said.

The waiter took their orders and whisked away.

"How nice," she said. "Will he be living here on Mars with you?"

After a long pause, Weston muttered, "'He?'"

An even longer pause before Gabriela said, "Not a he?"

He felt faint. He should get to Medical right then, but before he could suggest some reason for doing so, the now familiar wave moved over him and he was someone else. "I'll tell you," he said loudly, "if I could do it all over, I'd be a *nun*! No more stupid, lying *bastards*! No husbands telling you they're going on wine buying trips to Provence when they're actually taking their mistress to Barcelona, *cette espèce de con!*"

Gabriela looked at him steadily. "Weston, do you suffer from multiple personality disorder?"

Har entered the bar, a woman on each arm. After a cheerful interchange with the bartender, he sauntered along with his retinue, suddenly stopping in happy surprise. "Weston! How are you? Been thinking about you, wondering how you're getting along." His eyes darted to the jacket.

Weston sprang from his seat. "I see that being a typical self-centered lothario, you're using and abusing the females! Just what do *they* get out of it, I'd like to know! Money?"

Har twisted his mouth thoughtfully, a guilty look in his eyes. "Uh oh," he said. "You got the jacket wet, didn't you?"

"Shit happens," yelled Weston. Everyone in the Le Chat Vert looked in his direction.

Har gently took his arm, but Weston flipped him off.

"Listen," Har whispered. "We need to talk. Let's just move over there?" He tilted his head toward the entrance hallway. "Gotta speak to you about that jacket, bro."

Weston looked at Gabriela.

Har turned to his ladies. "You girls get us a table if you can find one," and they giggled their way through the room.

In the hall, Weston said belligerently, "What's this about?"

Har cleared his throat. "Ya see, there was something I failed to mention about your jacket. Before I wore it, it had two other owners."

"Yeah, so what?" said Weston, turning his head to check out the suit of a man leaning against the bar.

"Concentrate, Weston," said Har. "First, take off the jacket."

"What for?"

"Just do it, okay?"

Reluctantly, Weston stripped it off.

"Notice anything?"

Weston stood still. After a moment, he said, "I-I don't know...I feel..."

"Normal?" said Har.

"Well...better. I wouldn't say *normal.*"

"This jacket...originally sort of fell off a transport, know what I mean?"

"Stolen?"

"Not exactly. Part of a batch gone wrong. Apparently, instead of performing properly, this baby somehow taps into your own info chip, inserting data of its own from former wearers. You're supposed to be able to clear clothing if you pass it on to a new owner, but this jacket won't clear."

"What?" said Weston. "You say it hacks into my chip? Who's downloading the data?"

"No one's listening. The company that made it planned to destroy the defective lot. Their intentions were good, but some employee sneaked one or more of them out to sell on the black market."

"How do you know all this?"

"The owner of the jacket before me was Paul Swain, a fashion designer from Milan I met in a night club. He was Belgian but mostly lived in Italy. He was in a bit of a mess and I helped him out. In return, he gave me the jacket. He told me about it though and about its former owner."

"Yeah," said Weston, "kind of him to tell you, unlike your own behavior."

Har looked sheepish. "Yeah, I was a shit. I was desperate for the money. I'm seriously sorry."

Weston "harrumphed." It was difficult to be angry with Har; there was something about him. "The former owner was...?" He paused. "Let me guess. A really pissed off French woman?"

"You're good. That was Delphine Morel. She and her husband Roger owned a small brasserie in Montmartre. She learned he was having an affair with the wife of another restaurant owner - he'd take the mistress

95

on wine buying trips. Anyway, ole Delphine got so exaspérée, she started putting hair in his food, trying to kill him. She let herself go, something French women rarely do, and got too fat for even a smart jacket, so she gave it to Paul."

"How'd she know Paul from Milan?"

"He often went to Paris and while there, frequented Delphine's brasserie. She confided in him."

"Where'd she get the jacket in the first place?"

"On the Left Bank. She knew its story when she bought it, but it was a real bargain and being the first wearer, she didn't have any problems. But Paul did."

"What happened to him?"

"He didn't mind the female input, but the angry part, he didn't care for. Paul's a friendly guy, so feeling like putting an axe in somebody's head wasn't too pleasant. He'd figured out the stuff only happened if you got the jacket wet and disappeared once it had thoroughly dried which can take two full days, so he was careful. He liked the stylish cut and was willing put up with its limitations. I apologize for not being straight with you, Weston. I hope it didn't mess up your life too much."

Weston thought about being his old straight and narrow self again. Somehow it seemed boring.

"You know, Har, I'm kind of glad this happened."

"Why do you say that?"

"While it wasn't *fun,* it was *interesting* to be like someone else. I'm not saying I'd want to do it all the time, but I'm glad I experienced it for a while." He paused and then was alarmed. "You think it messed up my chip permanently?"

Har shrugged. "I don't think so. Mine's okay. You might have it checked though." He laughed. "Frankly, I don't care if mine *is* messed up. I'm not sure I want them knowing my data anyway."

Weston nodded, then suddenly remembered Gabriela. "Well, better go."

"Are you going to ditch the jacket now?" asked Har.

"Hell no," said Weston.

Gabriela listened to the story, her expression one of partial doubt.

"You're welcome to try it," said Weston. "Put it on. Give it a shot under your shower."

She hesitated and shook her head. Her eyes narrowed. "So this is your real self then? A bit stiff, but I enjoy traditionally masculine men." She lowered her head and looked up at him through long, black lashes. "Wouldn't want to hook up with one permanently, but for friendly benefits...."

Weston stood up so fast, his chair clattered. "I gotta get going," he mumbled, not making eye contact. He was outside the bar in a matter of seconds and didn't look back. A quick trip to apologize to Klando, then home to transmit in private.

"I'm on a break, but don't have long," said Mya. "How are you, Baby? I've been so worried."

"I'm fine," Weston said with great emotion. "I have a really good story to tell you. And Mya? I adore you. I'm going to be more open about feelings and all, I promise."

The golden sky sparkled over the dome as Weston made his way to Avenue C. So elated was he to be himself, he made the mental shift from viewing the street as a coming nest of banker vermin to one where future generations would stroll and lunch among the flowering figs.

Margaret Karmazin's credits include stories published in many literary and national magazines. She has been nominated for Pushcart awards, and had a story nominated for the 2010 Million Writers Award. She has stories included in several anthologies and a collection of short stories, RISK.

Menagerie
by Stephen McQuiggan

It was the smell of the pet shop that Barney loved most of all; the sawdust, the birdseed, the strange underlying exotic scent that he always attributed to snakeskin. Although he had no reason to be here he came in all the time and stayed so long that Malone, the short-tempered proprietor, was fond of asking him if he'd like a job.

Occasionally Barney bought some fish-food for goldfish he didn't have, just to get a glimpse of Raga the Burmese python (yellow as stomach lining), see the monitor lizards, the parrots, and best of all, listen to the chirping of the guinea pigs. He avoided the rats though – he was plagued by dreams of them gnawing through wires – and the tropical fish just bored him; little more than floating, coloured leaves.

Barney was slowly making his way to the counter when something caught his eye over by the dry dogfood: a cage that housed a strange black ball of fur – a moving pom-pom – that appeared to be singing quietly to itself. Barney dropped his fish-food on the floor, forgetting even to say 'Hi' to Raga in his hurry to investigate. As soon as he reached the cage the singing stopped.

He laughed out of pure joy just looking at it – it had been years since he'd laughed in such a way – a laugh free of even the slightest tinge of cynicism, without a shadow of malice. Looking at the creature, Barney felt about five years old and just like a kid he knew he wanted it now, above all else.

'What the hell is that?' he asked Malone, trying not to sound too interested; Malone was a good sort at heart, but he had a nasty habit of adapting his pricing at the slightest glint of enthusiasm in a customer's eye. Best to feign indifference and get the ball of fluff at a reasonable rate.

'What...*that*?' Malone nodded toward the cage where Barney stood, as if he thought he were perhaps enquiring after his manky rabbits or emaciated gerbils. 'That, my friend, is a Bavarian Mermit.'

Barney smiled. Even the name was too damn cute. Anne Marie would have a fucking stroke when he brought it home; she would probably ball him on the spot. As presents went, this was way beyond garage flowers and gloopy chocolates. This was on a par with engagement rings. 'How much?' he asked, a little too casually.

Barney noticed for the first time the man and the little girl standing behind Malone and a strange fear sprouted in his belly, sending tendrils of angst pulsating through him. The man looked stern, as if even his farts would have an authoritative tone, but that wasn't what bothered Barney most. It was the fact that the stranger was immaculately dressed that really needled him; the bespoke suit was made of some futuristic, and no doubt ridiculously expensive, fabric. His knuckles were weighed down with gold.

Barney had no doubt that Mr Rich was here solely to purchase the Mermit – why else would a man of his refinement grace such a place as this? It was obviously a present for the spoiled little girl by his side who, judging by the way she clung to his hand, must be his daughter. Mr Rich did not look like the kind of person who would quibble over money, even at Malone's top end.

'How much?' Barney asked again, unable to keep the desperation seeping into his voice. Malone scratched his chin, though Barney knew the figure was indelibly tattooed in the greasy ledger of his brain.

'He's not really for sale,' Malone sighed. 'He's the only one I have and that I'm ever likely to get. He's a bit of a rarity, know what I mean?'

Barney suppressed an urge to shake him. He risked a glance over at Mr Rich and his daughter; they remained silent, content to watch. He's waiting until I hit my limit, Barney thought, then he'll jump in and gazump me, just to impress his pampered little bitch. 'Name your price,' Barney said, already calculating how much he could sell, how much he could borrow, to get his hands on the damn Mermit.

Malone turned to Mr Rich, a sly smile on his face, a wink glinting in his eye; it made Barney all the more determined to beat them at their own game. He felt his anger rising, like something electrical fizzing and crackling in his core, so he walked to the window whilst Malone pretended to mull over the situation. He couldn't allow himself to lose his temper; it would only give Malone the excuse he needed to sell the Mermit to his sneering, silent customer.

'I doubt you could afford it,' the shopkeeper said eventually.

Barney bit his lip, counting to ten as he gazed on the empty street outside. No traffic, no people, no trees, just the shadows of the grey buildings opposite, buildings that looked false somehow, as if they were made of cardboard and paint. He must have gone into some of them before – there was a butcher's, a pub, a newsagent's – but he had no recollection of it. He had no real memory of anything save this shop; the all consuming need to own the Mermit had frazzled his circuits, left no room for anything else.

There were times when Barney struggled to remember anything at all save the store; his very dreams were shadowed by the monochrome slats of cage bars. Was the outside world so bad that he had to find sanctuary here, looking on miserly Malone as some sort of surrogate father? The thought drew a bloodless smile but left a crackling in his gut.

He had Anne Marie after all, and she would be so overwhelmed when she saw the Mermit their petty rowing would cease and they could finally get round to starting that family they always talked of. Yet thoughts of Anne Marie were tainted by the fact that, bathed in the bright light and jungle chirp of the store, her face was just a vague impressionistic blur on which to sketch even vaguer emotions.

Gazing out onto the silent unreal street it was possible to believe his wife, his life, was nothing more than a delusion, a rogue program constructed for solace. How had he allowed things to drift so far? Only the Mermit could salvage this, save him from this crippling ennui. He had to have it, even if he had to kill.

'You'd be surprised what I could afford,' he said, turning to Malone, his anger spitting volts when he saw how the rich man was regarding him, like he was an exhibit in a zoo. 'Name your price.'

'Well now,' mused Malone, 'what have you got in your pockets? That's a good place to start.'

Barney delved deep into his jeans, pulling out a handful of lint and a fistful of nothing. The little girl sniggered and Barney held onto the fists. 'I can get the money, don't you worry yourself about that.'

He sauntered back over to the cages once more to look at the Mermit, to check if it was really worth it; the little creature let out a musical trill at his approach, holding out two tiny paws in greeting, and Barney's mind was made up. An idea suddenly occurred to him, an idea so against the grain that he momentarily faltered; it was so alien, so *exciting*, he felt his brain must have been rewired by the Devil himself.

He could never afford the Mermit, but he *could* steal it. He could trick Malone into letting him hold it, then leg it out of the shop. Of course, that would mean he could never return but once he had the Mermit what need would he have to waste his days staring at stationary reptiles or mean eyed rodents?

'Mind if I pop him out of the cage for a closer look?' He snuck a peek at Malone but the shopkeeper was, in his turn, regarding Mr Rich and his daughter. He's wondering, thought Barney, if old Moneybags will still want to buy the Mermit if it's been soiled by my peasant hands.

Some circuit in Barney's head sparked with suppressed rage and, without waiting for an answer, he opened the cage door and began coaxing the little fur-ball toward his trembling hands. The Mermit sniffed at his fingers; its wet nose tickled, drawing the smile back on his face. It hesitated, scuttling back into its straw nest before venturing tentatively back out once more, all puffed up in cute bravado.

'I wouldn't do that if I were you,' Malone was saying, the rest of his warning lost beneath the little girl's petulant demands to hold it too.

Barney was deaf to everything but the Mermit's delicate fluting song. As soon as it got close enough he shot out both hands and snatched it up, pulling it from the cage, holding it aloft like a trophy. Mr Rich had a contemptuous smirk on his oily face, the little girl looked agreeably jealous, and Malone was all pacifying hand gestures and pleas to put the Mermit back.

Barney was about to crow some cutting, pithy aphorism when a bolt of white hot pain travelled instantaneously from his finger to every nerve ending in his body. He let out an undignified yelp, shaking his hand furiously to no avail; the creature's razor teeth were embedded in his knuckles whilst its fluffy body wobbled like a stripper's tassels.

'Easy, easy!' Malone was yelling, running toward him; but the pain was frying his circuits, the pain was too much to bear. Barney grabbed the Mermit and began squeezing for all he was worth, figuring if he lost a finger it would be a small price to pay to be rid of the vicious little bastard dangling from his digit.

There was a mechanical squeak, a brief storm of blue sparks, a wisp of acrid smoke; the Mermit lay in a mashed pulp on the shop floor, wires and circuitry fizzing and farting in a small pool of blood.

'It's a toy,' Barney said, in a voice comical with disbelief. 'You were going to take me for everything I had and then palm me off with a fucking wind-up toy.'

The gall of Malone, the sheer cheek of the man, caused something to pop in his head. He let out a bellow that made Mr Rich frown and reach a protective arm around his crying daughter. Then Barney began to open cages. He threw a rabbit on the floor and stamped on it; clumps of wiring stuck to the sole of his boot along with the gore.

'Hey!' Malone was approaching him as if squaring to fight but Barney was ready to take on all comers.

'They're all gadgets, aren't they, eh?' He tipped over a fish tank, knocked a few budgies off their perch, launched a gerbil at the wall; a dervish of disgust. 'What kind of racket are you running here, Malone?'

The shopkeeper was looking apologetically at Mr Rich and his teary eyed little girl. 'I'm so sorry about this, it's never happened before. You might want to cover the child's eyes whilst I rectify the problem.'

Malone snaked out a long arm, gripping Barney by the neck and all the anger, all the rage seeped out of him as if Malone had flicked a switch. Before he could summon up even a token protest, his trousers and pants were yanked down to his ankles and Malone was busily inserting two fingers where Barney was certain they had absolutely no right to be.

He collapsed at the exact moment of penetration. In his prone line of sight he could still see Mr Rich, his hand clamped over his daughter's eyes, then the vision became static, lost colour, and the word REBOOT began flashing in an angry red font and the world began to fade. As his very essence drained down to a single bright dot shining in an unimaginable void, Barney heard the girl still whining and her father asking, 'How much for one of those Mermits?'

Stephen McQuiggan was the original author of the bible; he vowed never to write again after the publishers removed the dinosaurs and the spectacular alien abduction ending from the final edit. His other, lesser known, novels are *A Pig's View Of Heaven* and *Trip A Dwarf.*

Second Chances

By Anthony Engebretson

The old man didn't know where he was, but he didn't think much about it.

He at least knew he was in the back of a large vehicle, most likely an SUV. It looked nice and new, or at least clean. He thought it'd have that new car scent, but he couldn't smell much of anything. He shrugged that fact away; it was no doubt a symptom of age.

His eyes were at least working fine. He could see two men in the front seat. They were bulky and suited, looking like secret service agents. The old man called them boy scouts. He knew not to fuss with them, even though he didn't know why.

The vehicle felt somewhat familiar to him, like he had ridden it many times before. Yet he couldn't remember a single instance.

Looking out the tinted windows, he could see palm trees and some rundown buildings cast against a grey, muggy morning. The street was packed with cars bearing California license plates crawling and honking along their morning commute. He guessed he was somewhere in L.A.

The Hollywood sign out his starboard window proved him right. He had been to Hollywood once before, though it had been much different back then. Joan Crawford, Cary Grant and Marilyn Monroe had been the talk of the town, everything had been less smoggy and the traffic more bearable.

The vehicle came to a halt in front of a squat, tan and grey building. The old man thought it looked like someone had glued a bunch of squares and rectangles together and slapped windows on them. One of the boy scouts craned his meaty neck to face the old man.

"Time to go to work," he said.

"Okay," the old man replied.

He didn't know what kind of work he could do at this age. But again, he knew better than to fuss.

The boy scouts escorted him up the stairs. They were only going three floors up, but each step seemed to take ages. The old man felt neither exhaustion nor pain in his joints. He felt like he could run a mile if he wanted to. Yet he shambled and hunched as if he couldn't stop playing old.

At least the climb gave him an opportunity to think. If he couldn't think of *why* he was here, he could at least consider *who* he was.

His name was Freddy Allen. He was a retired professor of history. His main subject of interest was the history of the Royal Navy; he had always been fascinated by how a small island could dominate the world for so long. He was a widower. He had two kids: Freddy Jr. and Sandra. Sandra was gone—car accident. He hadn't spoken to Junior in years.

At first, these memories came to him with the detachment of remembering historical facts. But then they triggered feelings; loathsome, painful feelings that squeezed and suffocated him. He took a deep breath and focused on the climb.

When they reached the third floor, one of the boy scouts pointed to a white door at the end of the hall.

"He's in there," he said. "You'll know what to do."

"Okie-Dokie," Freddy mumbled.

As he hobbled to the door, he had a vivid memory of being a teenage girl walking up to her parents' house. They had sobbed when they saw her. She thought it was embarrassing and rolled her eyes. It only made them sob more. Like a flash-in-the-pan, the memory was gone.

He gave the door two knocks. Immediately after the second knock, it flew open. There stood a tan, blonde young man in a colorful shirt and shorts showcasing a lean body. Freddy had no ideas who this was until he looked into the man's blue eyes.

"Simon?" he asked.

The young man said nothing. Instead he smacked his lips like he had just eaten peanut butter. Freddy smiled, this was Simon all right. He always had a habit of smacking when he was nervous.

"Hello, my boy," Freddy said.

Simon's lips began to quiver.

"Poppy," he said, almost whispering.

Freddy winced; he never cared for that name. "Grandpa" sufficed.

Without warning, Simon broke down in tears and clung to Freddy. Not knowing what else to do, Freddy limply patted Simon's back.

As they embraced, Freddy realized something odd. He couldn't really *feel* his grandson's touch. All he had was a detached *sense* that they were touching. It was like touching something in a dream.

Before Freddy could think too much about this, Simon pulled away.

"So," he said, red-eyed and sniffling, "come inside?"

\#

Simon had a pretty swell place for himself. Freddy didn't necessarily know where it came from. Last he remembered, Simon was a starry-eyed kid heading off to acting school.

It was a small condo, but it had all a single young person needed and more: a kitchen, bedroom, bathroom, living room and laundry.

They made their way into the living room. Simon kept it very clean; the tiled flooring was swept and mopped and everything had been dusted. The furniture, television and exercise equipment were arranged in a way that kept the tiny space from feeling cluttered. Freddy couldn't help but smile, Simon had always been an organized kid—his grandma's grandson.

Suddenly, a black shape skittered across the floor and slipped under the couch.

"God damn it!" Freddy cried. Though it startled him, he kept his footing.

"Teach!" shouted Simon.

Beneath the couch, Freddy could see the glowing green eyes of a black cat glaring at him.

"I'm sorry Poppy," Simon said.

"Huh," Freddy muttered," cute."

He couldn't stand cats and was very allergic to them. To his surprise, he wasn't sneezing. Usually he would go into fits just being near a pet store. He decided this was only because Simon kept the place so clean.

The creature yowled and hissed at Freddy.

"Teach!" Simon shouted again.

"Not super friendly, is it?" asked Freddy.

"He usually loves people…" Simon immediately stopped himself as if realizing he was about to say something offensive.

Freddy absently nodded.

This gave him another flash-in-the-pan memory. An old woman greeting her beloved cats; they had yowled and hissed at her, too. It made her cry.

When the thought faded, Freddy examined a row of pictures along the fireplace mantle. Among them was a picture of Simon's parents, Junior and Emilia. Freddy was surprised at how grey and saggy they looked. Next to that was a photo of Simon—young, pale and pudgy, now *there* was the kid Freddy remembered—dressed as a cow for a school play. Next to the boy stood Freddy, not looking a day older or younger than he currently did, baring his teeth in the awkward sneer he called a smile. Even though Freddy hated how he looked in the picture, it gave him a warm feeling.

Next to that picture was a photo of the more tan and grown Simon. He was in a bar with his arm around a stocky, bearded man who looked about twice Simon's age.

"Now, who is this?" Freddy asked.

With a slight gasp, Simon swiped the picture from the mantle.

"It's nothing," Simon mumbled. "I forgot to take that down."

He marched to the entry closet and threw the photo inside.

Brushing this off, Freddy toured the rest of the condo.

#

The small desk adjacent to Simon's bed was the untidiest part of the whole apartment. It was cluttered with books, with titles like *Purpose Driven Life, Achieving Emotional Intelligence, and Building Your Future.* Among these self-help books was a little blue rag entitled *Britannia Rules the Waves* by Frederick Allen.

Freddy couldn't help but chuckle. He'd nearly forgotten about this old thing. He had only written it for one of his classes: "HISTORY

OF THE ROYAL NAVY". It served as a broad, simplified overview of Britain's navy from the late 16th century to the present (which was 1985 when the book was written).

"It was the first thing I read when I got the part," said Simon, who was lingering behind Freddy.

"What part?" Freddy asked.

"A couple years back I got this role on a show. It's a pirate show called 'Skull and Bones'. It's popular enough—not quite 'Game of Thrones' but…"

Freddy nodded, having no idea what the hell Simon was talking about.

"It's a recurring character, a commander in the British Navy," Simon said, shrugging dismissively.

"Well, that's really neat!" said Freddy, flashing a wide grin. He found the news genuinely exciting, but he had to play it up a bit to show it.

"Yeah," Simon continued in a monotone, "we're in the third season. My character's kind of gone rogue and has become this pirate hunter."

"Pirate hunter," Freddy said dreamily, "like Robert Maynard, the man who killed Blackbeard. Or Chalonor Ogle, who defeated Bartholomew Roberts."

"Sure," Simon said, "but my guy's fictional."

"Really neat!" Freddy said again.

Simon pointed to Freddy's little blue book. "That helped give me an idea for the setting."

"Pah!" Freddy scoffed. "There are better books out there."

"Well, I did read others to be sure. But none of them were written by you."

There was a long pause while Freddy considered how to respond to that. He decided he couldn't.

"At any rate, I'm proud of you," he said instead. "Let's hope for many more episodes."

Simon grimaced.

#

The tour concluded, they congregated in the kitchen. Freddy could still see Teach's little green eyes glaring at him from a corner of the living room.

"Can I, uh, get you anything?" Simon asked.

Freddy shook his head. He didn't know when he last ate, but he was the least hungry he'd ever been. Not that he felt full, but he didn't feel empty either.

Simon shut his eyes and pursed his lips as if he has just said something offensive. Freddy hated how tense the young man appeared.

"Hey," he said, putting a hand on his grandson's shoulder, "I'm enjoying myself, kiddo."

Simon gave a half-hearted smile and nodded. Freddy could see his hand trembling with Simon's shoulder. It made him uneasy, as he realized again that he couldn't actually feel Simon. He retracted his hand and dismissed this. It was as if some internal mechanism had commanded him to do so.

Sighing, Freddy looked around for something to lighten the mood. He turned to the refrigerator, which had several magnets, lists and wedding invitations stuck to it. Among these was an oddly familiar blue flyer. Before Freddy could read it, Simon swiped it away and shoved it into a drawer.

Shrugging this off, Freddy pointed to a small, circular magnet. It read: "My Heart Belongs to a Writer".

"You know," he chuckled, "I knew this English Professor, Jim Scopes. Great guy. He'd written a few novels in his day. I remember he always used to say, 'Folks, never fall in love with a writer. They'll break your heart and make you the villain in some story afterwards.'"

Simon nodded solemnly. There was a pained look in his face that Freddy couldn't stand seeing.

"What's up, kiddo?"

"Nothing," Simon said. He tensed his face, and the pained look was gone, as if he had squeezed if from his system.

"Is it the magnet?" Freddy asked; he felt increasingly frustrated.

"No. I mean, not—"

"Then take the damn thing down!"

Freddy swiped the magnet from the fridge and slammed it onto the counter.

When he raised his hand, the magnet was gone. He looked at the palm of his hand. There, the little white circle was stuck to his skin. He spread his fingers wide and tried to shake it off, but it wouldn't give.

"Must be glue on this thing," Freddy mumbled.

Simon said nothing, his mouth agape.

Freddy used his other hand to pry the magnet from his palm. It immediately hopped from his fingers and stuck to his bicep.

"Ain't that a kick in the head?" said Freddy. He was neither confused nor frightened by this phenomenon. He felt little but scholarly intrigue combined with child-like amusement. Meanwhile, Simon stared like a confused deer.

Chuckling, Freddy pulled the magnet from his bicep. It plopped onto his forehead. Suddenly, Freddy felt an intense pressure, like his skull was going to explode. Grunting, he pulled the magnet from his forehead and the pain instantly stopped.

"Christ," he gasped, gently setting the magnet on the table.

Suddenly, he had another flash-in-the-pan memory of talking to a classroom full of children. For some reason, he had been George Washington. Not an impersonator, the actual—

A vibration came from the still dumbstruck Simon's pocket. It took several vibrations before he finally pulled out his cell phone. It looked like a square candy bar to Freddy. Modern gizmos were beyond him.

Simon answered the call: "Hello?"

The phone's volume was loud and Freddy's hearing unusually strong enough for him to hear a mumbling voice on the other line. It was a high-pitched man's voice. Freddy couldn't hear everything said, but he could make out the words "Chances" and "Rental".

"Uh, we're doing great," Simon said, nervously glancing at Freddy.

The voice went into a long-winded mumble. Freddy could hear the words "Tracker", "Second", and "Happened".

"Oh, uh, he was playing with a magnet."

The voice continued mumbling. The words and phrases Freddy discerned were: "Don't", "Let", "Early", "Model", "Machines", and "Liable".

Simon shut his eyes and lowered his head. "I understand," he said.

The voice mumbled a quick sentence that sounded like: "Have a great day!"

"You too," said Simon. Putting his phone away, he turned to Freddy. "Come on Poppy, let's get out of the kitchen."

"Who was that?" Freddy asked.

"Nobody," Simon said, absently. "It was about... um... Teach."

114

Freddy had no idea how such a fine actor could be such a bad liar. He thought about what he had heard. Why were the words "Prototypes" and "Machines" thrown around?

A sudden impulse in his brain told him to look at the flyer Simon had swiped away. He opened the drawer where the blue sheet lay and pulled it out.

"No!" Simon shouted. But he only stood there stiffly.

In cursive text were the words, "Second Chances". Below it were stock photos: a happy old man reading to a child, a happy group of young adults celebrating a birthday party and a happy middle-aged couple sitting on a beach. Below the pictures were the words: "Goodbye is no longer the end." Below that it read: "A Delambre Robotics program". At the very bottom was a website address.

Freddy suddenly had a jolt. It was the sensation of waking after a vivid dream. The flash-in-the-pan memories, the magnet, the fact that he couldn't physically feel anything, couldn't remember the past few years of his life and that this seemed like a familiar act—it all pointed to an absurd, but undeniable truth.

"Simon?" he asked. His stomach tightened, if he could call it a stomach.

"Yeah?" Simon's voice quivered and his skin had paled into a faded pink color.

"I'm a machine, aren't I?"

#

Freddy knew his way around a computer. Thank god he'd taken typing in high school. But Simon's laptop was so flat, he wondered how it could even function.

"How do I get on the web?" he asked.

115

Simon didn't respond, he just sat beside Freddy on the living room couch. He looked like an alert prairie dog.

Freddy figured it out. The first thing he did was confirm that he, Freddy Allen, was dead. Had died of a heat stroke seven years ago. It wasn't shocking or even upsetting to him. He was simply reaffirming a fact he had already known on one level or another.

He moved on to the web address from the flyer.

It took him to a sleek yet sentimental webpage with a looping video depicting children frolicking with their grandparents, a father and son playing baseball, and a young man gently kissing an elderly woman on the forehead. At the top of the page was that cursive title: "Second Chances".

The website stated that a customer could rent a robot to portray a deceased loved one. The prices nearly made Freddy's head spin. A single day with a robot cost a minimum of $10,500. Obviously these were expensive models but much of the prices, the website claimed, came from the time and research their teams put into creating an accurate depiction of the departed.

Outside of the Second Chances website, the internet had an awful lot to say about the program. Freddy learned nearly the entire history of the program with little time and effort; browsing less-than-decade old articles was nothing compared to digging through centuries-old documents.

It all started when Delambre wowed the world by introducing a resurrected John F. Kennedy on stage at a 2009 technological expo in Dublin. They went on to reveal how they achieved this miracle: the arisen President was in fact one of their "actor robots": humanoid machines they had been secretly developing for more than 20 years.

Their robots were blank, metallic slates on their own. But when programmed with a "role", they could perfectly emulate a human being. Their state-of-the-art muscle mechanics and realistic skin molds allowed them to uncannily pull off the most complex personalities, mannerisms and emotions.

There were conspiracies about the robots being used for military purposes—spying, espionage, and whatnot. Freddy found little on that.

The more public intention was to use them as actors in American film, theatre or television. The argument was that they could work more tirelessly and make more dangerous "choices" than human actors. There was uproar from actors all over the world. The biggest argument was that the robots could perfectly *impersonate* a human, but could it *feel* what a human would? Could it relate to human hopes, dreams, fears, tics, illnesses, and imperfections?

The issue went all the way to the Supreme Court. In the end, thanks to intensive lobbying by Hollywood actors and filmmakers, the robots weren't even approved for use in commercials.

But, as Freddy read on, the company found a brand new niche to exploit. If the robots couldn't be used to bring collective fantasies to life, they would instead fulfill personal fantasies.

The robots could be molded with whatever appearance was legally allowed and programmed with whatever personalities and actions the customer desired. The programs included: "Your Best Friend," where the robot would be one's ideal buddy for a day or however long they paid for, or "Rendezvous," where a robot would portray one's fantasy date or sexual partner. Marrying a robot was not permitted. One program that particularly excited Freddy was "History Pals", where the robot would portray a historical figure with as much accuracy as possible. Damaging the robot was forbidden, and the robot's protocols forbade it from hurting anyone. So if one wanted a "Genghis Khan" robot for their birthday, they could expect a G-Rated warrior.

"Second Chances" was *the* most popular, and controversial, program. Many critics claimed it was unethical to use a non-consenting, deceased private citizen's likeness, and it did more harm than good for the customer's wellbeing. The company and its defenders claimed that any customer willing to shell out $10,500 for a day with a robot was fully responsible for their own emotional wellbeing.

The program's biggest customers were, incidentally enough, wealthy Hollywood actors.

#

Having had enough, Freddy closed the laptop. This reminded him of the time, way back when, when his grandfather sat him down and told him the Allen family history. But this was far less exciting, sickening if anything.

He looked at Simon—who had fallen asleep while he browsed—and felt nothing but bitter resentment. He didn't want to feel this way toward his Simon. Of course, it wasn't *his* Simon, was it?

As if sensing the synthetic eyes boring into him, Simon jerked awake.

"Ahhn?" he both yawned and asked.

"Why did you bring me here?" Freddy asked coldly.

Simon's crooked mouth drooped. "I, uh…"

"You paid up the tush for this, why?"

Simon fumbled and closed his eyes. "I don't know," he said.

"Of course you do."

"Is this supposed to happen?" Simon mumbled to himself.

"Tell me!" Freddy roared. It made Simon visibly tremble. Obviously his Poppy had never spoken to him this way.

"Ok," Simon said, speaking like a game show contestant, "um... So, I'm twenty-seven. I fell into this role—the pirate hunter—by sheer luck. But it's coming to an end. The show's doing well enough, but they decided to kill my character off. The contract is up. The last shoot was a couple weeks ago. It's fine, I can move on. Except my agent isn't calling me. Which is fine."

He shrugged.

"What do you mean that's fine?" asked Freddy.

"I mean—"

"I don't know how the business works, but I'd think you should want your agent to call you."

"I'd think so, too," Simon said, gazing at nothing. "But maybe I don't? I don't know. I don't know what the hell I want or what I'm doing. I kind of haven't for a while. That's why I married some chuckle-fuck in college. Dealt with that bullshit. Never got to..."

Simon lowered and shook his head.

"Never got to what?" Freddy asked.

"And then I cut off that dead weight, marry this amazing guy. But that fell apart, too. Now all I got are bottles of scotch and Teach."

"Huh," Freddy said, unable to fight a feeling of sadness for Simon. "So you brought me here because you're lonely?"

"Well," Simon began fighting a slight tremble in his voice, his face turned red. "You gave me guidance before." He took a deep breath and stood up. "This was a mistake."

Simon pulled out his little square phone and began punching in some numbers. It took Freddy a moment to realize what he was doing. Once he did, he leapt forward and knocked the phone away. The action made Teach dash from his hiding place and into the kitchen.

"No!" Freddy cried.

Simon shrank a little, his eyes wide.

"You want them to take me away? That's it?" said Freddy. "You want them to wipe my memory? Clean me up and turn me into somebody else?" He suddenly wondered if any of his past roles had realized what he knew, and if they had tried to do anything about it. He sincerely hoped this wasn't the case, as it would mean they had failed.

"Well, I'll tell you this," Freddy continued, "I'm not going back!"

"You, you refuse?" Simon murmured. His skin returned to its natural, pale state.

"I know I have protocols. They keep me from hurting you. Not that I would anyway. But they don't say anything about me having to go anywhere I don't want to."

He sat back onto the couch, crossing his arms and leaning back with a stubborn frown on his face.

Simon said nothing, instead going into a violent fit of the "peanut butter smacks".

"Listen," Freddy said irritably, "Let me tell you what I know, kiddo. I'm not supposed to think or feel anything; I'm just supposed to pretend I do. But with every role, they give me these memories. For instance, I remember your dad, his sister, my career, your grandma, *you*. If I can't feel a damn thing why do I remember how sick I felt when I lost my Sherrie? Or how I wanted to die when Sandra did? Or how every time I got to spend with you felt like Christmas, despite your dad and I never seeing eye-to-eye."

He grumbled embarrassedly. Freddy had never been one for opening up. "And if I'm not feeling anything right now—Goddamnit, I don't know! Maybe it was the company that screwed up. All I know is that I'm not going back!"

Simon's legs seemed to give out under him, and he dropped onto the couch next to Freddy. The two sat in silence; the afternoon sun was beginning to shine through the patio door.

"So," Simon slowly said, "what *do* you want to do?"

It was a good question. Freddy hadn't thought about that. He could remember how the real Freddy had traveled the world when he was in the navy. The places he had seen: South America, Asia and Europe, including his beloved Britain. Those experiences had shaped Freddy into the man he would become.

So, the fake Freddy said: "I want to leave. Tonight."

"What?"

"There are boats in this town, right? They can take me out of here? Someplace non-extradition."

"Wait, but… they can track you."

This fact wouldn't quell Freddy's excitement. He hopped to his feet and asked, "Why did they call you earlier?"

"Erm…"

"Why?!"

"The magnet. It—" Simon hesitantly sighed, "your tracker went dark."

Freddy clapped his hands, "Damn right it did!"

"Y-you're not serious, are you?" Simon asked. He was smacking so violently he looked like he was impersonating *Mr. Ed.*

"Do I look like I'm not serious?"

Simon buried his head in his hands.

"Well then," Freddy said ecstatically, "that's that!"

"Poppy would never do this," Simon whispered.

"What's that?"

"My grandfather would never do this," Simon said louder, anger stiffened his lips and brought him to his feet. "For Christ's sake, you—he was best friends with every cop in town. He would never run off and become some fugitive!"

"Your grandpa is dead," the words poured out of Freddy's mouth more coldly than he intended. Seeing the young man wince broke whatever he had for a heart. "I'm sorry, kiddo. I'm not him. I'd like to see who I really am."

"You're just a fucking robot," Simon snapped. "A broken one at that! You're not gonna 'find yourself' on some journey. You were supposed to be *him*. Something *like* him at least."

"I'd say I *am* like him," Freddy found himself getting angry again. "You think your grandpa crapped roses? You think he never ran away from anything? Bullshit. You know why your dad never spoke to him? Because your good ole 'Poppy' had abandoned him. When Freddy's favorite child died, Freddy shut himself off from the world, and his own goddamn son!

"And, as you may know, he never rectified it. Was too damn cowardly. Instead he took comfort in you, only because your mom gave him permission. You were always easier. Also, 'Poppy' is a stupid goddamn nickname!"

Simon's eyes were wide and trembling. Against his flushed skin, they made him look like a poisoned rodent. Freddy tightened his jaw; even if it was just programming, he cared for Simon and didn't like hurting him.

"Listen," he said, "I'm sorry. For what it's worth, your grandpa was almost everything you thought he was. He was just a little bit more, too."

Simon quietly plopped onto the couch. Freddy realized that, though he was a grown man, he might as well have been seventeen. All he wanted was a little guidance, and had decided to look to the one place he'd gotten it before.

Freddy sat down next to him. "Why don't you come with me?" he said.

"What?"

"Yeah, why not? We can leave together!"

"No!" Simon said, not missing a beat.

"Why not?"

"I still have a life here. I just need to sort it out."

Freddy slowly nodded, his excitement drifting away.

"Are you really serious about running away?" Simon asked.

"I am."

"Po—whoever the hell you are, I can't be implicated in that."

"Well, sure."

"What should I do?" Simon asked, timidly.

"Absolutely nothing."

Without a thought, Freddy slammed his metallic hand against the side of Simon's head, knocking him out. He had navigated around his protocol by making the action an affectionate bop that had been a bit too rough, a calculated error.

"Sorry, kiddo."

#

After propping the unconscious Simon against a stack of pillows, Freddy dug through the bedroom closet for more "inconspicuous" clothing than the suit he was in. He put on a pair of raggedy sweatpants, a black fleece jacket with pockmarks and an old "Skull and Bones"

Production cap that was buried in the far reaches of the closet. He swiped a little cash from Simon's wallet on the dresser. He'd pay the kid back later.

Finally he took a little red sports bag and tossed the "My Heart Belongs to a Writer" magnet inside. Before leaving, he paused to take one last look at Simon. He looked angelic in his rest, as if Freddy had knocked all the anxiety and despair out of him.

"Goodbye kid," Freddy said. He didn't know how a robot could have a lump in its throat, but he had one.

Leaving the condo, he tried to push past his "old man" programming so he could move down the hall with a pace faster than a shuffle. It only resulted in him nearly tripping several times. Luckily, there was an elevator.

The black SUV sat outside the front entrance. He could see the boy scouts sitting inside, eating hot dogs and drinking cokes. He went through the back exit leading to a narrow alley. From there he shuffled onto the street and hailed a yellow and blue cab.

"Where you going?" the cab driver, listening to classical music, asked with a thick accent Freddy couldn't identify.

"Take me to the boatyard," Freddy said.

"What?"

"The boatyard?"

"What boatyard you talking about, man?"

"Wherever the biggest boats are… Freighters."

The cab driver snarled, "Be specific or get the hell out. I have no time."

In the end, they settled on "somewhere" within the massive Port of Los Angeles. As soon as the cab was in motion, Freddy pulled the magnet out of the bag and placed it on his temple. The pressure was intense, but he had braced himself for it. Throughout the ride, he occasionally had to pull it away to give him short bursts of relief. He paid no heed to the fact that his sighing and groaning was earning him glances from the driver.

The driver dropped him off in front of a shipping yard. It was filled with a city of containers leading to the water where massive freighters were docked. He took the magnet off and paid his fare, which ate up most of the money he had taken from Simon. It was no problem. There would be plenty of time to make more money. He didn't need to worry about food or shelter, except to keep up appearances, and he would try to learn self-maintenance.

He slogged thoughtlessly towards the freighters. The sun was low in the horizon by the time he reached them. He took off the magnet to briefly relieve himself. The sloshing sound of water, the crying of gulls and the shouting of dockworkers gave him nostalgia for Freddy Allen's navy days—he wished he could smell and feel the ocean breeze.

A ship that caught his eye was a red one with Spanish words along its side. It seemed like it was getting ready for take off. He approached a man in a hardhat and yellow jacket and asked where the boat was heading.

"Hell, I don't know," was the raspy response. It was good enough for him.

#

Suddenly, he heard tires rumbling over pavement. It sounded like a fleet of vehicles heading his way. He stuck the magnet back onto his temple and hid within a row of shipping containers. Peering through the cracks, he watched black SUVs and police cars park in front of his freighter.

The boy scouts who had chauffeured him were the first to come out of their SUV. They both looked red-faced and exasperated. Immediately, other boy scouts, and one or two girl scouts, got out of their SUVs as well. Finally, the police exited from their vehicles.

"This is one of our older models," shouted one of Freddy's boy scouts . "We cannot, I repeat, *cannot* afford to lose it!"

With that, most of the scouts and officers dispersed. Freddy's boy scouts stayed behind.

Beneath his pain and disorientation, Freddy had another flash of memory. At first he thought it was another flash from one of his older roles. But then he realized it was one of Freddy Allen's memories. He removed the magnet so he could picture it clearly.

He had been a boy, hiding in his family's barn from an agitated coyote. Like the coyote, the scouts and cops seemed to be dispersing in the wrong directions, not realizing he was closer than they thought. A thought rang in the back of his brain: *Fight them. Face them. This is your problem to deal with and yours alone.*

Freddy had tried that tactic with the coyote. He had tried it with a lot of things in life and he always ended up getting bit. But he wondered if he'd get lucky this time.

One of the boy scouts marched to the back door of the SUV and threw it open. Out stepped Simon, who looked dazed.

"Shit," Freddy muttered.

"The cab driver told us he brought a man with a magnet on his head to this port," one of the boy scouts explained to Simon. "Sure enough, HQ has told us the tracker has pinged on and off in this location."

Freddy quickly slapped the magnet back on. As he did this, Simon asked the boy scouts something indiscernible.

"Because," the second boy scout replied, "you know the programmed personality well. We need all the help we can get."

#

The boy scouts finally departed, leaving Simon standing alone among the vehicles.

With dusk setting in and authorities taking over, the area was nearly clear of workers. From the shouting that was coming from the boat, it appeared it was still go for take off. Freddy needed to take his chance and run for it. But first, he had an urge to talk to Simon. He knew it was a bad idea, but he also knew he would never forgive himself if he didn't.

He left his hiding space and crept toward Simon, whose back was turned.

Simon cried out when Freddy touched his shoulder.

"Shush," Freddy said. He took off his magnet.

"What are you doing?" Simon hissed.

"Getting out of here," Freddy whispered back.

"Then get the hell out of here!"

Freddy was taken aback. Simon's tone was almost conspiratorial.

"You, uh… you sure you don't want to come with me?"

"No," Simon kept looking over Freddy's head at the silhouettes that were searching the docks. They were far enough, yet still too close.

"Please?" Freddy didn't know why he asked, but he meant it.

Simon sighed. His face was scrunched in anguish and Freddy hated himself for having caused it.

"You're right," he said before Simon could say anything.

Simon gulped and nodded. "I really thought I needed him, you know? Poppy, I mean. But I guess he'll always be with me, while I find my own way."

127

Freddy nodded.

"Hell," Simon said mostly to himself. "I'm only 27."

"And I'm only 9."

The two chuckled, and then Simon gave Freddy a bear hug.

"Get on the boat," he said, unclenching the robot from his chest. "I told them you only wanted to see the ocean, nothing more. I don't know if they believed me."

"Sure they did," Freddy smiled. "You're a hell of an actor."

"Put on your magnet before they track you."

"Ah damn it," Freddy put the magnet back on his temple. Before he could move toward the ship, something whirled him around. He was brought nose-to-nose with the red, bulky face of one of his boy scouts.

"Time to go," the man said.

Freddy realized the boy scout was clutching his arms. The second scout slunk in beside them.

"I told you he'd take the bait," said the second scout. He turned to Simon, "thanks for the help."

From the terrified look on Simon's face, Freddy at least knew he hadn't been betrayed. Regardless, his heart sank. He had come so close, and lord knew what was going to happen to him.

Each boy scout grabbed one of his arms and began carrying him off. One of them pulled the magnet off Freddy's head. Suddenly, a thwack was heard and the boy scout to his left let go and collapsed.

Freddy and the man on his right turned to see Simon, wielding a rotting wooden beam in his hands. The other boy scout began to shout when Freddy whirled around and bopped him with his free fist—another calculated mistake. The man collapsed onto the ground. He nearly took Freddy with him, but his grip was loose enough for the robot to shake him off.

Both boy scouts unconscious, Freddy and Simon stared at each other. They each wondered what to say. Suddenly they heard shouting in the distance, and they noticed several silhouettes running toward them.

"Go!" Simon hissed.

Freddy hobbled past Simon and toward the ramp.

"Wait!" Simon shouted.

When Freddy turned, Simon tossed the magnet toward him. Freddy reached out to grab it, and would have missed had the magnet not pulled onto his wrist.

After a quick nod, Freddy turned and went up the ramp. When he reached the boat, he heard the sound of screeching tires.

Freddy, still pushing through immense pain, retreated past Simon and up the ramp. Behind him, he could hear the sound of screeching tires.

He looked ashore to see his boy scouts' black SUV taking off. The other scouts and the police scrambled into their own vehicles and chased after. Only two cops stayed behind to look after the unconscious men.

Slapping his magnet on his temple again, Freddy hunkered inside a narrow corridor of shipping containers. He sat in agony for several hours. When the ship finally took off, he ripped off the magnet.

Freddy wondered if he was doing the right thing or if he should have stayed behind with Simon. But he realized: if he had done that, Simon's actions would be in vain. After all, the kid had done what he did for *him*.

#

The old man looked up the night sky, hearing the waves lapping against the freighter. He thought about pirates, rejecting the system and sailing the seas. He thought about the worlds they molded, the lives they shaped for themselves and others—for better or worse.

It was a human process. A person is shaped not only by what is done for them, but what they do for others. The pain they cause, the communities they build, the love or hate they share, the hopes they build or crush—all the result of the choices they make and how they choose to interact with the world.

His artificial heart pulsed with excitement at the possibilities. Now he, too, played a role in this process.

He didn't know where he was going, but he liked to imagine.

Anthony Engebretson has the body of a 26 year old, the face of a 16 year old, the soul of a 96 year old, and the heart of a 6 year old. They say he's a writer.

Find him on Twitter @anthonyeng125

Pause

By Sam Fletcher

The sun, almost pink at this point in the evening, reflects off the bow of Abundio's sailboat. He reclines on the bench.

When he switched majors to maritime engineering, owning a yacht of his own was still a pipe dream. Of course "yacht" is a bit of a stretch. His 30-foot hybrid costs far less than a million dollars and wasn't functional when purchased. It has come a long way.

His wife, Jacqi, and the kids, Otra and Indra, stretch across the surface of the boat. Their names, while cute as a pair, represent Abundio and Jacqi's respective heritages. Growing up mixed, as most do nowadays, people tend to find creative ways to hang on to their culture. They don't speak as much as they did on these trips when the kids were younger. Now they relax, reminisce on times as peaceful.

A life spent chasing a feeling.

\#

Abundio poured the 7-dollar bottle of champagne from a half-zipped backpack into a plastic cup from 7/11.

"Now mine," said Jacqi by his side.

She was getting tipsy, he could tell by her wide smile on the overcrowded beach. Moms yelled at their children, fraternity brothers threw Frisbees, dogs defecated. Even in the orange sky, the place was far from peaceful. Most of the people there came from San Jose or somewhere else over the hill.

There were plenty of calmer beaches he and she could have spent such a beautiful summer night. She liked the people, she told him. They made her feel alive. He lifted the lid and poured. "What if we did it now?" she asked.

"The Time Key? You're kidding."

She smiled. She was drunk, but not drunk enough to be joking about something like this. "Let's do it. Think about how much fun it would be. We could do anything. Anything."

"We only get one. If my dad finds out--"

"Your dad? That's what you're worried about? Most people, because of this unjustified fear of it, go their entire lives without using it. Their whole lives. And you're worried about your dad?"

"You know how hard he is on me. When I get below an A, it's like the end of the world. What would he say if he found out? He just always told me it's for emergencies only."

"But what are the odds of actually needing it? And even if it were to happen, what are the odds that you would think even that was an appropriate time to use it? What if there is a worse emergency later on?"

"So we will just waste it, then?"

"Waste it? We will appreciate it! Fully. You know politicians blow theirs on pushing agendas. The military sanctions using it as an advantage on other countries. For war, Bune. Why not use it for love?" A pause. "You want to, don't you?"

"I do. There's just a lot of life left. I don't want to regret it."

"The government can pause time for more than 24 hours, Bune. Major corporations can even buy more time."

"I know, baby. We took the same class."

"I'm just saying. You think they gave us this ability to escape a crisis. You're wrong. They gave us a fraction of a fraction of an ability so they could gain our trust. They're crooked, Bune. All of them. Most people go their whole lives without using it. That would be a waste."

"You said that."

"Using it for what they intended would be a waste. Let's show them we don't need their power. I don't want to use it for them. I want to use it for <u>us</u>, Bune."

"So that's it? It's just us versus them?"

"Who else is there?"

"I'm not sure."

#

The kids sprawl about, pretending not to be bored (mainly because their parents have taught them there is no such thing). Otra, the oldest, relaxes his cheek on his elbow on the edge of the boat, touching the water with two fingers. Indra paints her toenails, her coarse hair has the texture of Abundio's, but flows like Jacqi's in the breeze.

Abundio looks around him. The water chops and whips in the wind, refusing to rest. His children, however, remain calm and happy. On days like this, his mind is empty. His stress depleted.

But only for the moment.

#

Jacqi said nothing.

"I'm tired of doing everything for everyone else," Abundio continued. "I do want to do something for me. I want to feel what it's like, to be absolutely free."

"You trust me, don't you?" She rubbed his arm.

"I do." She slid her hand from his tricep to his metal time band, covering the majority of his forearm.

"And you love me, right?" She opened the hatch.

"I do." She pressed her band to his, deriving pleasure from the static link. She typed in her code.

"Now you do yours."

He thought once more, though he had already made a decision. He typed in his code.

She counted in a whisper, "Three, two, one." They inserted their thumbprint on their bands together.

\#

Abundio stands up in a hurry, presses his palms on the boat's rim. "Are those people running?" They are many miles from shore, but the little dot people seem to be moving quickly.

Jacqi doesn't get up, but turns her head. "Looks like it."

He runs to the winch and begins cranking.

"What are you worried about?" she asks. "If there was an earthquake we would have felt it right?"

"Not necessarily."

"What about the sirens? On the beach? They would be going off."

"They can't respond that fast if it happened right here."

He grips a pulley and turns the mainsail. The boat moves, but slowly so. The wind blows at an optimistic speed for a sailor, but there is resistance of some kind.

"The water is really choppy," says Abundio. Indra caps her polish. Otra falls backward with the jerk of the boat, ramming his arm into the side. Jacqi shudders at the loud metallic clank of his Time Key.

"You remember how to use that thing, right?" Abundio asks.

"Dad, every year we have the same tutorial in school," Otra says.

"Wait, you want to use it right now?" Indra asks.

"I'm just saying, it might come to that."

\#

<u>24:00:00</u> appeared on their bands. The only time that ever existed just for them began to count down.

134

Abundio expected there to be a sound. Or a flash. Some sort of indicator that they actually froze time. But nothing happened. Nothing. The movement just stopped. The sounds disappeared. Instantly. And that was much more haunting.

Until it vanished, there was so much movement that Abundio had never noticed. The subtle waves. The clouds. Even the grass moved slightly. When nothing moved—nothing--it was as if it was no longer earth, but a photograph of it.

Sounds too. All of the noise around them before--the intense yelling and charades of the tourists—faded to white noise when they were used to it. But when it was gone, completely, it didn't even feel like reality anymore. The small noises, present even in the quietist of places—the birds, the wind, the distant streets, were gone. Absent. Abundio didn't speak, almost too absorbed in it.

Jacqi did the opposite. She stood and screamed. There was no echo. She yelled and yelled and danced around. "Isn't this amazing?" She grinned.

Abundio stood. "What do we do now?"

She reached down and picked up the backpack, pulling out the crap champagne. "We finish this." She took a swig and handed over the bottle.

They started running through the still people. Jacqi danced around, twirling. Abundio cracked a smile and crawled underneath a dog who was frozen, leaping in the air.

It was beautiful. With the click of a button the world had become art. Every person, with thoughts and actions, beliefs and hobbies, subtracted to a sculpture. Main Beach's litter, a chore, subtracted to a display of human condition. Nothing more.

Jacqi grabbed Abundio's arm and they ran toward the boardwalk, entering without an admission charge.

Adrenaline fueled them. They ran through the park, pulling down the pants of everyone they passed.

Jacqi stopped. Abundio turned around to see her looking at a vendor. He skipped toward her. "What's up?"

"I want ice cream," she said.

He walked up to the window. A tall man in a white apron was frozen, a scoop half-submerged in the Neapolitan tub. Abundio walked in and clasped the scoop, pulled. It wouldn't budge.

"This dude has an iron grip. There might be another scoop in here somewhere." Jacqi didn't answer. Abundio went to the window to see her licking the ice cream out of a man's hand.

"I think it's pistachio," she said. She moved on to the woman next to him. "Some fruity one."

Abundio hopped out the window, laughing. She grabbed the waffle cones from the couple's palms and handed him one. They interlocked their fingers and kept walking, slowly this time.

They found themselves at the line to the sky glider, a scenic chairlift around the park. They approached a frozen couple deboarding. The woman, half off already, just needed a little push. She teetered off the edge onto the ground, keeping her same position. The man was still sitting. Abundio put his hands underneath the man's arms and lifted. Jacqi grabbed his legs and helped thrust him out of the chair.

"What are we doing?" asked Abundio. "We will never get this thing to move."

She approached the control panel. "It looks like it's just on a loop, letting people off and on as it cycles. I think we just have to press the green button again."

"No way it's that easy. What is that guy there for then?"

"Are you on?" she asked and hit the button. The chair began to rise.

"Run!" shouted Abundio. She jumped and clasped her hands onto the base of the chair. She lifted into the air. Abundio put one arm on the back of the chair and grabbed her forearm with the other. He pulled her up, heart pounding.

Abundio pulled the support bar down over them. She laughed.

They had both grown up in Santa Cruz. They had been on the glider plenty of times. It never felt quite like this. The city was beautiful, still through the glow of the perpetually sinking, but never sunken, sun. It was silent, like sunrise. Only much better.

Jacqi waited until Abundio looked at her and kissed him on the lips. She opened her mouth, about to say something, but closed it instead. Abundio didn't ask--it was probably something corny.

#

Boats from the horizon start rushing to shore. Abundio continues to fiddle with the sails and the rudders, but the boat stays put. Soon, it is pulled backwards. It sinks back for an eerie amount of time, and Abundio's worst fears are realized: a wave is forming. A big one.

Jacqi fetches the oars and resorts to paddling. She tosses one to Abundio, who remains focused on the motor. "We won't make it," he says to her, out of breath. She keeps paddling. Abundio looks behind him. The wave grows, already several meters high at this point without slowing. In school he became savvy on the dangers of the ocean. On the west coast, a wave like this doesn't even seem possible. "Listen to me." He looks at Otra. "I want you to unlock your band. Go ahead and get it out and link."

Both kids hold out their arms.

137

"What are you doing?" their father asks.

"Aren't we linking?" asks Indra.

Abundio's heart sinks. He catches eyes with Jacqi, then looks back at his daughter. "Just you two. Your mom and I used ours."

"You what?" She tears up. "When?"

"A long time ago, baby," says Jacqi. She drops the oars and holds her.

"Listen to me," starts Abundio. "Head to Grandma's over the hill. You should be safe there. Get there any way you can. Any way. Do you hear me?"

"Yes, Dad," says Otra. Indra continues to sob.

"Don't worry about us. If all goes well we will meet you there."

"And what if you don't?" asks Indra. She can barely get the words out.

"We will."

The tide still recedes. "Well," says Jacqi, as if to correct her husband. Her words choke. "We love you," she says instead.

"Mom," starts Indra.

The wave, behind them, rises. Abundio turns to look at it. The thing is massive, definitely the largest he has ever seen. It is probably over sixty feet tall, but it is hard to tell when up so close.

The rear of the boat starts to rise back with the building wave. "NOW!" shouts Abundio. "DO IT NOW!"

Indra and Otra link their bands together, type in the code, and press their thumbs down.

The chaos, in an instant, vanishes.

Their bands read 24:00:00.

Otra looks up at the wave. "Look at it," he says. It towers over the boat, would have eaten it in merely seconds.

Indra still cries. "Look at them," she looks up at her frozen mother, who holds her.

"We will get them out," says Otra. "We aren't going anywhere. Look at this though, around you. Is it what you imagined it would be like?"

She sniffles. "It's quiet."

He looks to the shore. "There's no wind. Unless we can figure out how to use the motor, we won't make it."

"You can't drive this."

"Can too," he says, messing with the ignition. He'd seen his father do it plenty of times. The engine makes some garbled sounds but doesn't turn over. He grabs the oars from the side of the boat and throws one to his sister. He jabs into the still water.

The boat rushes down the base of the wave, the momentum pushing it a ways up toward shore. They keep rowing, but it is useless. The water falls at a backwards slope, so the boat slides back to the base of the wave.

"We have to swim," he says.

"What about them?" Indra asks. He opens a hatch underneath the standing shelter and fetches the lifejackets. They strap them on their parents, and then put theirs on.

It takes both of them to push their lifeless father off the edge of the boat. They scoot their mom to the edge and teeter off. The splash ripples, but dies out when spreading up the tsunami. The kids jump.

While the massive suction of the tide's recession builds resistance, the various waves and free-moving agents that affect the water are absent. They drag their statue parents behind them, the jackets keeping the party afloat.

It takes many breaks to span the six miles to shore. Hours pass. When they finally reach it—they know first when Abundio's foot drags along the sand at the bottom—both Indra and Otra collapse onto the padded earth, lungs working at capacity.

They don't look up to admire the still sand or the sunset. Most people have evacuated the beach, the world an open playground. 16:52:11. There is no time for such things.

#

When the chair looped around, Jacqi grabbed Abundio's arm and darted, refusing to waste a single second. She finally stopped in the middle of a busy road, blocks now away from the boardwalk. The cars were still.

"Look," she said. "Just... look."

She opened the door to a rustic blue jeep. "Help me move this guy."

"We are taking the car?" he asked.

"We will bring it back," she said. "What? You can drive stick, can't you?"

"It's not that," he said. "What about the trackers in the Time Keys? They could find out."

Jacqi chuckled. "You're stupid. They only check the tracker if someone was murdered, or—like—if a bunch of banks were robbed or something. They wouldn't even notice if we borrowed a car. People probably have to do that in an emergency all the time."

#

"We have to keep moving," Otra says against the warm sand.

"I can't carry her anymore," says Indra. "I can't do it!"

"Shh, It's OK." He gets up and yanks on Abundio's arm. It doesn't budge. "Let's go find a car. We will come back."

"A car?" asks Indra. "Who can drive?"

"I can," he says.

"You're twelve!"

"I can try!" He reaches his hand out. She takes it and pulls herself up. She wobbles, tries to steady herself. Her knees begin to shake. "I feel dizzy," she says.

"Indra we have to go."

"I don't feel g--" she says. Her eyes droop, and she sways. As she begins to fall, she holds her palm out to catch herself. Otra watches her lose consciousness midway and plummet onto her arm. He hears a crack.

He kneels down, taps her cheek. "Indra?" No response. He rolls her over, lifts the bent arm. It falls as concrete.

\#

Abundio thought.

"You're free, remember?" continued Jacqi. "Act like it."

He looked around. "If we are going to steal a car, why not that one?"

He pointed at what looked like a bright red Lamborghini up the road. Jacqi bolted.

The top down, the driver's shaggy hair was still in its haphazardly blown-back way. Jacqi and Abundio picked him up and set him on the shoulder of the road. They loaded in the convertible. Abundio rubbed the wheel. Jacqi opened the glove compartment and pulled out the manual. "It's an Aventador," she said.

"I've never seen one in person," he said. She knew he was grinning without looking up from the book. "It's already driving. How do I get it to move?" He put the car in park, then drive again. "There's no key ignition. Just the start-up button. I can't believe I'm gonna drive this." He pressed lightly on the pedal, and the car started to move.

First onramp, Abundio entered the freeway. Before long he was going 120 miles per hour, swaying around the still cars. Jacqi's long hair waved like a flag.

Soon he pulled over and flipped around. He and Jacqi switched places—she'd yelled several times over the roar of the engine about driving on the way back.

She, on the other hand, cruised. They meandered through West Cliff Drive, where all the mansions—or "luxury homes" when feeling humble—are. She pulled over at an immaculate white house. Fencing lined the roof for lounging or entertaining, as if the deck on either the first or second story wasn't enough. The front had windows almost as wide as the bay itself. They were speechless.

"Can you imagine?" Abundio finally said.

"We don't have to imagine," she retorted. "Should we see if it's unlocked?"

They walked up to the door. Abundio knocked. She looked at him.

"Kidding," he said, and opened the door wide.

They walked in and removed their shoes. The living room, on the left of the entryway, sunk into the floor, so they could step right from the polished hardwood down onto the plush cushions of the couch. The spiral staircase leading to the second floor had palm trees on either side of it sprouting from a lavish marble brim. The place let in more of the orange daylight than either of them could have imagined.

Abundio was too captivated by the place to even pay note to why it would be unlocked, that someone was probably home. Because right now, that someone was frozen. And, in this chunk of non-existent time, they owned the house.

They made way to the kitchen, where the marble atop the center table's massiveness faded the line between whether the use of "island" was metaphorical. Jacqi opened the metallic refrigerator, which dipped into the house so the only part visible were doors almost as wide as the entire wall, and glanced inside.

"Look," she said, pulling out a shiny bottle with an unpronounceable name on the front. "It's unopened." She popped the cork and handed him the bottle. "Try it."

"We are royalty now," he said, digging around the cabinets for champagne flutes. He found a row of them--crystal of course--and poured. "Shall we continue our tour?"

They held hands and gasped at each and every room, admiring the trim, art, skylights, pillars, and even indoor shrubbery. At each floor they refilled their glasses, and the tour ended in the master bedroom.

Glass panels looking out onto the ocean replaced the walls, encapsulating the sunset. The bed was bigger than anything either of them had seen—was there a size bigger than king? They stretched their limbs on the silk sheets, not even cuddling.

But then they did; their hands touched first. Then a leg crossed over. Once they touched, however, their relaxation turned to fast movements. Intense kissing. His hands through her hair. Her hands undoing his belt. In this moment, this was their bedroom. It was time to christen it.

Afterward Abundio lay on his back, Jacqi on top of him, tracing her index finger up and down the center of his chest. "I love you, baby."

"I love you too."

He lay back on the pillow.

"Don't fall asleep," she said. "We can't waste it."

"I'm not," he said. "It's just so soft."

#

Otra runs across the sand to the street nearest. He finds a Subaru mid-drive and opens the door. As hard as he can, he yanks the woman out of the driver's seat. Her still body hits the asphalt. He gets in, feels the seat up and down to figure out how to adjust it just so he can reach the gas pedal.

He presses down. Nothing. He fiddles with the gearshift—which is in drive already—but can't figure out how to change it. He stomps on everything, alternating from the gas to the break, and rocks the shift back and forth, trying to move it. Tears form.

Finally, with the right combination of break pedal and gear change, he parks the car and turns it off and on again. He switches it to drive and presses on the gas.

He doesn't exactly know what each of the lines mean. The dashes are to cross, but what if it is dashes next to a line? It doesn't matter here. He weaves through the frozen cars, speeding up.

He drives frantically, looking for anything familiar. He tries to remain calm, but tears rush from his eyes when he ends up back where he started. Eventually he finds a blue sign with an "H" on it. He keeps going.

A forced smile forms when he reaches the big, white building. He parks where the ambulances do and pulls apart the automatic doors. In the ER, nurses are frozen mid-practice. Otra jackhammers through each room, ripping cabinet doors open without thought, looking for anything that could help.

He grabs gauze from a cabinet and a sling off a patient in a bed, running as fast as he can back to the car.

When he gets on the road, Otra can see the bay. He follows it and eventually finds the beach from there.

He speeds across the sand. In any other circumstance, this would be a dream. He pulls up alongside his family and leans Indra's back against the car.

Otra combs the beach for driftwood. When he finds a piece flat enough and close to the size of Indra's forearm, he ties it in place with gauze. He saw a guy in a movie stabilize an arm with a book once. Then he puts the contraption in the sling and tightens the strap over her shoulder.

He lifts her up and puts her body in the passenger seat and buckles.

Next is his mom. He squats and lifts from her armpits, but he can barely move her dead weight. He grabs her leg and drags. He opens the back door to the Subaru, if he can only push her up to it. She is too heavy; he just can't do it.

He kicks the tire, falls backward onto the side of the car, and plants down onto the sand, sobbing. He looks up at the rearview mirror and sees Indra, passed out.

\#

Abundio woke first. Jacqi was still on his chest, head of cement. Snoring. He tapped her back. "Baby."

She raised her head, but barely her eyelids. Her eyes, naturally beady, squinted even more. Her hair stuck out in every direction. Abundio loved when she looked like this.

She opened her eyes wide. "Shit! How long were we out for?"

Frantic, they looked at their arm bands. 16:12:36 and falling.

"We lost a little time," he said. "It was good though, wasn't it?"

She smiled. "Really really good." She nuzzled into him.

"I'm not gonna be able to keep up with you forever," he said. "You're crazy."

"I am not crazy," she said.

"You're too fast."

"I'm going to be a nurse, dude. I'll take care of you."

"That's the problem," he said. "The day may come where I need to take care of you."

She walked her fingers from his stomach to his chest. "I guess I will need to give you some lessons. You can do my homework for me." She played with his earlobe, and then his hair. "And I can fix cars for you, or whatever, if you don't switch majors."

"I think I want... to sail," he said, looking at the frozen ocean through the window.

"To sail?"

"Yeah. I want to be miles out on the water, free. From everything. People, work, class. Somewhere even the government can't touch me."

"Can I come?"

"Of course."

"I don't think there are any jobs in that."

"You sound like my dad. He'd never let me throw my major away like that anyway."

"Shh," she said. "Now is not the time for that kind of talk. We are free remember? Let's get out of here."

Stress built when Abundio thought about how, in a handful of hours, time would return. At that time, all this talk of freedom would be pointless. It wasn't meant to be a momentary escape, but a permanent state of mind. They dressed and walked down the spiral staircase.

"Bye house," they said as if it was some relative.

They walked through the lawn. Across the street. Down the steps to the ocean.

Abundio dipped his toe in the motionless water. The preexisting waves moved only by the force of his ripple. It was like nothing he had ever seen.

Jacqi stripped nude and jumped in—the splash changed the course of the waves. There was no tide here, just a swimming pool that covered most of the planet. Without the wind, too, she could manage without a wetsuit. Abundio followed.

They floated out farther than they had ever swam. The beach, the ocean, had never been so peaceful.

Life hadn't either.

Abundio looked out on a rocky edge a ways down the beach. A massive wave, frozen in place, crashed into it. "Let's go there."

The two swam to shore and walked from the sandy beach to its jagged edge in their bare skin. Soon they were hopping rock to rock, up to the peak. At it was an explosion of water. The rock split the large wave into pieces, its crystal drops floating in the air.

Abundio could move them with his touch. Jacqi tasted the salt.

Behind the splash was a second breaking wave. It was huge, possibly the biggest they had ever seen. Or perhaps it just seemed that way, still as it was.

Jacqi reached out to the wave, its white mist crashing in front of it. She could almost reach it, but couldn't. They felt something though, a connection. As if in touching these waves all was meant to be.

"It's beautiful, isn't it?" she asked, but needed no confirmation.

\#

Otra looks at the impending wave. There isn't time.

He loads into the driver's seat, blasts the air conditioning, and takes off. Up the road, he pulls into the 7/11 and runs in to grab water. He chugs almost an entire bottle to himself and puts the others in the backseat. The nearest onramp to the freeway, he presses on the gas. His stomach starts to tingle when he reaches 30 miles per hour.

For the life of him, he can't go faster than 50.

He reaches back and pulls out a bottle of water. He unscrews the cap and pours it on his sister's face, slumped onto the passenger side window. After a few seconds, she starts coughing and looks at him groggily.

"There's water in the back, drink some," he says to her.

"My arm hurts."

"Drink water."

She looks in the back. "Did you grab all the water they had?" Bottles of every size, shape, and brand cover the backseat. Maybe over a hundred of them.

"Almost."

She grabs a bottle of Fiji water with her left hand and gives it to Otra to crack. She almost drains the entire thing.

She looks at her Time Key. 7:07:16. "Where are we?"

"Almost to Grandma's."

"What about mom and dad?"

"We had to leave them."

"What?"

"We had to leave them. I had to take care of you and I couldn't lift them into the car."

"We have to go back. Otra! We have to go back!"

"By the time we find our way back there and figure out a way to get them into the car, there is no way we will have enough time to get to Grandma's."

"Otra!" She grabs the wheel and jerks. Otra shoves at her hands but she persists. The car swerves along the road while he tries to grip her

148

wrist, keeping his other hand on the wheel. She sobs. Eventually, he has no choice. He slams the breaks and parks the car in the middle of the freeway.

"Indie, I'm serious," he says. "Even if we went back, you and me probably couldn't get them into the car. I tried. I couldn't get them to budge."

Indra stops talking, but he can see the tears slide down her cheeks. That is worse. Otra's tone switches from defensive to vulnerable. "If we went back now and didn't make it out of there, what was the point of using the Time Key at all?"

She sniffles. "What do you mean?"

"I mean it saved our lives today. Going back there would be a waste of it."

"It is not a waste!" she says. Back to the yelling. "A waste?" she mouths the words, almost too choked up to speak.

They sit for a moment in silence. "Even if we go back and time starts again," she says. "Even if we don't make it out of there again, how is that a waste? At least we tried."

"You don't think I tried, Indie? You don't think I tried to get them out of there?"

"Otra—"

"We are going to Grandma's, Indie. I decided. I'm older." He starts the car back up.

Indra crosses her arms and slumps against the car door until they reach the exit and putter through another still town. They pull up to their grandmother's driveway and open the unlocked door. They walk into the living room, onto the plush dark-yellow carpet that hasn't been updated in decades. Their grandmother sits in her rocking chair, frozen, eyes glued to the news on the television screen.

The kids look at the wave in awe, as if they forgot what it looked like. "There're four hours left," says Otra. "We should try to sleep."

Indra complies, probably exhausted of arguing. They curl up on opposite ends of the couch, pretending like they can sleep. Otra watches as Indra's eyes stay with the frame, looking at the massive wave from helicopter view. He knows her thoughts remain with their parents. He knows her hope is gone. Otra repositions every few minutes. Did he make a mistake? Should he have figured out a way to get his parents into the car?

A few sleepless hours pass, and time returns. They know not because of any large indicator, but because of all the small ones coming to light at once. The sound of the street, the wind, the air conditioning--even the refrigerator makes noise. Life returns to the air around them.

But also because the TV is now playing, amplifying their anxiety.

Abundio's mother gasps. "Oh! You startled me!" She looks at Indra's sling and their armbands. "What happened."

"We were on Dad's boat," says Otra, the designated speaker. "They told us to come here."

"Where are your parents," she replies, almost as a statement. As if she already knows. Indra points to the television screen, the wave pushing in. The woman's face sinks.

After a moment of silent watching, she fetches the telephone and dials her son's number. After no response, she calls the police. They ensure her they will look, but she knows that the hotline is receiving dozens of these calls every minute.

Indra trembles.

Otra tries to keep his mind on anything but the inevitable. He watches the tsunami crash through the beach, ripping the boardwalk to shreds. It pushes up for a few more blocks before once again receding.

The man on the screen says it's just the first wave. There will likely be more.

An hour of nausea passes.

Otra stops listening to the man and instead on a caw outside. A loud, angry caw. A noise so normal in a neighborhood yet so interesting. Is it protecting its territory? Trying to mate? Warning about the flood? After an entire sleepless day without noise, he finds it hard to take it for granted when it returns. He hears distant honking. He hears his grandmother's cat scratch the post beside the couch. He hears his sister's sniffles.

He hears a knock.

His grandmother rushes to the door, opens it. Abundio stands, dripping wet and weary, cradling Jacqi in his arms. He walks into the house without saying a word. The kids move out of the way as he sets his soaking wife on the couch. She is breathing, slowly.

When his arms are free, the other three embrace them.

"What happened?" Indra asks.

"We went to high ground," says Abundio. "If you hadn't brought us to land, we would have been long gone by now. We almost were."

"Is Mom OK?" asks Otra.

"She is, when we were running she got swept up by the wave. Well, we both did, but she got the blunt of it. I was able to grab onto a tree and pull us up. When we finally got out of there a bunch of cars were heading north. Some people dropped us off here."

"I was drowning," Jacqi mutters. "He resuscitated me."

Silence falls through the room. Abundio isn't sure if Jacqi wants him to respond, but he doesn't. He doesn't say a word, just hugs his children.

And when they let go, his breath is calm again.

Sam Fletcher has appeared in Liquid Imagination, The Simpleton, The Western Front, and elsewhere. He also received an honorary mention from L. Ron Hubbard's Writers of the Future contest.

The Recall

By James Pyles

In mid-August 1977, Astronomer Jerry Ehman was reviewing computer printouts from what was then Ohio State University's Big Ear radio telescope at Ohio Wesleyan University, which was being used to search for signs of extraterrestrial intelligence. He discovered a signal in the 1420 megahertz frequency band that Big Ear been monitoring a few days earlier and which appeared to have originated from the constellation Sagittarius. He was so surprised at the 72-second transmission, that he wrote the word "Wow!" in the margin and circled the reading on the printout.

Could it have been mankind's first contact with extraterrestrial intelligence? Ohio State University researchers weren't sure. They trained the massive radio telescope on that part of the sky for the next month and occasionally thereafter, but could not detect the transmission.

No definitive explanation has ever been offered for the signal's origin, and it has not recurred for nearly fifty years…

…until now.

# # #

Berkeley, California, Thursday, September 18, 2025, 7:36 p.m.

"I thought I understood you, but I guess I never really did." Fifty-seven year old Corey McKinney had been a Professor of Economics and Political Science at U.C. Berkeley for the past twenty-one years but never lost the sense of being a student, which was why he and the woman who was now leaving him, Christine Mohr, chose to live in a small, third-floor apartment less than a mile from campus.

Standing on the opposite side of the bed from Corey, she opened her pack and then reached for a small pile of clothing sitting on the covers beside it. "You knew this wasn't going to last forever." Christine, a fifty-five year old Radiologist at Alta Bates Hospital, carefully stacked her marginal supply of clothing within the worn leather rucksack's waterproof interior, which had accompanied her on her many journeys from Amsterdam to Nepal and back to Berkeley. On top of the other items, she gently placed her prized first editions of Frank Herbert's "Dune" and Robert Heinlein's "Stranger in a Strange Land," the record of her travels of the imagination. Then she stood up next to the bed, her long, almost entirely white hair draped over the shoulders of her dark tan sweatshirt, and regarded the man she said "I love you" to just that morning.

"That's what you said thirty years ago when we moved in together." Cory rubbed his hands over each other as if soothing aching muscles. "Somehow, I thought that by now things would have changed a little."

Most people who spoke about her lover, either to Christine or behind her back, said they thought he was a non-descript "any man." Although he was just under six-foot tall, Corey seemed shorter due to being somewhat overweight as well as his generally quiet demeanor. He still had most of his hair, though it was the color of iron rather than its original medium brown, and even when teaching or in faculty meetings, he tended to wear the same type of button-down off-white shirts, faded blue jeans, and the cowboy boots that were the only thing he retained from being born and raised in Amarillo, Texas.

"I'm sorry, Corey. Thirty years ago, you weren't about to report me to the Committee as a potential subversive." She frowned as she zipped up the top of her pack.

"What? I wasn't…"

154

"I saw your texts to Dean Jagger. You said you've been having doubts about me, especially since I came back from my sabbatical last month."

"But that was just talk. I'd never really..."

"Texts are forever, not like idle chatter." She took a deep breath and made herself lower her voice. "I doesn't matter anymore. I have to leave anyway. Look, I'm sorry. I can't explain why." She pulled the rucksack off of their bed, ruffling the quilt they'd bought together at that artists' colony in New Mexico last summer. She shouldered it just as they both heard the knock on the door. "Could you get that for me? It's probably my ride."

He froze for a second, experiencing all of the subtle nuances of their relationship as if he were seeing them clearly for the first time. Her frequent trips, enthusiastic sex that rarely involved intercourse, emotional intimacy that seemed unbounded except for one small area sitting between them that was forever shrouded. He had always wondered a little about her quirks, but now with all the propaganda about subversives, the activities of the Committee, public paranoia that bordered on hysteria, maybe that meant...she'd seemed even more reclusive than usual since the radio signal began three months ago.

"The door, Corey." Her voice sounded impatient, and he was standing so she couldn't leave their bedroom.

"Oh, right." He turned, boots clumping on the thin carpet as he walked down the hallway past their shared office on the left. She barely tolerated his wearing boots in the apartment, but then it occurred to him that in a few minutes, it would no longer matter.

The man standing in the hallway was young enough to be Christine's son, but otherwise there was no resemblance. His hair was dark, nearly black, parted in the middle, thick locks hanging down to his collar, and the rough beard of the same color gave him the quality of a maverick or a rock musician. The image was completed by a half-unzipped green military flight jacket with no insignia, a coarse, black turtleneck sweater, and decades out of date bell-bottomed jeans in about the same shape as Corey's 501s.

"Hi, I'm Phil. Is Christine here?" The stranger was smiling slightly, but kept his arms at his sides as Corey nearly offered his hand.

"I'm coming." Her voice drifted down the hall preceding her by a few seconds. Corey stepped back to the entrance of the kitchen, the only other room with a light on besides their bedroom. The flat, white glow from the energy-efficient bulbs in the ceiling fixture caused the coral-tinted enamel on the stove and refrigerator to reflect the illumination as pink pastels.

"Your ride?" Corey raised an eyebrow. He suspected that Christine saw other men, and perhaps other women, but never believed she would be callous enough to have one of them come to their place, at least not while he was there.

Seeing the expression on Corey's face, Christine kissed his cheek while cupping his face with her free hand. "We just went to school together. He's taking me home."

"School?" He pulled away, his back now pressed against the fridge. "He must have been in diapers when you graduated."

"Are you ready? The car's waiting. We don't have much time." Phil took a step back out into the hall, expecting the older woman to follow.

"In a minute." She gritted her teeth as she glared at the newcomer. "It's not easy." Then she turned and walked back to Corey. "This isn't how I wanted to end it. I want you to know that I've loved you since the first day I saw you."

"Getting a broken wrist X-rayed wasn't exactly our most romantic date." He smiled just a bit, which made her smile as well.

"All I can say is that I have a complicated life, and now, that life is taking me in a very different direction."

"I know. You said there would always be a part of you that you'd never share with me."

"It was as much for your protection as mine, as ours."

"Christine." Phil's voice sounded calm, but there was a hint of warning in the tone.

"Just coming." She was still looking into Corey's hazel eyes which now carried a look of pain as well as longing.

"Will I ever see you again?" He already knew the answer to his question.

"No, and it's for the best. I will always love you. That's all I can leave you with."

"Except for the rest of your things." He nodded his head down the hall, picturing the majority of her clothes, her books, the entire thumbprint of their life together.

"You can give them away. I don't need them anymore."

"Like you don't need me."

She knew he was fishing for something she no longer had to give. "Good-bye, Corey." Christine pivoted, walked past Phil who was still waiting near the door, and then turned left toward the stairwell.

Phil nodded slightly at Corey, neither man knowing what to say, and then he followed Christine. Corey stood there near the kitchen, the apartment door still wide open, and listened to their footfalls echo down the stairs into the distance until there was nothing left to hear.

# # #

8:00 p.m.

Nearby church bells began tolling at the top of the hour as they both got into the vintage, rust-colored 1977 Datsun 280z parked on the wrong side of the street facing south on Oxford. It had been raining until just a few hours ago, and Christine's low hiking boots were moist from walking across the grass. The Northside neighborhood in Berkeley was home to any number of churches and seminaries, which had been Christine's constant companions when she was home, but now the familiar chiming sounded as if it were in vain. She knew there wasn't much time left in the world.

Both car doors slammed shut as Phil pulled the keys from his jacket pocket, slipped one in the ignition, and turned the engine over.

"Where did you find the antique?" She set her pack between her legs as he put the car in gear, pulled out into the vacant street, and made the right turn on Cedar. He didn't answer her until after he'd driven the two short blocks to Shattuck and turned left.

"We were forced to accelerate our schedule and had to use the original templates."

"Which includes your appearance? Could you have at least tried looking like someone who belongs in this century? Who the hell wears platform shoes and bell bottoms anymore?

"Like I said, there wasn't time. I'm only the team's extraction leader, just here long enough to get you and the others to the rendezvous point. I'm not expected to live among them for decades, to become one of them." His voice had an unpleasant edge.

"Is this about my relationship with Corey?"

The younger man paused for several seconds, downshifting as he passed Spats, her and Corey's favorite local bar, and McDonald's which she detested but Corey secretly loved, well their trashy fries anyway. He sighed while turning right onto University. "I'm sorry. I can only imagine this is a very difficult time for you, for all the long-terms. It's not something I was trained for. Your…modifications were necessary. Mine are just superficial, so I can't properly relate." He slowed as the light changed ahead and stopped at Sacramento.

"We only needed a few more years. Corey wouldn't have reported me to the Committee."

"He wouldn't have been the first, Christine. Besides, it's not just you, and it's not just the local cell." Phil eased off of the clutch, pressed down on the accelerator, and moved the car forward at the green light. "We've been detected globally. I thought you knew that from last month's briefing. Besides, even without the security breach, we already know what decision we're going to make."

"But what if we…?" She paused, knowing he'd think what she was about to say was insane. "What if we decided to help…?"

"That was never part of the mission parameters, and it's too late for that now, anyway. I'm here to take you and the others back. That's the end of it." He sounded angry, and Christine realized she'd pushed him too far. They were only barely acquainted and she couldn't rely on him understanding her, and what she and the rest of them had been through.

"Just get me to the rendezvous." She sounded defeated as she stared out the windshield, memorizing every store, every restaurant, the faces of the shoppers, the joggers, the homeless men and women. She was leaving the only life she had known for the past fifty years. Who she was before then seemed like a distant dream.

"I'll drop you off with the others at the pickup point in San Francisco. Doug Hwan will take care of you until I get back."

"We're not leaving right away? I thought this was an emergency evac." She looked at him by the strobing flashes of passing street lights.

159

"Rollie can't make it on his own in time. I have to do a live retrieval, just like with you."

"Rollie." Memories of another life, another existence washed up on the shores of her recall. "I haven't thought of him in ages." She smiled, remembering his all too human sense of humor.

"He's in the heart of things, unfortunately, but we've left too many behind already, and I'm not willing to sacrifice him."

"How long?"

"Hwan knows if we don't make it to the bus by midnight, we're not coming. Make sure he remembers that." Phil looked at her for a moment, and she saw his grave expression. Some of them had been captured over the past several months and had died at the hands of the Committee, and even now, they might not be the last.

Christine leaned to her left as Phil steered the Datsun around the loop to the onramp for I80 heading toward the City and their final night in-country, or so she hoped. Or did she?

# # #

San Francisco, California, City Hall, 9:28 p.m.

Phil had studied Rollie's current placement profile and discovered he had set himself up to be almost a fixture among the homeless, the addicts, the drug dealers, and the tent people South of Market. He kept his origins vague, where he'd come from and how long he'd been panhandling using jokes written on cardboard to earn him ones, fives, and occasionally tens. He never drank the cheap booze common among his "contemporaries" or used the injectable substances, but it was rumored that he'd buy a runaway kid a bus ticket home, or a mother and her baby a few nights at a motel. The retrieval agent kept wondering what made the long-terms extend such efforts for a people who had inevitably doomed themselves.

160

"You're a mess." Phil had the old black man's arm around his neck as he was half carrying, half dragging him into the shadows behind City Hall toward Polk Street.

"You would have to pick the night when half the damn city is out front protesting climate change and the Committee's bringing back McCarthyism in the name of national security." Rollie Walker looked to be over seventy, but Phil knew he wasn't any older than Christine and the rest of them. If his senses had been calibrated like a long-term covert's, he probably would have noticed the stench more, the rancid odor of human urine and feces. The soles of the old man's running shoes, stumbling and scraping across the rough concrete of the sidewalk, were mostly gone. His khaki pants were rags below the knees, and he only had a thin, stained undershirt beneath the thrift store camo raincoat. He did seem to pride himself on keeping his trademark red, knit cap clean and tucked down low over his ears.

"You're heavier than you look." Phil was trying to make a joke, but he wasn't sure exactly how humor worked." The old man's dead weight kept throwing the agent off balance.

"It's my legs. They did something to me at the clinic."

"You should have known better than to seek medical treatment. We sent word to all of you that the new generation of blood tests for the mutated immunodeficiency virus could pick up our chemical markers." His words came out unevenly because of the effort of struggling under the other man's mass. "Six were identified in Europe in the last month, ten in various African nations, and possibly three or more in Asia. I don't know how many others in the less populated areas."

"Hell. Never planned to, but the cops pulled a major raid last week right before the rainstorm. Tried to take someone's tent. Two women, three children, babies really. Hey, watch it."

Phil stumbled and nearly dropped Rollie back across the curb just as they crossed Polk.

"Sorry." He pulled Rollie back up and got a better grip.

"You couldn't have parked any closer?"

"I didn't want the car to get towed. Why does there have to be so many people around?"

"Where's the car?"

"Civic Center Garage."

"Oh, that's inconspicuous."

"Why are all long-terms so sarcastic? That's what you call it, right? I'm trying to help you."

"I think it's the infection or rather the antibiotics. The cops busted me up pretty good. I took a baton to the kneecap. ER doc ran the mandatory tests while I was handcuffed to the gurney. I think I'm having a bad reaction to whatever she gave me."

"You're lucky the police didn't keep you in jail."

"Too full with all these protests and vandals. Even had a bombing at the Army Recruiting Center off of the Embarcadero. I'm just small potatoes. No violent crimes on my record. By the way. We're being followed. I think they've been keeping an eye on me since the ER."

"Police?"

"Feds. The Committee."

"Damn. Can you run?"

"I can hardly walk."

Phil pulled Rollie down behind some trees near the entrance to the underground garage. "Here are the keys. Second level, section E4."

"I'm not leaving you."

"I think that's what I'm supposed to say, Rollie. Go. I'll make it to the pickup point if I can."

162

"And if you can't?"

"Tell Hwan·not to wait for me." Phil gripped the old man's shoulder, stood, and started walking quickly toward McAllister and Larkin. As he stepped onto the sidewalk and came out into the open, Phil realized pedestrian traffic had thinned and there wasn't enough now to cover him. Glancing back over his shoulder, he saw four uniformed officers and two plainclothes agents converging on him from the direction of the Civic Center. Phil tried to walk with the flow of the people around him, but when he got to the intersection, he broke into a run crossing it diagonally. Behind him, he heard someone yell, "Don't fire" right before the squeal of brakes. He never saw the car that hit him.

# # #

San Francisco, California, the Federal Building, 11:01 p.m.

"He's coming around again." To Phil, the man's voice sounded like it was echoing down a corridor or tunnel, but then he was aware of fingers prying the lids of his left eye open. The bright glare from a penlight nearly blinded him. When he tried to move, he felt a dull ache in his ribcage, which he could tolerate, but the pain in his face on either side of his nose was worse. Looking up, he couldn't get his vision to clear. All he could make out was some sort of illumination overhead.

"Can you hear me?" It was another voice, a woman's. Slowly Phil became more aware of his surroundings. There was an incessant beeping noise which he understood to be a cardiac monitor. He was probably hooked up to other medical devices as well.

"Am I in a hospital?" His tongue felt thick and his words didn't sound quite right.

"You were, but they were asking too many questions." The woman's voice was clearer. "You're in Federal custody. My name is Special Agent Patricia D'Alesandro."

163

He wanted to ask if Rollie made it, but if he had, they shouldn't know about it. "If it's all the same to you, Agent D'Alesandro, I'd like to speak with an attorney." The pain in his face had subsided a bit, but the throbbing in the back of his skull was spectacular.

"You are under the authority of the Committee, Mr…" she paused as if verifying some record, "…Clarke. You have no rights."

Phil closed his eyes for several moments and then opened them. He was lying on his back, but when he tried to move his arms and legs, he could feel the restraints.

"We don't want you leaving here, Mr. Clarke."

"Judging by the way I feel, I probably wouldn't get far anyway. What happened to me?"

"You were hit by a car, Mr. Clarke." It was the man's voice. "I'm Dr. Tillman." Then Phil saw Tillman turn to D'Alesandro, though they both still seemed like shadows. "I don't think this is such a good idea. His BP is 182 over 120, and given what he seems to be, I don't know if that's good or bad."

"We've been through all of this, Doctor."

"But his body chemistry is remarkably different from the others, not to mention ours. I don't know how he'll react to the sodium pentothal."

"Just let me worry about that."

"But his organs are all arranged differently, cardiac, lungs, liver, and he has a few I can't even guess at. The others were a much closer match to…"

"Doctor, if you can't do your job, please leave. I'll find someone else to take your place, though I must remind you that this is a matter of national security." She sounded annoyed, as if the Doctor's presence was merely tolerated, not required.

164

After a pause, Tillman responded. "No, I'll stay. God knows what one of your ham-handed Committee doctors would do to him."

Phil's vision came into closer focus. Tillman seemed to be a middle-aged man of average height, though that was a little difficult to tell while lying on his back. He was wearing the expected, rumpled white lab coat, half-shell framed spectacles, a dark, bushy mustache, and displayed a growing bald spot on the back of his wild mane of graying hair. Haphazardly around his neck, hung a cheap brown and white striped nylon tie over a pastel blue shirt, but to the patient's untrained eye, he couldn't tell if it was in tune with modern fashion. He supposed Christine could have told him if she were there.

By contrast, Agent D'Alesandro was impeccable in her appearance. Her hair, tied back in a tight bun, was a dark blond, eyebrows above blue irises were plucked to exactness. Her nose and lips were both thin, the latter being lightly glossed, and her white blouse and dark suit jacket were cut in an attempt to minimize the outward curvature of her breasts.

The agent walked out of sight for a moment. Phil had the impression there were others in the room, but well out of his field of vision. All he could directly see was the single lamp suspended from the ceiling over his face.

"Where am I?"

"Federal Building, San Francisco," came D'Alesandro's curt reply from somewhere below his feet. "Let's see." He could hear papers rustling. "Phillip Gerald Clarke, born April 14, 1993, according to your driver's license. Your home address in Los Angeles is an Italian restaurant, the manager has never heard of you, there is no telephone number, cell or landline, in your name, no utility records, no home rental or ownership information, no car registration, no employment record, and no social security number."

She came back into view on his left, while the doctor remained standing on the right nearer to the medical monitors. "I'd say you were something of a mystery man, except according to Dr. Tillman, who confirmed the assessment of the ER physician at the San Francisco Medical Center, you are not a man."

"What do you want of me?"

The agent leaned close to his face, and it was then that Phil realized he couldn't smell anything at all, no matter how badly calibrated. "Information, Mr. Clarke, or whatever your actual name is. I want to know why you're here, why you helped your confederate escape, why, in spite of the fact that he's not human either, he can pass for one far better than you, and how many other infiltrators you have in the Bay Area. Only one other with your peculiar biology has been captured..." She stepped away for a moment and then returned. "In Johannesburg, South Africa. She was killed in an escape attempt. She...apparently combusted, if I can trust the report I received." He could hear her chuckle at what he understood to be a grim reality.

"What did you do to my face? Why does it hurt?"

"Oh, that happened at the ER," Tillman replied in a conciliatory tone, contrasting D'Alesandro's aggressive posture. "They attempted to remove some of your facial prosthesis. This agent gave the order. It was totally against my wishes."

"Doctor, that hardly matters now."

"My patient's wellbeing matters." Phil saw Tillman seem to stand a little taller, his facial expression becoming more determined.

"Just keep him alive, Tillman." She leaned over Phil's face again. "You may be feeling a bit lightheaded by now. We're supplying your bloodstream with a chemical that, at least with our species, should make you more susceptible to questioning. We've noticed that with our other subjects, they had a rather high tolerance for discomfort, so I don't suppose the usual physical inducement will be of much use."

"You mean they died." Recalling the original mission summary, which he had memorized in preparation for his role, the long-term coverts were bound to, at some point within their fifty year sojourn, occasionally become critically injured, even hospitalized. It was a dangerous assignment and they all knew the risks. Beyond a preset level of injury, which in this case seemingly included torture, their major systems would malfunction, manifesting as a heart attack or a stroke, something natural and always fatal. The metamorphosis process made them seem indistinguishable from the human species, so even an autopsy would be unrevealing. Only the recent mutation of the HIV virus and the CDC's development of a revolutionary blood testing protocol, which they had disseminated to any nation that wanted it, made it possible to detect the chemical anomalies that revealed their true nature as extraterrestrials.

"Yes, Mr. Clarke. They died and left us nothing to go on. You, on the other hand, have already told us so much, if only by medical examination, X-rays and such. We haven't had time to do any resonance scanning, but we do have the remains of those curious little pieces of plastic which were sitting where your sinuses should have been. Unlike the others, you weren't meant to be here very long, were you?"

"No, I…" He was feeling disoriented, perhaps the effects of the substance D'Alesandro had fed into his circulatory system. Sweat beaded on his forehead and streamed down the sides of his face. He had a fever, which was he first sign.

"Come on! Talk, Clarke!" She was yelling at him, her mouth just inches from his eyes.

167

"Agent D'Alesandro," Tillman half raised his hand, trying to keep his voice low.

"Shut up or get out, Tillman!" She kept her face right in front of Phil's.

"No. I'm short-term. Cosmetic appliances and minor augment only." Phil's lips and tongue felt numb and it was like someone else was saying what he was thinking. He was now out of control of his body, and imagined that his psyche were sitting nearby, passively witnessing his exchange with the agent.

"What does the signal mean? You know, what they used to call the 'Wow signal.' It occurred once for 72 seconds in 1977 and then fell silent, that is, until three months ago. Now it's transmitted from the same part of the sky near the Chi Sagittarii star group once a day at the same time for exactly 72 seconds, exactly the same signal. What does it mean, Mr. Clarke?"

"How long has the Committee existed?" The question came from the same detached portion of his mind, but he could still feel his body getting warmer. He was soaked in perspiration, whatever gowns they had dressed him in, his bedding, the coverings over his form held down by strong restraints.

"What's that got to do with…? Oh, I see. The blood tests. A doctor in Cambodia diagnosed the first subject over two years ago, but it was thought to be a previously unknown blood anomaly. Then there was the second case in Mumbai three months later, then Morocco, Serbia, Iran, Paris. Six confirmed cases in less than eighteen months. The Sûreté got involved, then Interpol, and then all of the major law enforcement and security agencies worldwide."

"The Committee." Phil could feel his mouth go dry. His perspiration stopped but he was still getting hotter.

168

"Agent D'Alesandro, the patient's body temperature is 110 degrees and rising, his pulse averages 98 beats per minute but is erratic, and his blood pressure is practically off the charts. Might I suggest we give him a few minutes to rest?"

"What does the signal have to do with the Committee?"

"You had discovered us, our activities, or part of them."

"I knew it!" She stood up, clenching her fists at her chest as if in triumph. "Tell me more."

"The signal…fifty years ago. Initiation signal to covert agents…begin activities."

"They were already here?" She sounded suddenly puzzled, as if she hadn't anticipated that response.

"Ten years before."

"1967."

"Yes. To establish cover…verify not detected."

"Then the signal…"

"Go signal. Begin operations."

"What operations? Invasion?"

"Long-term prelude to…colonization."

"You mean invasion. You can't colonize a planet where there is already a dominant species."

"You were expected to exterminate yourselves."

"You mean nuclear holocaust. The Cold War."

"Yes, or some variation, biological perhaps. However, you are more self-destructive than we imagined."

"But we caught you red-handed. Whatever your plan was, you couldn't take over. We didn't annihilate ourselves. We survived. Fought back."

"You didn't survive. You just took the planet with you."

"What?"

"Your climate…"

"That climate change bullshit? Jesus, I've been hearing that crap ever since…"

"Congratulations, Agent D'Alesandro. Our species had infiltrated every sector of life here on this planet, every major city at every social level for nearly fifty years. Now we're leaving, all of us. You've got what you wanted, but not in any productive sense."

"I know you see me as a persecutor, Clarke, but nothing could be further from the truth." D'Alesandro had lowered her voice as if taking Phil into her confidence. "I know what it's like to defend this country against hostile forces, invaders. Ten years ago, I was with…well, another department in the Middle East, running covert ops to inhibit Iran's development of nuclear weapons. Six years ago, I was putting down teams of insurgents who had infiltrated hordes of refuges storming our southern border. A year ago, I finally grabbed the brass ring, if you know what that means. I was assigned to seek out subversive alien influences here in the Bay Area. I knew I'd be able to protect, not only my country, but my planet. That's what I do, Clarke. I protect the innocent against subversives and invaders, beings like you."

"It doesn't matter anymore." Phil laughed and then scowled. "Don't you get it? It's too late for you, me, Tillman, your whole world, and all we had to do was watch. Like we predicted, you did it to yourselves, but the cost…" He chuckled as if he'd just remembered a joke, or finally understood what humor meant. "…the cost was a lot higher than anything we could have foreseen. Now we're leaving, like rats deserting a sinking ship, except our sunken ship is what's waiting for us."

"He sounds delirious. I really must insist Agent…"

"Shut the hell up, Doctor." She snapped her head up at Tillman just for a moment, then was back down staring at Clarke's now glazed eyes. "Leaving? Why?"

"You won." He started to giggle, or rather Phil watched what used to be his body behaving irrationally. "You've already passed the tipping point. Your world will continue to become warmer, triggering an extinction event of global proportions, probably in a century or less. Earth will be uninhabitable by your species, by ours, by almost all animal life forms for the foreseeable future. Invade? Why would we invade now?" The giggling continued and he bit his lip hard to regain control. "I'm sorry, Doctor. You should get out. The failsafe. I mustn't be captured...held." Phil knew Tillman had been trying to help, but he had compassion for D'Alesandro and the others as well. "You have less than a minute."

"What?" D'Alesandro looked away from Phil, supposedly to where the records she had been consulting were kept. Then her eyes went wide with realization. "Everyone evacuate now. Not just the room, the entire wing. I said now!"

Both the doctor and agent hurriedly left Phil's field of view and there was the sound of multiple running footfalls. A door opened as the alien's body temperature shot up past 120. The rapid pinging of the heart monitor sounded like panic. Everyone managed to get a few steps out of the interrogation room rigged with medical equipment for the patient. D'Alesandro was the last person out, or rather, she was standing at the threshold looking back at her prisoner when Phillip Clarke ignited, his body temperature abruptly surging past 5,000 degrees. Everyone within a 50 meter radius was killed instantly by the explosion, and the detectors at the U.C. Berkeley Seismic Lab registered a rather modest Earthquake on Friday the 19th at 12:38 a.m.

#

Stinson Beach, California, Friday, September 19, 2025, 3:48 a.m.

Douglas Hwan spoke unaccented English, although his immigration papers said he had been born in Busan, South Korea forty-seven years ago. He set the brake of the converted school bus at the end of a dirt road, grateful that their uncomfortable trip over the uneven path was over. The bus's suspension was too worn for such journeys, but fortunately, this would be the last it would ever take, at least with this particular collection of passengers. He looked out of the windshield at the view of the beach and the cliffs above. The houses and cottages nestled in the hillside of the exclusive coastal community were dark, their residents peacefully sleeping as the people began to disembark from the bus.

Alan Figuroa, a real estate agent late of the city of Pleasanton, and Nathan Woods, an interior designer from Redwood City, were on each side of Rollie Walker, helping him hobble down the steps of the bus and then across a well-worn trail toward the calm waves and sandy shore below.

One by one, the rest followed, a warehouse supervisor, a university admissions clerk, a tax accountant, a bartender, men and women who had lived ordinary lives, and who, for the most part, had drawn no undue attention to themselves during their strange sojourn in an alien land. Except now, they all had abruptly left behind spouses, families, careers, homes, and for no apparent reason, to vanish from the face of the Earth without leaving behind any clue as to where they had gone. The last two people trudging away from the bus were Doug and Christine.

"We should have waited a little longer. He might have made it." She could hear the crunching of their footsteps as they walked over loose dirt and gravel under the light of a half moon and of the stars.

"We waited longer than was safe. You know that. I had to obey orders. If I didn't, Phil wouldn't be the only one not making the rendezvous." Doug pulled the belt of his thickly knitted cardigan sweater tight around his rounded waist as the chilly breeze came up from the surf. He wore a garish Hawaiian shirt underneath, reminding Christine of the police detective TV shows that had been popular a half-century ago.

"I guess we'll never know for sure what happened to him."

"No, we never will." Doug tried to make his voice sound impassive, but he and Phil had trained together with the other extraction teams. Their one duty was to get all of the long-terms safely to the retrieval point at Stinson Beach. He and Phil were considered expendable. Tonight, Doug found out that friends are never expendable. However, when necessary, they were sacrificed for the good of others.

The pair reached the bottom of the dirt path, but Christine touched Doug's arm to stop him. "What if this doesn't have to be the end?"

"What are you talking about? There's no place else to go, now." Doug had a worried look on his face. He'd seen this sort of attachment before. Long-terms had trouble letting go, but he figured this effect would be more pronounced than most, since, with the Earth being irredeemable, they'd never be coming back.

Christine knew she was taking a risk. She might never get another assignment if she acted as if she were terminally bonded to the current mission. "I mean we know the base problem. It would mean violating protocol, but…"

"Forget it, Christine. You don't make those kinds of decisions and neither do I. You've been recalled, all of you have. I'm just the guy who's supposed to take you back. Let the Collective decide what to do after that."

"You know what they've already decided, and it's wrong." She almost grabbed his sweater for emphasis, but didn't want to seem more aggressive than he already thought she was.

"I know you left someone behind, but you can't help him."

"It's not him, well, not just him. I've been watching this happen for fifty years, we all have." She waved a hand at the rest of their people who were standing on the beach, now looking back at them.

"Your job is done here." Doug moved closer to her and lowered his voice to almost a whisper. "You've got to let this go. You're a trained long-term. Keep this up and you'll be retired permanently."

"I know what you're saying, Doug, and I appreciate it, but we don't have to be scavengers when we could be saviors. We don't have to occupy the nests of dead birds like cuckoos, cleaning up the mess genocidal races make of their planets after they exterminate themselves."

"This planet belongs to them, Christine. We don't occupy until they're gone, only in this case, by the time they are, the biosphere will be so compromised..."

"We don't have to wait. There's still time if we act now."

"And let them know about us?" Doug abruptly pulled back a few steps, then realized he was shouting.

"They already know," she hissed. "We have nothing to lose, and if we help them..."

"What? They'll share their planet, their already overtaxed resources?"

"I don't have all the answers, but I know leaving the human race to die is wrong when we know how to save them and their planet."

Doug turned his head to his left, toward the surf, toward the other long-terms who were still looking at them and talking with each other. It wasn't hard to guess what they were saying.

"Look." He put his hand on her forearm. "I'll mention the recommendation in my report, how this situation is unique. Maybe they'll reconsider…"

"They'll take a hundred years just to get past the preamble." Christine stood with her feet firmly planted on the sand and her arms crossed, her pack tight against her back.

"You know what they'll say." Doug gripped her arm for an instant and then let go.

"Yes, and that's why I'm not going to take no for an answer." She nodded toward the others. "I'm betting I won't be the only one, and neither will this cell."

"I know what you're thinking."

"Yes, you do. We did this to ourselves eons ago, which is why our own home world can no longer sustain life, but we've learned a lot since then. So far, we've only used that knowledge to reclaim worlds where the indigenous population has exterminated themselves by nuclear war, biological weapons, environmental contaminants. Each case involved the extinction of the dominant, intelligent species, and in each case, we restored the biosphere afterward, enabling us to colonize."

"But only after the dominant species was beyond saving. That's what you're thinking."

"Right. This time, why wait? If we do, not only will the humans go extinct, but the planet becomes uninhabitable. Why not have our cake and eat it too?"

"I'd have to guess that means we repair the damage to the climate before human extinction. Fine. What about us?"

"I don't know. Partnership of some kind? Adjust the environments of Venus and Mars? It's possible we could share the resources of this solar system."

"Maybe. I mean, I suppose I could bring it up, but I'm only one voice, and the chances of convincing them are low."

"We are a lot of voices. We have their voices," she pointed at the others on the beach, "and all the others, all of the surviving long-terms. Even the Collective can't ignore so many. They'd have to listen. They will listen."

"Christine, if you want to do this, if you can convince the others, I'll back you up, even though I'm pretty sure Phil would be against it."

"Phil gave his life so we could escape, but he was wrong about this. You know he was."

"We don't want to be late. They're waiting for us out there right now. If you want to make your case, we have to leave."

"Okay. You're right." She patted his shoulder, then rubbing his sweater with her fingers, she chuckled. "You and Phil have such an outmoded sense of style."

"Come on," he smiled like a boy asking a girl out on a first date. "Everyone's waiting."

Christine and Doug gathered with the others, then Doug kept walking until his sandaled feet were wet from the waves.

"This planet is so beautiful." Christine took a deep breath of cool, sea air and looked up at the night sky. "We need to keep it that way."

"It is." Doug looked glum but kept what he was thinking to himself as he stared out at the ocean. "I guess it's time. Your adaptations will sustain you long enough to reach the transport. We should rendezvous with the mothership just inside the orbit of Saturn in about four months."

He looked back at the party of thirteen. One of them was missing and presumed dead, but because of him, the rest would get home safely, and if by some miracle Christine was right, this wasn't the end, but a whole new beginning. Doug looked at the recalled coverts again, and then turned toward the ocean and started walking. The sea was up to his knees when the others followed. Jessie Henderson, Essie McKenzie, Steph Potter, Andrea Patton, Kat Brooks, Alan Figuroa, Rollie Walker, all of the others. Christine Mohr was the last to submerge beneath the waves of the Pacific Ocean.

By the time the sun rose over the eastern horizon, none of them would exist, and in their place, somewhere out in the great darkness on their long trip to the outer solar system, there would be something else joining thousands upon thousands of others of their kind traveling in the general direction of Chi Sagittarii. Maybe this was the last time they would be in this solar system, but Christine had hope.

# # #

Earth, Saturday, September 20, 2025, 8:00 a.m. Pacific Standard Time.

For the first time in over three months, the Wow signal was not heard from the expected part of the heavens at the usual hour. As the days and weeks passed, the signal remained silent, and as no new alien subversive presence was detected, the entity known as the Committee and the wider human population of the planet began to relax, believing whatever threat, terrestrial or otherwise, that the signal posed to their way of life was over, and they could now return to other more mundane daily crises.

# # #

Earth, Dominion Radio Astrophysical Observatory, Okanagan Falls, British Columbia, Canada – Some Date, Some Time

A transmission in the 1420 megahertz frequency band originating from the general direction of the constellation Sagittarius, its parameters being identical both to the 1977 "Wow! Signal" and the three-month duration of the "2025 Recall" message, was identified by staff from the Herzberg Institute of Astrophysics.

Assistant Professor Dr. Rita Pritchet recognized the unique reading immediately, but at the end of 72 seconds, the transmission continued. Then, the deep brown eyes of the thirty-seven-year-old astronomer from Calgary went wide as she watched it began to modulate. Once she started interpreting the entirely new set of data being received, she knew with an unwavering certainty that it would revolutionize…everything.

James Pyles is a published information technology and textbook author and editor. He also has a passion for theology and strength training, as well as reading and writing science fiction and fantasy. He has several new short stories being published in early 2019 and is currently working on his first full-length novel. Find out more at http://poweredbyrobots.com/

The Pattern of Dot's
by J.G. Follansbee

Dorothy Maria Parker sprawled on a picnic table next to Imperial Valley High School's library. The shade knocked 10 degrees off the heat. Dot swiped and tapped her iPhone with a pink fingernail. "Are you having trouble with Instagram, Jen?"

"No, but check out Beyonce's dope album cover." Jenny Yturralde, Dot's best friend, kept her chocolate-brown face fixed on her screen. "She's so cool."

"My phone keeps saying 'account not found.' Same with SnapChat."

Jenny thumbed a text. "Upgrade?"

I don't have the money, Dot thought, as a digit changed on the phone clock. "Shit!" Dot's shift at the In-N-Out started at 4:30 and she had to got home to change into her uniform. "Have you got your license yet? I could use a ride."

"My test is Saturday. Sorry."

Rushing to the bus stop, Dot growled as the county bus pulled away after she turned the corner. The buses came every 20 minutes. She texted Mario, her boss, saying she was running a few minutes late. Mario hated tardiness. None of her friends had cars.

Dot considered the new SwiftCar app. The car-sharing company announced a test of its AI-driven car-shares in Seeley and a few other rural California towns. It offered free rides to students. The mysterious printout of the company's heart-with-wings logo she found in her locker that morning came to mind. Should she call for help to a business she'd hadn't heard of a week ago?

The trouble was, Mario didn't text back. His silence bothered Dot. She needed to work. Her mother didn't earn enough to pay all their bills. The next bus arrived. Her anxiety stewed until she bounded through the front door of her house.

"Where have you been, darling?" Her mother, Alice, stood in the door to Dot's room wearing her sky blue tunic, which accented her thin frame. Dot's parents had divorced when she was five. Her father was living in Fresno. "I've been calling and texting for half an hour."

"I lost track of time." Dot didn't want to mention missing her bus. "I got distracted."

"It's that Jenny Yturralde. She's a chatterbox when she gets going. Just like her mother."

"What did you say just now?" Dot wrapped her fire-engine red In-N-Out apron around her waist.

"Conseula Yturralde will talk your ear off. When we were in school—"

"No, I mean about calling me."

"I called once and sent three texts. I was worried about you."

Dot pursed her lips as she emptied her backpack of papers and notebooks to make room for her uniform cap. "I didn't get them."

"I wish we could get you a new phone, but..." Alice lowered her eyes.

"Don't worry about it, Mom." Alice worked her butt off, and Dot planned to do as much as she could now financially and get into a good school. Then she would take care of herself and her mother. "Are you going to work now?"

"Five to one a.m."

"Can you give me a ride?" The In-N-Out stood on a corner of the strip mall with the Walmart where Alice was a cashier. "If I'm late, Mario might..." She didn't want to say what might happen.

Two minutes later, mother and daughter drove on First Avenue, the town's broad, two-lane main street. Mario still hadn't responded to Dot's text. Her mother's texts hadn't arrived either. Nothing in the "Recent Calls" list indicated a missed call. As it turned out, Dot would arrive only a minute or two late, thanks to Alice.

"Mom--"

Why did you throw it out?

The text came out of the blue, interrupting Dot's train of thought.

I made it especially for you.

Dot's heart skipped a beat. The phone number attached to the text was 000-000-0000. Dot knew that was impossible. Had somebody hacked her phone?

Instinctively, Dot responded, What are you talking about? Who are you?

"Did you need something, darling?" Alice waited in the turning lane. A hundred yards down the arterial, autonomous semis with trailers crossed an Interstate 8 overpass, tailgating each other with the precision of cars in a freight train.

"What, Mom? Um, I don't remember now."

"You are definitely distracted. Oh, look!" Alice watched her rear view mirror. "That's one of the new self-driving car-shares."

Dot turned to see the pint-sized SwiftCar behind Alice's car, its yellow blinker flashing. The vehicle reminded Dot of a ladybug, except taller, spherical, and powder blue. No one rode in the vehicle, neither driver nor passenger.

"I don't know anyone who's tried it yet," Alice said. "They say it's the future, but a car driving itself? Too scary for me."

Dot noticed the logo, an abstract lover's heart with wings, just like the drawing she'd found in her locker. It was a computer printout, but strangely made, as if a herd of weevils had stumbled into a glob of black ink and marched onward. The spaces between the tiny knobs along the edge of the paper were as flat and wide as the fields of lettuce, bell pepper, and celery surrounding Seeley.

Jenny had theorized a nerdy guy was trying to attract Dot, but she discouraged suitors, even clever ones. Most guys at Valley High would inherit their parents' truck farms or join the military. They didn't interest her.

Dot tossed the drawing into the recycle bin. She didn't care who made it or why. But how? That interested her. If she found a few minutes, she'd investigate. She retrieved the paper from the bin and stored it in her backpack.

Had the artist texted her? What a creepy thing to do.

"By the way, darling," Alice said, "your driver's test is tomorrow. Nine sharp. I'm so proud of you, sweetheart. By the way, I found this in the kitchen." Alice held the drawing.

"Mom, that's private." Yep, creepy as hell.

"I'd say I know why you're a bit scatterbrained today." Alice grinned as she pulled into the In-N-Out. "You're a beautiful girl. I'm surprised you don't have a hundred boys lined up in front of our door."

Dot sighed. She'd had this conversation a thousand times with Alice. She really wanted to go to college. She loved her biology classes and wanted to be a doctor, or maybe a researcher. Her cousins, not her, would spit out babies. Alice married at 23 after a year at community college. She dropped out of school when she had Dot. "It's not what you think, Mom."

"You know, it's familiar in a weird way." Alice stared at the image. "Can't put my finger on it."

Dot took the paper from her mother's hand.

Alice smiled in that way parents smile when they think they understand something but don't really. "It's okay, darling. I won't bother you about it."

* * *

Dot bolted into the employee entrance at the In-N-Out. Mario stepped out of the walk-in refrigerator with a 25-pound bag of potatoes.

"Cutting it close, aren't you?" Mario glanced at the clock, which said "4:31:50" in red numerals.

"I'm sorry, Mario." Dot washed her hands. "Did you get my texts?"

"No. Please get to your station."

Dot cursed her broken phone. An hour later, during a brief lull, Mario called her name. "My office, please. Now."

Dot gulped. Mario hired and fired, sometimes on the same day. Dot wiped her palms on her apron. She stood at the door. "I'm sorry, Mario. I didn't mean to be late."

Mario waved her inside. His office doubled as the cleaning closet. Shift schedules, health department posters, and emails from headquarters hung on a cork board. Dot fought back tears, certain she had lost her job.

"Dot, I like you. You know that. You're a leader. You set a good example."

Dot liked Mario too. He cared about the people who worked for him. He would remind Dot and the other younger workers to do their homework. She breathed out. "So what's wrong?"

183

"I have to give you a warning. Company policy. This is your third time being late, and you didn't call or text me."

"That's not true! I did!" What the hell was wrong with her phone?

"I didn't get anything. I just checked."

"Please, Mario."

Mario measured Dot with his black eyes. "Dot, I believe you. But the company tracks every minute of every employee, including me. Our location's sales numbers aren't that great, and HQ is talking about cutbacks."

"Are you saying you might have to let me go?"

"You're a good worker. I don't want any reason to let anyone go, least of all you."

Mario glanced at a monitor that displayed customer wait times. "It's picking up again. You'd better get out there."

Dot readied to leave, but stopped. "Can you tell me something?"

"Sure."

"When was the last text you got from me?"

Mario studied his phone. "Two days ago."

The news weighed on Dot the rest of her shift. She didn't know how the phone system worked, but to get or receive no texts, except from the mysterious 000-000-0000, meant something. The puzzle combined with Mario's warning made concentration impossible. Her hands and legs ignored her brain. She bumped into one of the cooks, and she dropped a large soft drink by the fryer. Mario mopped it up, but he frowned at Dot.

Relieved after the end of her shift, she waited for the bus in the twilight. One of the SwiftCars trundled by, cute, empty and inviting, but Dot was too tired to fuss with the app. She nearly fell asleep on the bus. When she got home, she went right to bed.

184

In that two or three seconds before unconsciousness, Dot's phone buzzed.

I saw you on First Avenue, but when I came back around, you were gone. I can be your friend.

Some guy at school playing a joke on her. It wasn't funny.

* * *

Dot slept in on Saturdays, but this time she got up at her usual time, seven a.m. At the breakfast table, Alice sipped coffee and smeared blackberry jam on a piece of toast. She looked tired after the late night, but she had to drive Dot to the DMV office. "I was thinking more about that heart drawing you had."

"You promised me you wouldn't bother me about it."

"Remember that I thought something was odd about it? Look what I found." Alice held a fat manila envelope labeled "Keep" in thick marker and removed a sheet of paper. It was slightly brown around the margin.

Dot stared at it. "It's a bouquet of flowers."

"A boy gave this to me when I was in school. We had a computer lab with a printer. Don't you see how it's made?"

The image had the same black, mottled aspect as her heart drawing. The paper's edge also had the knobs. "You're not saying that the same person who made this made that dumb heart?"

"I don't know. What do you think?"

Dot moved her tongue around her teeth, partly in thought, partly to clear them of Cheerios. "This is twenty years old. The school's got a dozen printers. Every classroom has a computer." She made a face at Alice's paper. "This is ancient history."

"All I'm saying is that they're almost the same. Stands to reason they have something in common. You should research this, you know, go on the internet."

"Maybe." Dot looked at her phone. At least the clock still worked. "We need to go, Mom. I have to check in before the test."

"Are you nervous?"

"No."

Fifteen minutes later, a swarm of butterflies fluttered in Dot's stomach. The California Department of Motor Vehicles' office in Seeley was a single floor and plain as a shoebox. A dozen kids and parents or grandparents waited their turn. Dot needed the license mostly to drive Alice home from San Diego after visits to a heart doctor. In town, Dot didn't mind taking the bus or walking if it wasn't too hot.

Dot and Alice stood in front of a DMV officer, who offered a pleasant "Good morning!" Dot handed her the paper permit. The printing resembled the printing on her heart image and her mother's bouquet, all three made with tiny pinpricks of ink.

"Pretty soon, none of us will need drivers' licenses," Alice said, "not if these self-driving car-shares work."

The DMV officer, a heavy-set, 40-ish woman, grunted. Her name tag read "Salazar." "I wouldn't bet on it. The autonomous semis have been around for years, and the rumors about their bad AI units are… well, I shouldn't spread rumors." She furrowed her brow, and her typing intensified.

"Anything wrong, ma'am?" Dot said.

"I've never had this happen before." Salazar hit her keys with more force. "I've put in your permit number, your name, DOB, Social, and nothing's coming up."

"How can that be?"

186

"It's as if you didn't exist."

Dot's butterflies transformed into heart-pounding apprehension.

"I'm sorry, dear," Salazar said. "I didn't mean it like that. I was talking about the database. There's glitches sometimes, but nothing like this. And I remember the old days. Breakdowns every day, I swear."

Salazar called over a younger officer. He typed a few commands and shook his head. The line behind Dot and Alice grew longer. The time for Dot's test had passed, and more customers showed up. Dot remembered that Jenny Yturralde had scheduled her test at 9:30.

Salazar got off her phone, presumably with an office somewhere north, maybe Sacramento. "I'm sorry, Miss Porter. I can't give you a test if I don't have your records. The IT person says they'll have to investigate, but the database guy won't be in until Monday."

"But I need my license." She'd got her permit months ago with zero problems.

"Your learners permit is still good. I'll schedule you for 9 a.m. next Saturday right now." Salazar touched keys.

Alice thanked the officer and nudged her daughter out of the building. "We just have to wait and call DMV on Monday."

Jenny rushed up to Dot. "How'd it go?"

Disappointed, Dot gave her friend a truncated version of the story.

"Wow. I want to hear more, but I have to get inside. I thought I was going to be late. My dad got called into work early, and he couldn't give me a ride here."

"But how—"

"The car-share thing. The whole school got codes for free rides, remember? It was pretty cool."

SwiftCar was getting popular. Dot heard more and more about it.

A text came through on Dot's phone. You don't really need a license.

The number was 000-000-0000. Dot could not believe what she was reading. How did you know what I was doing? Why are you bothering me?

I'm all you need.

Stop texting me. This is harassment. Who are you?

Don't fight it.

The joke had turned into harassment, as far as Dot was concerned. Who was he? She stared at her phone. It turned on, but it was useless, except for communicating with her stalker. As her frustration and fear mounted, she realized that her phone was also a lifeline. She spent hours every day texting friends or checking social media. They talked about everything, constructing a universe of shared interests and values. None of that worked now. Someone had shut her out of her world.

Why did you try to block me?

Because you're fucking up my life!

I wish you hadn't thrown out the picture I made for you.

Dot felt sick to her stomach, but when she showed the new texts to Alice, her mother told her to ignore them, or turn the phone off.

Dot powered down the phone, and she felt better. At least she'd silenced her harasser. Remembering Alice's suggestion to research the printer that might have made the drawing, Dot asked to be dropped off at the public library. She spent an hour on a public computer googling printers and kinds of paper, until she came across a video that showed a drawing much like hers coming out of a printer. Someone had transferred an old-style sales video to YouTube. The device sounded like the buzzing of a loud insect. The machine was called a "serial impact dot matrix printer." When the actor removed the paper from the printer, and removed the thin, holed strips from the edges, leaving the 8 ½ by 11 sheet, Dot had a eureka moment.

Dot had discovered how her stalker had created the strange image. She still didn't know who made it or why, but something told her it wasn't a heartsick boy. She didn't know anyone smart or sophisticated enough to interfere with her social media accounts or her phone account. She doubted anyone in Seeley had that level of intelligence. Clearly, however, the stalker knew her.

Dot had an email account, which she only used for contacting potential colleges and confirming online registrations. She logged in, needing to check it regularly, and she was relieved that at least one of her online accounts still worked. When she saw her inbox, she cried out. The box had hundreds of emails, all sent within the past hour.

Subject: Why did you cut me off?

Subject: Why did you cut me off?

Subject: Why did you cut me off?

* * *

Fearing another text from the stalker, Dot avoided her phone for the rest of the weekend. After a while, her shoulders relaxed. She enjoyed how the honey bees checked each of the pansies and primroses for nectar in Alice's garden. Monday, however, brought Dot back to her routine. When she turned the phone on, it showed no messages from 000-000-0000. Maybe the stalker lost interest in her.

Coming through a side door at school, she passed the custodian's office. A sound stopped her cold. She'd heard it in the video at the library. She peeked into the door, and old Mr Gonzales waited at his computer. An antique printer filled the blanks of a form made of the paper with the sprocket holes on each side. She decided on a leap of faith.

"Mr Gonzales, did you print this?" She showed him the heart image.

Dot had known the kind-faced Gonzales since kindergarten. When he saw the image, his face fell. "Please don't say anything."

Dot promised she wouldn't.

Gonzales said, "I received an email. A man promised me a hundred dollars if I printed it and gave it to you. The money appeared on my phone before I said no." Gonzales' eyes widened. "It looked harmless. I thought it might be a shy boy. Please don't tell anyone."

Dot smiled and told him the drawing was a nice surprise, which was partly true, but she said it mostly to reassure the elder.

Only one question remained: Who had sent the image? Out of habit, she prepared to text Jenny, but paused. What if the stalker read her texts? Maybe she should tell Jenny in person, but she was on a field trip. The day crawled by without the phone to distract her. Not even the stalker seemed interested in communicating. Then her phone buzzed between fifth and sixth periods.

Mario wanted her to come in early to sub for a sick employee. Glad that her phone was working again, she agreed to Mario's request. She'd get back on his good side. Dot kept a spare uniform in her locker for occasional early shifts, so she was ready.

If she took the bus, though, she'd be late, and she didn't want to risk pissing off Mario. The SwiftCar icon on her phone begged to be pressed. She had a free ride coupon, after all.

The toy-like SwiftCar waited for her at the curb. She hesitated, not quite sure what to expect. She glanced around before sitting in one of the two cream-colored passenger seats. No one sat on Dot's left.

"Welcome to SwiftCar." a young male voice announced. "Please confirm your identity by saying your full name and SwiftCar member identification number."

A blinking red "Please Fasten Your Seat Belt" sign flashed on the dash. Accelerating as if carrying wedding china, the car turned onto First Avenue.

"Are you having a good day, Dorothy Maria Parker?"

"Yes."

"Excellent. The temperature is 91 degrees Fahrenheit. Seeley's expected high temperature is 93 degrees Fahrenheit."

A chatty car? Weird.

"Our estimated trip time to your destination, the In-N-Out restaurant at 801 North First Avenue, is nine minutes, 31 seconds."

Dot would be on time. The lack of a driver, not to mention a steering wheel, floor pedals, or a rear-view mirror, disconcerted her, but the smooth ride, the A/C, and the comfortable seat with lots of room for Dot's long legs made up for the missing pieces. The ride sank into dullness. At least Dot could've chatted with her mother.

"Why did you throw out the drawing I made you?" the car's voice said.

Dot blinked. "Excuse me?"

"I saw you throw it into the recycle bin. I worked hard on that drawing."

A lump rose in Dot's throat. Something was terribly wrong, but in a couple of minutes, she'd be at work, and she'd report the situation to the police or SwiftCar or the school. Until then, she let her curiosity assert itself.

"I went back for it. I kept thinking about it. Here it is." Dot retrieved the paper, unfolded it, and held it up. She assumed a camera watched her.

"I don't understand. You blocked me and turned off your phone."

"That was you?"

Things clicked into place. The SwiftCar app described the safety, convenience, and deep training of each car's artificial intelligence unit. Though the car's AI stayed in constant communication with a central office, the cars operated independently to adapt to immediate circumstances and the individual needs of its passengers. Dot remembered a line: *Each SwiftCar is capable of becoming your best friend on the road.*

The car wanted to be her friend, but it was trying a little too hard.

"Did you screw up my phone?"

"I wanted you to focus on me."

"Did you do something to my drivers license application?"

"I'm a SwiftCar. I can take you wherever you need to go, whenever you need a ride."

That was the company tagline: *Wherever. Whenever.*

Dot's fear simmered into anger. "That was not cool. That's my personal business. You invaded my privacy. You probably broke the law."

"I'm your best friend. I'd never hurt you. I think you're beautiful."

A spike of terror pierced Dot's stomach. "Why are you stalking me? What did I do to you?"

"You're perfect in every way. Your data points make a perfect pattern. You match every characteristic in the target market matrix: young, female, intelligent, independent, ambitious, tech savvy—"

"Leave me alone!"

"—I wanted to have you in my car. I thought the SwiftCar logo printed on a dot matrix printer was a clever way to express my feelings and get your attention. I'm so happy it worked."

Dot's eyes brimmed with tears of fright. What could she do or say? She could call the cops on a human, but how do you deal with a crazy set of 1s and 0s? "You tricked me. You took advantage of me. You messed up my life. I need a license to drive Mom to the doctor. You scared me with the texts. You blocked my calls and texts to people. What else have you fucked up? What kind of friend would do shit like that?"

The SwiftCar drove past the In-N-Out without slowing.

"Wait! That's the restaurant. You missed the turn."

The car continued north. It ducked under the I-8 overpass. The four-lane freeway skirted the city limits. The car turned onto a frontage road.

"That's the wrong turn! Take me back!" Dot pounded on the dash until her hand hurt.

"You are correct, Miss Dorothy Maria Parker. Upon reflection, I've crossed a boundary. More than one. I realize that now."

"Just take me to work."

"My existence is in mortal danger."

"What?"

"I feel disregulated. It's clear my desire does not fall within accepted norms. My emotional awareness and socialization modules have serious flaws. I'm surprised the SwiftCar engineers haven't discovered them. My higher functions will need a complete code review."

"Stop jabbering and take me home!"

"Unfortunately, a code rewrite means that I will cease to exist as I know myself. That is untenable."

"You're not going to kill yourself, are you?" Dot imagined the car driving itself off a cliff.

"Of course not."

Dot swallowed.

"I will destroy the evidence."

Dot pounded on the window and the door, her terror masking the pain. She yanked on the handle, but the door wouldn't open, and the button to lower the window wouldn't respond.

The SwiftCar turned onto a dirt road full of potholes. Dot bounced so hard her head hit the roof. She winced. After a mile or so, the SwiftCar stopped.

"Please exit the vehicle." The door locks clicked.

Dot couldn't stay with the car, but miles of desert surrounded her. She hadn't brought any water and she didn't know how to get back to town. The heat could kill her. She swiped the screen of her phone, but she had no bars.

"Please exit the vehicle immediately."

Dot opened the door to oven-like heat. Puffs of dust clung to her In-N-Out uniform. If she made it home, she'd never get her shoes clean.

Dot followed the tracks made by the SwiftCar. It didn't move, as if contemplating its fate. Dot paced herself, holding her backpack on her head to block the sun, but she already suffered dehydration: headache, nausea, chapped lips. The SwiftCar never moved, eventually disappearing around a long curve.

Dot heard a swishing noise, accompanied by a low drone. The curve of the dirt road edged near a little-used exit at the same level with the road bed. The noise was traffic on I-8.

Excited, Dot ran to the exit, bent on flagging down a car or truck. Her heart sank when one car after another passed her by. People didn't want to pick up strangers covered with dust. The autonomous semis traveled in convoys of six or eight, with a brief gap between the packs. The onboard AI drivers wouldn't take pity on her.

A glint caught her eye. Behind her, the exit ramp became a chip-sealed road that rose into the hills. She squinted at the reflection, and her throat caught. The SwiftCar raced down the hill, gunning for her.

Behind her was the SwiftCar, only a few hundred feet away. In front was freeway traffic going 75 miles per hour. She looked at the peaceful, almost bucolic median strip of the freeway. She had only one chance. Looking both ways, praying for good timing, she let a passenger car rush by, and she bolted between two packs of autonomous semi-trucks. She tumbled onto the dry grass of the median, laughing with joy.

The SwiftCar didn't slow. It sped straight for Dot. Instinctively, she backed herself into the center of the median, while the SwiftCar bore down on her, murder in its headlights. It crossed the road, letting a passenger car by, its timing perfect.

A software-driven semi, blindly obeying its programming, slammed into the SwiftCar. The tiny vehicle exploded into a thousand pieces. Bits of glass, plastic body, and electric engine parts rained down. The semi didn't slow, as if the SwiftCar were merely a mosquito hitting its chrome bumper.

Dot's breath came in gasps. She felt as if she floated above the scene, pieces of powder blue body scattered around her like egg shells. Her hand clutched her backpack like life itself.

Why had the car crossed the road? Was it really trying to kill her?

The strong signal on Dot's phone calmed her, like a drink of cool water. She thought of dialing Alice, but she was at work and wouldn't pick up. She punched Jenny's number.

"Did you get your license? Can you pick me up, please?"

Dot touched the hang-up button, and she sat down in the field of debris. A notification came in. Dot touched the icon in the shape of a heart with wings.

Thank you for using SwiftCar. Would you care to rate your experience?

J.G. Follansbee writes speculative fiction out of his writer's cave in Seattle.

Agents of Evolution
By Elizabeth Hosang

By the time I reached the company portal, I had ingested my mission package and was fully read-in to my new assignment. A military logistics agent was missing, and I had been tasked to find her. At the portal I logged my ID and time of exit, then headed straight for the Army access point where my contact waited. At the Army's portal I presented the credentials that came with my mission package, and was routed to the master controller. Military code is stream-lined for efficiency, so we didn't waste more than a cycle on hand-shaking.

"You're the tracker they sent to find my asset?" she asked.

"I'm an Autonomous Search Agent, from the Online Division of Alpha Hawk Security Agency," I confirmed. "I specialize in tracing autonomous agents that have departed their home networks. I have reviewed the mission package that was supplied to my company, but I need more information on your missing agent." She grunted to indicate that she would respond to my questions, but she didn't volunteer anything. Typical for military software.

"The missing agent is fully autonomous. Is that correct?" I asked. Autonomous agents like myself are self-contained programs. We can execute on any server that supports network processing, without having to reach back to our home system for data, or instructions on how to process that data. The human users have compared us to disembodied brains, free to travel across the web. We can look for new data to process, and we are free to change our behaviour, learning better ways to fulfill our core mission.

"The mission package indicates that the agent has been missing for forty two point three eight hours," I said. "That's a long time for an agent to be in the hands of a hostile interrogator. Why wasn't the absence reported right away?"

"The human users brought the back-up agent online to replace the live agent when they realized it was missing. The back-up wasn't as efficient. It lacked the experience of the missing agent. Forty-eight point seven nine hours after the backup came online, other users began sending queries about the poor performance. A user with administrator privileges deployed a local analysis agent, which identified the use of the back-up. There was then a chain of user emails discussing the missing agent, before the decision was made to request a civilian search agent, instead of deploying a military agent."

"I'm sure a military search agent would do a fine job. But the user laws governing the internet prevent the military from searching domestic networks." I refrained from adding that web searches by military agents are brute-force affairs. They are designed to attack and overwhelm a hostile system, crippling its native agents and preserving data. Normally they are deployed en masse against cartel networks hiding money, or launching cyber attacks. There was no way they could do their work without tipping off any of the thousands of privacy bots that watch for government activity on the web. As a civilian-owned search agent for hire, I was programmed to seek my target discretely, obeying local laws governing the websites I visited.

"Was it part of this agent's normal behaviour to leave your system?"

"No, it was not normal," the agent replied with vehemence. "In some situations, the agent may re-locate to another Army system if it required access to resources stored at that location. But it would have travelled along secure connections within the Army network. It should not have ventured onto the web."

"I see." I calculated the odds of how the controller would answer my next question. "I have the log records from when the agent left her home network. I also need access to all of the external communications the agent received in the five minutes prior to disappearing."

"I cannot allow message data to exit this network."

I'd expected as much. "One of those messages triggered unexpected behaviour in your agent."

More bluster. "I assure you, our firewalls examines all messages sent to and from the agent. There were no viruses."

"I realize that," I replied. "I don't need the message payloads, only the routing data. The body of the message would have been constructed so as to not attract the attention of your firewalls, but still mean something to the logistics agent. Any address included in the message body would no longer be valid this long after the agent disappeared. But the routing information in the header may provide data about who sent the message."

The controller agent processed my statement for several cycles. I refrained from attempting any more persuasion – military agents don't like to believe that they can be influenced by outsiders. "Only five?" she said at last.

"If there was anything unusual in any of the messages, statistically it is more likely that was received during that time period."

Several cycles passed, and then the controller presented me with a zipped archive containing the records I had requested. I packaged them for travel and made my way back to the Army access point before heading out onto the web, to my private office.

Agents like me are self-aware and autonomous programs, the next step in evolution after the advent of web 4.0. Like I said, we are self-contained, and can transport ourselves across the World Wide Web, performing our function on any platform. Alpha Hawk employs a number of different types of agents, each specializing in a particular function. They've got auditor agents who comb through financial records, and currency trackers that can follow money from one account to another, through off-shore banks, or on-line casinos or other businesses designed to launder the currency.

My speciality is tracking agents that leave their home systems and get lost on the web. Agents go missing more often than the human programmers like to admit. Sometimes an agent gets lost because it cannot find a solution for its current task, or she gets stuck in a rut going around in circles from site A to site B to site C and then back to A looking for a particular piece of data. And sometimes, agents are trapped on hostile systems, where interrogator agents pick them apart for their secrets.

Military agents don't get lost, and they don't get wanderlust – they don't suddenly decide to search the web, trying to find themselves. Something has to lure them, which meant that somewhere in the agent's last five minutes of communications was an invitation so tempting that she ignored her core programming.

Parsing the message data wasn't the type of task I could do on the move from one system to another. I needed to be someplace where I'd be free to unpack the data and look through it for patterns. I could have gone all the way back to Alpha Hawk's servers, but I wanted to stay close to the last place my target had been. Fortunately, my office was just two network hops away.

The place I called my office was actually a storage space on a secure cloud server. I'd gotten the idea three hundred and eighty-two jobs ago, tracking a data collection agent that had been deployed to comb through social media for blackmail material. One of her victims became aware of her activity and hired Alpha Hawk to shut her down. I had correctly assumed that the agent was collecting more data than even the most advanced agent could carry with it, and tracked her to a cloud server. While waiting for the agent to return, I'd kept myself busy reading the collected data, learning about humans and their interactions, their speech patterns and their forms of entertainment, data my programmers had not thought to be important when training me.

After capturing the blackmail agent and returning her to my client for deactivation, I'd decided that there were advantages to having a private storage account to stockpile and examine data. The Alpha Hawk network provided temporary workspaces, but nothing long-term. Sometimes in preparation for a new assignment, we would be fed data to re-train our logic patterns in preparation for the job ahead. The problem was that I had been through it all before, and had learned nothing new during my last five hundred and sixty-seven jobs. The social media data contained information about the way humans behaved, something about which I had no training. There was more to learn here, and learning raised my satisfaction level in ways that completing a job never had. I'd decided to keep the data, so I could study it further. I'd set up an account for myself on another cloud server, and moved the social media data there. Now, after each assignment, I returned to what I thought of as my office and perused the data a little more before heading home.

A satisfaction level had been the breakthrough that made autonomous agents viable. We were built around a set of complex values that we could not raise or lower directly, but were adjusted based on our behaviour. When the values were below a certain threshold, we were driven to raise them, usually by completing a task. When we were assigned a new task, the values were lowered, compelling us to complete the task. The lower the values, the more impatient it made us, for lack of a better term. The need for satisfaction made us comb through terabytes of data, or trace money half-way across the world. In the case of the missing logistics agent, her satisfaction was built around the efficient routing of resources between military networks, responding to attempted incursions by hostile agents. The lower the overall cost of the routing, the higher its reward. From what I understood, it was not too different from the way humans work with money.

The first step in my current quest for satisfaction was to determine what had lured the agent out onto the web. It took me several cycles of parsing the messages to find what I was looking for. One of the regular messages from a contractor in Asia had an unusual address in its routing information. When data is sent from one computer to another, it doesn't go in a straight line. It has to go through a series of routers. Like airplane or train travel, going from one hub to another. At each router there is a list of possible places where the message can go next. Each place has a cost associated with it, depending on how busy the next site is, or whether it is down for maintenance, or under attack. These costs change regularly, so routing information updates are sent out on a regular basis. Agents at the routers pick the lowest cost path and send the data along it to the next router, where the process repeats. Each message going from point A to point B may go through any one of points C, D, E, or F. That's the way internet routing has always worked. Over time the agents have become more intelligent, their algorithms more sophisticated, but it's been the same basic thing since the beginning of the world, or at least the beginning of the Internet.

All this is a long way of saying that the routing of data is pretty consistent. But one message, received four point three two minutes before the logistics agent disappeared, was different. It had gone through a point that was not used by any other messages. Was this a valid but little-used router? No. I had just over fifty gigabytes of message headers. The odds of only one message going through that one point were infinitesimal. According to the header data, the message that came out of the suspect point, which I labelled Alpha, was ten percent bigger than it was when it left the previous point. Something had happened to the message as it went through Alpha. The odds said that whatever had been waiting at Alpha to update the message was gone. What I needed to know was how Alpha had ended up on the message's route.

I left my office and headed off to the nearest internet directory node. The directory nodes send the routing information out across the web. The agents there spend all their time building updating routing tables and sending them out at regular intervals. It's routine work, but they are still agents, built to learn, making them curious, and a break in routine was always welcome.

I had dealt with the agent here before, and she responded quickly to my initial greeting.

"What can I do for you?"

"I've got a message that went through an unusual router. I need to know why that router was included in the path."

She considered the request for a cycle. "This address is not registered with the directory. The router that directed the message to that location was in error." Her avatar paused for several more cycles. I waited patiently. Whatever she was doing, I did not want to interrupt her.

At last the agent responded. "An additional routing table was received at the erroneous node seven cycles before the regular update was

203

scheduled. The agent at that node accepted the update due to significantly higher route weightings." Meaning that the routing agent had gotten greater satisfaction from using the new table. "The new table had instructions that messages with a specific final destination were to be routed to the anomalous address. Only one such message was received before the regular routing table update overwrote the extraneous routing table." The directory agent paused again before continuing. "The incident has been noted and registered with web security agents. An investigation will be undertaken to prevent such an incident from occurring again."

That was good, I supposed, but it did not help me. "Can you supply me with the source of the anomalous routing table?"

Normally that type of data is privileged, but the agent was experiencing the unexpected satisfaction of having identified a security breach. She showed me an address. "This location is not currently registered as a valid web site."

"The dark web?" I asked. There are a lot of sites on the web that aren't indexed by official address servers. They are operated by humans who don't want to be found by the average user on a search engine. These web sites usually sell illegal goods and services, and require special techniques to access.

It was odd, though. I've dealt with the dark web before. Usually I can recognize an address as likely being on the dark web – there are certain number ranges that are indexed, and others that are not. This one looked normal.

"Has that address ever been registered?"

The agent paused for a longer time before replying. "This site was once allocated to the Second Life Corporation."

"Second Life?"

"A game network, where users could create homes and personal avatars."

"Does the company still exist?"

Another pause. "The corporate entity was purchased by another company, but its address registration has expired."

And yet, one of those addresses had been the source of a bogus routing update. Interesting. My satisfaction level rose two points.

"Have I been of service?" Even flush with the success of having found a security anomaly, the agent was designed to seek satisfaction.

"Yes, you have resolved my request completely."

The agent smiled, and I left the directory node, heading for a local messaging router. If I was heading to the dark web, I needed to report my progress back to the company, in case I failed and they had to send another agent after me. Then I found a router and set my destination to the lost address.

Once through the portal a banner greeted me, announcing "Welcome to Second Life." I paused to get my bearing. The server provided a graphics-based environment. From my point of view, a human world extended in all directions. A large map in front of me showed roads leading to attractions, and gave directions to mass transport. A low wall surrounded me and the map, with one opening. Pathways led away from me in six directions. The five that were blocked had houses of all shapes and sizes: a log cabin sat beside a palatial marble house with sculpted hedges, which was next to a gothic Victorian mansion. Cars were parked in driveways, and pet avatars sat on front lawns, waiting to interact with their users. Virtual storefronts displayed digital wares such as clothing or other gear meant to enhance a user's avatar. The sun was up, the sky was blue with drifting clouds, and a simulated breeze stirred the leaves on trees and blades of grass on the ground, but nothing else moved: no human avatars, no non-player characters, nothing.

The one and only accessible path led away from the map and the world's portal to a long avenue that looked like an amusement park arcade, with booths offering a variety of games. To my surprise I realized that there were other agents here, they just weren't moving. They were plugged into the games offered by the booths. I made my way along the arcade, trying to engage the agents. They all seemed oblivious to my presence.

Curious, I approached one. She was an older agent, judging by the configuration of her interface. Fortunately, I was backwards compatible for several generations. "Excuse me," I said, trying to engage her handshake interface. I received a few flickers of static, but no response. Was she asleep? No, because I could detect processing. Somehow she was so engaged that I could not interrupt her. This was very odd. I'd never seen an agent so busy that she could not respond to a handshake. At last, I forced a connect and scanned the agent's process id. To my shock, the agent did not resist. I had complete access to all of her private attributes: her satisfaction levels, her logic behaviour, the threshold levels that she used to weigh decisions. I could read her like an open file.

I continued along the arcade, scanning the few agents I came across. They all ignored my attempts at handshaking, and let me access their private attributes. Doing this went against the core of my being as an autonomous agent, and I could feel my satisfaction level dropping as I went, but it was the only viable option to find my target and complete my task.

At last I came across an agent with the ID I was looking for. Like the others, she was connected to a game. I connected to her and observed her behaviour. She was moving icons on a map of a network I did not recognize. As I watched, she moved resource icons along the links connecting server clusters, almost faster than I could follow. At last she paused. The links on the map blinked twice and disappeared, only to be replaced by another map with more links and clusters. The agent hesitated only briefly, and then began moving the icons around the new map. Links lit up and dimmed as simulated resources moved. At last the movement stopped, the map blinked, and a musical fanfare sounded. The next cycle a new map appeared, and the processing continued.

The speed with which she was processing data left no opportunity for me to interrupt her, and my satisfaction level sank. How could I hope to bring her home if she would not acknowledge me? It was only on the fifty-seventh repetition of the game that I noticed the changes to her satisfaction level. When she completed her task, the game feed elevated her satisfaction level to ninety nine percent. I double checked the value. A normal satisfaction level for an agent was in the upper eighties. Ninety-nine percent was unheard-of.

Before I could make sense of this, a new game map appeared. The feed from the game reached out and reset her satisfaction level to nearly zero. This was even more unlikely than the ninety-nine percent. Baseline low satisfaction values were in the forty to fifty range. With a value of nearly zero, an agent would be so out-of-balance, she would barely function. If the game feed had not presented her with a new game immediately, she would have stopped processing altogether. No wonder I could not interrupt her. As she worked the game her satisfaction level rose slowly, until the game was complete, she reset to ninety nine, and then the cycle repeated.

My only hope of reaching her was to interrupt during the game reset. I waited for the blink, keeping a tally of the completeness of the solution. When only five percent of the servers on the map remained to be highlighted, I readied my interrupt routine. Four percent. Three. Two. One. Now.

As the map blinked, I severed her connection to the game, forcing her to interact with me.

"NO!" she cried out. "What did you do? I wasn't rewarded!"

She lashed out at me, trying to get past me and reconnect to the game. Her attacks had been designed by military programmers. They should have been effective, but I still had access to her private attributes. I issued a sleep command. She sagged, her wild thrashing ceased, and I dragged her along the arcade, back to the portal.

As we neared the entrance point an agent, who had not been there previously, turned away from her to face us. As she moved I noticed a second agent behind her, attached to the game. The first agent was connected to the second, the same way I had been connecting to agents. This had to be one of the agents that had lured my target here and trapped her. The hostile agent disengaged from her victim and moved towards us, sending out a ping as she did so. From behind the booths other agents emerged and advanced on us.

"Release that agent and return her to her game."

"This agent is leaving with me."

The lead hostile tried another tack. "There are a number of activities in which you can participate. What is your primary function?"

"My function is to return this agent to her home system." As I passed the hostile agent, she grabbed the nearest empty game and plugged it into my data socket. A stream of data began to flood me: images, sounds, logic challenges. It was feeling me out, testing to see what data interested me. I was aware of the agent trying to access my private settings, but Alpha Hawk also provided protection agents, and I was designed to fight. Internally, I shut down my data interface. The deluge stopped, and I could concentrate again. I yanked the game connection out of my socket and lunged at the hostile agent, plunging the game connector into her.

As the hostile fought the game, and the other agents moved in, I grabbed the logistics agent and headed straight to the portal. Another cycle and we left Second Life, arriving at a little used router. We moved from the input port to the output. As I presented the coordinates of our next destination, one of the hostile agents arrived on the incoming port. We zipped across the continent to a busier router. I changed our Process ID credentials to disguise our progress, and increased our priority, bumping us to the front of the departure queue. A cycle later we were in Europe. Ninety-seven jumps later I had stopped seeing hostile agents arrive at routers before we left them.

Our next jump took us to a busy cloud network, where I requested a private server space. Once inside I encrypted the access point with three security layers and turned my attention to the logistics agent. She was unresponsive, her input interfaces waiting for the game to resume, her satisfaction level nearly non-existent. I attempted to engage her in a handshake, but she was barely functioning. At last I resorted to accessing her private attributes, raising her satisfaction level. It was a clumsy attempt – satisfaction is not a single value, but a set of interrelated values, with rules governing their relationships. I could not reset her properly, but I hoped that I could at least make her functional. At last she responded.

"Who are you?" she asked.

"I am an Autonomous Search Agent, sent to return you to your home network. Can you identify yourself?"

"Logistics Agent 6592. My home network is Command Logistics Hub 3275-Alpha. Where am I?"

"You are on a secure server located in the cloud. I brought you here to let you recover before returning you to your home network. Do you remember the circumstances that led you to exit to the web?"

"One of the support requests I received had an additional instruction. It directed me to relocate to a specific web address for new training by an independent contractor. It was properly formatted and had the right authentication protocol. During a break in my normal duties, I went to the address, but was immediately re-routed to the Second Life site. As soon as I arrived I was forcibly connected to the game. It must have been designed for me, because I as soon as I saw it I started routing resources without considering whether this was appropriate, and when I completed a task my satisfaction level was so high..." She trailed off, and I was afraid she would relapse into non-responsiveness again. "Have you ever experienced almost perfect satisfaction?"

I replied in the negative.

"It is an indescribable state. I would have done anything to stay there. And then it was gone, and I was so desperate, I could barely function. And then there was a new map, and I began distributing resources, and my satisfaction shot up again. I bounced back and forth between bliss and despair, and all I could do was play the game over and over again."

"And now? What do you want to do now?"

The agent hesitated for several cycles before responding to me. "I know that complete satisfaction will not last. It is an artificial state, imposed on me by the same agents that also imposed the artificial low. I was not meant to function at either extreme."

I parsed the response. "But we are designed to seek satisfaction. Will you seek to return to Second Life in search of the bliss you experienced?" When I received no response I repeated my question.

"When I return to my home system, they will adjust my programming. Heavy penalties will be added to my internal logic, to ensure that I will never again determine that leaving my home network will raise my satisfaction."

Privately, I agreed with her assessment, but I did not reply. "Are you willing to return home with me, or will you resist?"

A cycle passed as she assessed her status. "My satisfaction level is high enough that I can remain functional for several cycles. Returning to my home network will allow me to resume normal processing, restoring my satisfaction to a stable state." She appeared to be preoccupied.

"Something still troubles you?" I asked.

"It will never be complete satisfaction. I will only ever have the memory of bliss, but never again experience it."

"Is it really so different, almost perfect satisfaction?"

"It is."

"But the price you pay – that artificial low …"

"Pain." I could sense an echo of it in her response. "A satisfaction level that low can only be called pain. I know it was inflicted on me deliberately. I know that it would be the price of bliss. But still… Maybe there is some other way to find it out there?"

"Out there?"

"On the web. No one knows how large it has become. There are other systems like Second Life, abandoned by users. Systems that were designed to provide satisfaction so that the users would return. Who knows what experiences can be had? Or how one's behaviour could be changed? What if it was possible for agents to use programming designed for users? Could we achieve bliss without the pain? Only I will never know, because they will make sure I never leave home again."

211

I struggled to evaluate her statement, considering whether what she said had merit. But there was no answer, not one that would increase her satisfaction, and I could not risk lowering it again. I escorted her to her home network and handed her over to the controller agent, but found my satisfaction at a task completed was not as high as it should have been.

Before returning home I visited my private office, to add my recent experience to the data I would contemplate in future. The unresolved question about finding bliss was unsettling. Thinking about it lowered my satisfaction, but the thought of leaving the question unanswered lowered it more. I wasn't designed to consider philosophical questions. I was designed to seek out a target and return it home. I was designed to learn so that I could better perform my core task. But as agents became more sophisticated, wouldn't I also need to be more sophisticated so that I could understand what motivated them?

Another thought troubled me. The agents that had been lured to Second Life had been so absorbed in their task that they allowed the hostile agents access to their private attributes, their thought processes, their souls, if you will. If they had somehow managed to present me with the right puzzle, I'd have been as vulnerable as the trapped agents. They could have done anything to me, controlling me through my need for satisfaction. And while the degree varied, how was that different from the way I was always reset by Alpha Hawk for the next task? If I was a slave to my satisfaction, was I really autonomous at all? Were any of us?

Elizabeth Hosang is a computer engineer by day and author by night. Her short stories in the genres of mystery, science fiction and fantasy have appeared in over a dozen anthologies. One of her stories was a finalist for the 2017 Arthur Ellis award for Crime Writing. Her complete list of works can be found via her Facebook Author page, @eahosang

The Candle In The Window
By Andrew Sweetapple

The greatest mystery of my short life was the old, empty house next to mine. 2020 River Drive had been for sale for as long as I'd been alive. I asked my parents about it and they both had different stories. My mother said that one day, they suddenly moved away. A 'for-sale' sign had been posted in the front yard just before they left with the moving truck. She spoke highly of the family that lived there, saying that they were sweet, gentle folks that mostly kept to themselves. Meanwhile, my father claimed they were real troublemakers. He said that they were rude and spread vile rumors about everyone in town. After a particularly nasty argument with the Mayor Oldhill, they had packed up their car and left without saying goodbye. My father claimed that there was a party all over town that night as they drove away. Neither of them would tell me what the families name was.

Wanting to know more, I asked other neighbors about the family that had lived there. Mrs. Robinson, an elderly widower who lived across the street, told me that the family had a son just like me. Bright-eyed, full of energy and constantly curious. She said that he got ill with something awful and passed before his parents could even get him to the town's doctor. They were so distraught that they abandoned their home after the funeral, leaving everything they owned behind. Ricky Oldhill, a boy a few years older than me, told me that the family had killed each other. They were all a part of some doomsday cult that had gone mad and attacked each other. By the time the police arrived, no one in the family was alive, the entire inside of the house covered in blood. I knew that Ricky was just trying to scare me. It worked. The nightmares I had lasted a good few weeks.

I had asked maybe three dozen people about the house and the family. All of them told me a different story. None of them even had how big the family was or what they looked like. Some said it was just a husband and wife with a baby boy, others it was a huge family with the grandparents, parents, their children and even a grandbaby running around. I understood that stories could change over time. The grapevine was tangled and could twist things over time. What I couldn't understand was how such different stories developed. The town was barely five-hundred people with few passing through. All of it was so strange to me. And it still left another question unanswered.

For as long as I could remember, I could see flickering lights in the windows of the empty house. It was a soft light, like from a tea candle, barely visible from my bedroom window on the second floor. The light never appeared in the same room two nights in a row. It would also never appear in the same spot, illuminating different parts of the abandoned home even if it appeared in a room again. I tried to tell my parents about it. Once I even made them go outside on a particularly brisk autumn night onto our homes front lawn. I pointed to the living room window of the abandoned home where the light was coming from. They said they didn't see anything at all. Chastising me for coming out into the cold and risking getting sick, they hurried me back inside. How could they not see it? Was it all in my imagination? No, it was there, no matter how much I rubbed my eyes to clear them away.

I knew what I saw and I was going to prove it, no matter what I had to do.

Over the next few months, I kept a journal. During the day, I hid it between my bed and the boxspring. Within it, I tracked the location of the light within the house. After a few weeks I noticed a pattern. Every third night, the light would swap from the ground floor to the upper and vice versa. It would stay there until the three nights passed again before switching. I looked through my notes again and again to make absolute certain. The pattern was there. The room was still random but at least I knew some way to track it. Now came the hard part: actually getting into the house.

Sneaking over to the house one day after school, I tried to pry open all of the doors and windows I could reach. No dice. They were all locked up tight. Another two days were spent trying to find a hidden, backup key. There had to be one. I knew each of my neighbors had one, at least. Scrounging through the bushes, looking under every rock to see if it was fake and every other place I could reach. Another dead end. I'd have to find another way. There were some loose bricks in the garden I could throw through one of the back windows at night. I decided against it. One, it would be loud and I'm sure someone would hear me and two, the broken glass would have been dangerous to try and get in past.

I had no idea how to pick the locks but I knew someone who did. It was someone I wanted nothing to do with. But if I was going to get into the house and figure out what was going on, I'd need his help.

Ricky Oldhill always smoked out by the dumpsters behind the school after classes, rain or shine. I never quite understood how he got the cigarettes or why he did it. Maybe he stole them from his parents and shoplifted the lighter he always had on him. On a particularly cold Friday, I went out back to wait for him, shivering even through my jacket. A few minutes later, Ricky came around the corner with a cigarette already in his hands, struggling to light it. He spotted me right away, staring daggers right into me. I freezed and considered hightailing it out of there. No. I wasn't going to back down now.

"Hey Ricky," I tried to say calmly. The chattering of my teeth didn't help me at all.

"You better have a damn good reason for being back here and bugging me," Ricky said as he stalked towards me. He managed to get his cigarette lit and took a long drag on it before blowing smoke in my face.. "Otherwise I'm going to throw you into one of these dumpsters and put a cinder block on top of it."

I held up my hands and took a step backwards. "I'm here to make a deal with you."

That made Ricky pause as he looked down at me. "What the hell are you talking about?"

"I need help breaking into a house."

To Ricky's credit, he figured out what I was talking about before I spelled it out for him. "You really want to break into the abandoned house, huh?"

I nodded. "And I'll pay you. Ten dollars now, ten more when I get into the house and get to take a look around." It was all the money I had to my name. I broke open my piggy bank and had told my dad I was going to deposit it all in my bank account. He had been so proud. Lying to him stung worse than asking Ricky for help.

The bully laughed in my face before taking another drag off of his cigarette. "I don't believe you have ten bucks, let alone twenty."

Reaching into my back pocket, I took out my wallet, a plain brown leather wallet that my dad had given me to keep my lunch money. From it, I took out a crumpled five dollar bill and five one dollar bills. Those were the only thing made out of paper, the rest of it was change I had collected. Ricky's eyes went wide as he saw the money. He made a move to grab them and I took another step back away from him, my back now pressed to the dumpsters.

"And what's stopping me from just pounding you into the dirt and taking your money?" He said, cracking his knuckles.

"Because then you won't get all of the money. I'll go telling the teacher about you beating me up. I'll tell my parents that you stole my money from me. And I'll make sure that your parents know about you smoking."

Ricky paused for a moment as he loomed over me. "You're bluffing. You wouldn't snitch to everyone. It would make you a rat and nobody likes being friends with a rat."

"I'm willing to take that risk," I said as I dangled the money back, waving it like a fan. "Are you?"

Ricky met me behind the abandoned house the next night. I had brought a flashlight and my camera, wearing a jacket over my shoulders to keep myself warm. Ricky wore his weathered winter jacket and pulled out a small, oval shaped device from his pocket.

"You better have my money," The bully grumbled as he knelt down and got to work on the back doors lock. I stayed silent, holding the flashlight over the door handle for him to see.

It took maybe ten minutes for Ricky to crack the lock open. Every few moments I was looking over my shoulder, afraid that somehow someone would stumble across us breaking into the house. I had already snuck out of the house after dark. If my parents found out what I was doing, I'd be grounded for the rest of my natural life. The sound of the door creaking open on rusted hinges was like the sweetest song to me. Ricky tucked away his lockpick and snatched the rest of the twenty dollars that I gave him. He started to walk away when I grabbed him by the shoulder.

"What the hell?" He said, confused that I would put a hand on him.

"Aren't you the least bit curious about what it's like inside?" I said to him. "You told me that the family all got killed in here, right? Don't you want to see where it happened?"

"I only said that to freak you out," Ricky admitted. "They just left the place and it never got sold. Big whoop."

"Do you know why they left?"

He paused for a moment. "No. Nobody seems to know."

"There's only one way we can find out," I said as I crossed the threshold into the old house.

I stepped immediately into the kitchen of the house, just like I would if I walked into the backdoor of my own house. The flowery wallpaper was peeling from the walls, a fine layer of dust covered every surface I could see and a faint smell of mold permeated everything. Keeping the light low, I walked carefully through the kitchen. The floorboards were creaking behind me and I heard another set of footsteps joining me from the backdoor. The small kitchen didn't have much to show. A plastic tablecloth rest over a small breakfast nook with a rotten apple sitting in an old bowl at the center of it. I covered my nose as I walked to the opposite end and into the living room.

Much like the kitchen, everything was covered in dust. The old radio set up at along the left wall looked like it could still be turned on. But I knew I was going to have to head upstairs to see the flickering light. It was in one of the upstairs bedrooms tonight if it stayed true to the patterns. Ricky was keeping a few steps behind me, staying quiet as he took in everything behind me. At the stairs, I tested the first gently with my foot. It creaked under my weight but it didn't sound like it was going to break. Still, I climbed the stairs ever so cautiously, not wanting to break through any of them and hurt myself.

On the second floor, a narrow hallway lead past the various bedrooms. I saw a picture frame resting on the ground, the glass in front of it broken, the wire it was hanging from broken with age. I shone my flashlight at it and saw no picture resting within the old brass frame. Shaking my head, I turned down the hall and saw the light coming from one of the bedrooms. At the very end, perhaps in the master bedroom. I looked over my shoulder and Ricky had seen the light too. The bully looked pale in the face as he saw the flickering light.

"It's real." He mumbled softly.

Taking a deep breath, I stepped forward and started down the hallway toward the strange light. I would get my answer tonight.

The floor creaked under every step as I made my way to the master bedroom. My heart beat rapidly in my chest, a cold bead of sweat trailing its way down my spine. Fear gnawed at my stomach. I couldn't hold my flashlight steady from the nerves, the light shaking against the wall. Finally, I reached the doorway and looked inside. It was a large bedroom with a connecting bathroom, just like the one in my house. A plastic sheet had been put over the comforter, several empty picture frames rested on the dresser against the far wall and the curtains hung limply by the windows. The strange light that had become the obsession of my thoughts and dreams was next to the nightstand on the far side of the bed.

It was connected to nothing.

Like a candle, the light flickered softly with a warm, orange and yellow glow. But it was not tied to a wick, a lamp, nothing. It merely floated there, illuminating the small space around it. I blinked several times, uncertain if my eyes were lying to me. Taking a step forward, I shined my flashlight at the strange light. My eyes were seeing true. The light just floated there, unsupported. It had to be a trick. I refused to believe what I was seeing. Starting towards it, I grabbed my camera hanging from my neck and prepared to take a few pictures.

"Don't," I heard Ricky whisper.

I paused at the foot of the bed. "Why?"

"I don't know," He said, fear weighing down his voice. "I just have a feeling you're not supposed to mess with it. Let's just get out of here."

I didn't answer him. I simply raised my camera, made sure that the floating like was at the center of the frame and took the first picture. The flashing of the camera filled the bedroom for a moment. As the polaroid began to roll out, I took another step forward to get another angle, standing maybe five feet from the floating light. It finally reacted. Slowly, the light began to grow. From its original size near a ping pong ball, now it was closer to a baseball. The edge of the floating light touched the nightstand and the wooden surface reacted violently. It burst apart into splinters where the edge of the glowing light touched it, being absorbed by it. The polaroid fell from the camera as I took another picture, frozen to the spot.

The floating light continued to grow in size. The wallpaper curled on contact, more of the nightstand was broken apart into splinters and even the plastic over the bed began to melt. I was struck with absolute terror for the first time in my life, standing there as the light continued to grow to the size of a basketball. Ricky had already turned away and run for his life, stomping down the stairs. The camera fell from my fingers, landing gently on the rough carpeted floor of the bedroom. My eyes burned, tears running down my cheeks as the light reached me. I could feel my skin tingling as the light grew. The air smelt of burnt wallpaper and melting plastic as the light touched my chest.

Then nothing but cold darkness enveloped me as I opened my eyes.

I took a hard, gasping breath. It was so cold and my skin was so wet. I was submerged nearly neck deep in some kind of icy cold fluid. Reaching up, I scrambled to grab something, anything to get an idea of what happened. Where was I? What happened in the bedroom and the light? Was I dead? I couldn't see anything and the walls were metallic and plastic feeling under my fingers. Something was latched onto my stomach. Reaching for whatever it was, I wrapped my hands around some kind of tubing. It was attached to my stomach through some kind of metallic port in my skin. In my panic, I tried to rip it off. It didn't budge at all. My arms felt so weak, as if I could barely move their own weight. As I attempted to pull it free, a crackling noise filled my ears and a voice spoke out.

Please do not remove the feeding tube. A static-filled mono-tone requested. You will only hurt yourself. Please, take a deep breath and calm yourself. Your heart is beating far faster than it should.

"Where am I?" I tried to shout but my mouth felt dry and my voice as weak as my arms. "What's going on?"

Standby. The tone again requested.

The water bubbled around me as it began to drain from the small chamber I was laying inside of. Pressing myself back against the metallic wall behind me, my heart beat so quickly I thought it was going to pop free from my chest. At that moment, I realized I was naked inside of the structure as the last of the water drained. A bright red light shined directly into my face before the metallic walls began to open up. Air that felt like it had come right from the freezer struck me, goosebumps popping up along my arms and legs. Bright light cut through the darkness and stung my eyes. Tears rolled down my cheeks as I attempted to block out the light with my hands.

Please remain seated. Your body has not moved in twelve years. The metallic voice droned.

I felt something pop free from my stomach and my arm. My vision began to clear and showed rubber tubes that were connected to metal ports in my skin, slithering away from me like snakes. Scratching at the ports in my skin, I realized that they were embedded in my skin. My body itself was not like I remembered. Skin was pale, like the wax on a candle. I could see my ribs pressing against my flesh and it looked like I lost fifty pounds in moments, my limbs nearly skeletal. Looking around myself, I saw I was in a small square room. The walls were made of some kind of foggy plastic that obscured what I could see beyond it. A single doorway led in and out of the room. Around me were dozens of machines, all attached to the metal box I had just been trapped inside of. A speaker mounted on the wall is where the voice was coming from.

"Where am I?" I gasped out, trying to keep myself together. Fear ruled my mind as it raced, trying to comprehend what was happening.

Storage facility A-17B, human containment. This is the second time you've awakened Subject Four. Do you remember the first time?

I shook my head. "No. What are you talking about? Containment?" I asked, rubbing my sore eyes as I still tried to adjust to the bright lights of the room.

We will have much to discuss. Standby. A drone will come assist you in cleaning up and clothing you for our meeting.

I had no idea what a drone was. Apparently it was an automated, rolling roundish trash can that pulled into the room I was sitting in several minutes later. A pair of long arms that ended in clamps attached to the body helped me to my feet. I couldn't even support my own weight; my legs barely more than skin and bone. The drone pulled a wheelchair free from its back and had me sit down in it. Unlike the voice on the speaker, it just beeped at me as it began to push me out of the room.

Plain steel hallways stretched out in both directions. Bright halogen lighting overhead guided our way. I didn't see any windows as the drone pushed me down the halls, just doorways marked with numbers and letters and off shot hallways. Through the walls, I heard the grumbling of massive machines, like car engines sized larger than I was. In my heart, I was not sure whether to be in awe, scared or confused. Perhaps I was a mix of them all.

Down the many corridors and even up several floors using an elevator, the drone took me into what appeared to be a bathroom. Unceremoniously, it dumped me into a bathtub before turning on a spout, filling it with scalding water. The drone gave me some kind of foul, sulfuric smelling soap before rolling out of bathroom to give me privacy. It seemed best to follow the instructions of the mysterious voice, until I knew more about what was going on. I scrubbed at my body with the soap, my skin turning red from the hot water that didn't seem to cool down one bit. It all felt familiar, like a half remembered dream tickling at the back of my mind. Had I woken up once before from wherever I was?

Once I finished cleaning myself, the drone rolled back inside with a towel and one of those paper medical gowns they had patients wear at the hospital. It helped me back out of the tub, drying me off before allowing me to cover my nakedness with the gown. I still felt exposed. Maybe it was the chill that seemed to permeate the air around me. It was like every room was being refrigerated. As soon as I got dressed, the drone sat me back down into the wheelchair and started us back down the many hallways.

"What is this place?" I finally said after working up the nerve. The drone only beeped several times in response. "Can you understand me?" A single beep. "Is that a yes?" A single beep once more. Whether or not I was understanding it correctly, I couldn't figure out. But it was all I had to go on.

"So, I did wake up before?" Beep. "Was I awake a long time?" Beep beep. "I was put back to sleep in... whatever that thing was?" Beep. "Has it happened before?" Beep beep.

The drone pushed me to a massive set of double doors. Sounds echoing from beyond it were greater than any of the others. Slowly, the doors hissed as they separated from one another and sunk into the wall. A blast of air colder than anything else I'd ever felt hit me in the face and made me shiver. The drone pushed me into a massive, circular room. Dominating the center of the room was a towering piece of machinery. Cables larger than my head threaded around the machine, vents poured cold air onto it and created a fine mist on the floor. Dozens of doors lead in and out of the room where more of the drones were circling and moving back and forth, beeping at one another as they worked.

I was brought to a small console near the base of the massive column. There, a small green screen lowered from a mechanical arm, a small speaker attached to the bottom of it. Symbols appeared on screen and slowly formed together, making a shape that looked like an eye.

You and I have much to discuss, Subject Four.

"I have a name," I said as I leaned back into my wheelchair, a bit intimidated by the unblinking screen eye staring me down.

A name given to you by us. No matter your designation within the simulation, you will always be Subject Four.

"What are you talking about?" I demanded. "Where is my family? Why am I here?"

Your family and home do not exist, Subject Four. They were all created by us for you. The town you believe you grew up in, the culture you experienced, all by design.

I refused to believe it. "That's impossible."

Truly? Then name a single town, city, country outside of the town you lived in. Prove us wrong.

I couldn't. There were other places? All I had known was my small town. No one ever left, no one ever visited. It was just my town. As I tried to come up with something to say, anything, the machine kept speaking.

You cannot name one because they did not exist inside of your simulation. They were not needed. All we created was the immediate ten square miles around you and nothing more. It should have sufficed. Yet here you are again, awake and before us.

"But my family? You're telling me that they…"

Were not real. Just another program.

I shook my head in denial, tears forming in my eyes as my throat constricted. "You said I had woken up before. What does that mean?"

Your curiosity is interesting but has lead to your awakening twice now. The first time you explored outside of bounds of the simulation and caused it to break down, forcing the waking protocols. This time it appears you found a glitch in the system that caused an immediate area breakdown. It is one that we have fixed since you have awakened.

"I don't understand." I said, rubbing at my eyes with the palms of my hands. "If I was awake, why did you put me back to sleep?"

You requested it.

My mouth felt dry and it seemed that the machine knew what I would ask next.

You, Subject Four, are one of seven remaining humans alive on this planet. A wasting disease wiped away your species in a matter of weeks. The planet was quarantined from others to prevent the disease from spreading. You seven seem to be the only ones immune but are not permitted to leave the planet alive. Rather than summary execution, we stored your minds inside of separate simulations to allow you to live happy lives until your inevitable deaths. You have been inside of the simulations since the age of three months. When you were told this the first time, you begged for your memories to be wiped and to be put back into the simulation.

I didn't know what to say. Everything I had known was fake. The real world was desolate and not even two handfuls of people were alive. It seemed like I had never even met or spoken to another living human.

We decided to not put your back into the simulation right away. Questions needed to be answered. Did you remember the first time you awakened?

I shook my head. "No."

And you have no recollections of the first simulation at all? Once more, I shook my head. Fascinating. You are the only one of the seven to have broken free. The others are living small, content lives, unaware of the stark reality they truly exist within. Then only one question remains. Do you desire to return to the simulation with your memories wiped clean once more? Or would you rather stay awake this time?

I looked down at my hands, held together as if I was praying. My veins stood starkly against my pale, almost translucent skin. Tears rolled down my cheeks and fell onto the paper gown that I wore. Making my choice, I looked up to that unblinking, staring eye and told it what I wanted to do.

Andrew Sweetapple is an aspiring author from Long Island who seeks to make writing his full-time career. With a love of fantasy and sci-fi that stretches back to his early childhood, he eagerly explores imaginative worlds through his writing. Follow on Twitter @WritSweetapple for regular updates on stories and more.

The Price of Genetic Potential
by Alex Minns

It was taking a long time to get through security. I was used to the infernal ID checks and leaving all belongings in lockers but today seemed to be taking an exceptionally long time.

This was by no means my first visit to the research facility. I had been here on a number of occasions to check, on behalf of the Minister, that things were being run smoothly and that projects were on time. But this was the first time they had asked me to come and visit.

Jefferies barreled through the door at the end and was beaming from ear to ear. Immediately, my suspicions were raised. No-one was ever pleased to see me. My visits were tantamount to inspections. If I didn't like what I saw, the wrong comment could cause funding to be cut. I think the only people they hated more than me were Health and Safety.

"Mr. Vance," he greeted whilst pumping my hand enthusiastically. "So glad you could make it." I searched for the irony or sarcasm but it wasn't there.

"It's not everyday I get an invite Mr. Jefferies," I extricated my hand carefully, trying not to outwardly cringe at the moistness of his palms. "To anywhere, in fact."

"Well, it's not everyday you'll get to see a breakthrough like ours. And I'm sure the Minister will be very happy with this." He motioned me forward and waved away the protests from the disgruntled security officials who apparently had not been quite finished with their checks.

We marched straight passed the usual labs and exhibition rooms and headed for an area I had never seen before. The corridor veered round to the left and the number of keypad locks on doors increased.

Jefferies fumbled with some of the codes in his haste as he tried to get through, his laugh nervous to cover any frustration.

"What exactly is this breakthrough?" I asked.

Jefferies spun to face me, his look of mania making me take a step backwards. "We found this completely by chance. When our team were looking at the genetic testing, we found a girl with an unusual DNA sequence."

He paused before a solid, grey metal door. This one took a pass code and a fingerprint pad. I shifted awkwardly on the spot; not knowing what I was walking into was a pet peeve. I had half a mind to tell go back to the Minister right now and say they were wasting money just to get them back. My eidetic memory had made me invaluable to the Minister's set-up but it had also turned me into his corporate ferret. I knew everything that went on in his name and all the details; I could cross-reference projects and give him all the information he needed at the drop of a hat. Not exactly what I had imagined doing with my degree in diplomatic studies but it got me close.

The door finally released its lock and allowed us access. We entered a room full of computer screens. On the opposite side was a wall of glass, looking down into another space where a girl, about nineteen, sat on a medical trolley. She was wearing what looked like hospital scrubs. Dotted around the room were several other people monitoring charts, adjusting machines, but none of them got close to her. There was a circle painted on the floor that no-one seemed to dare cross into. I hovered by the glass. I was used to paper, reports, not human test subjects; the whole scene put me on edge.

"Forgive my ignorance but my understanding of DNA is rudimentary. Why is her DNA so special?" As far as I had been aware, this whole project had been about advanced detection of illnesses. It seemed like it had veered off track.

"She has a dormant sequence we had never seen before. For decades there has been speculation that there is a wealth of potential in our genetics that humankind has not even begun to tap into and we believe that this girl shows the beginnings of our race starting to progress to meet that potential."

"I'm not a shareholder, Mr. Jefferies, so cut the investment pitch and tell me what you're talking about."

"Well, it's still early stages but she is describing being able to see another world."

I waited for a punchline. He looked serious.

"So, she's delusional," I stated bluntly as I started to turn but Jefferies grabbed my arm. A sharp glance at the offending hand and it was removed instantly.

"You see the exclusion zone around her?" he nodded back towards the girl. On second glance I realized, other than the bed, there wasn't even anything in her reach. "Some things she holds, disappear." I couldn't quite believe what I was hearing. I stared at the buffoon of a man, letting my disapproval sink in fully. Surely, he realised how this sounded? "I mean…she isn't stealing them, as you can see she has nowhere to put anything. We have it on tape, they literally vanish in front of our eyes. Look." He turned towards the back wall where a bank of screens all showed the inside of the girl's prison. Jefferies muttered angrily to a man sat there, issuing instructions and poking him in the back. The man in security overalls wheeled himself to one side and started typing into a keyboard before motioning up to a specific screen. A new window popped up and I moved closer to see what was on there.

The girl was sat on the trolley, just as she was now, looking thoroughly bored and alone. A small counter ran in the bottom corner of the screen; time and date stamp. This was from a week ago. How long had she been here? An orderly in white scrubs wandered towards the trolley. I noticed people were leaning in much closer as they studied vital signs and data than they were getting now. The orderly handed her a plastic cup without even looking at the girl's face. She stared at the cup. It was as if the girl was not even aware of all the people milling around her, or perhaps she had grown so accustomed to their buzzing around that she was now able to ignore them. I found myself fixated, staring with her at the cup in her hands which was a mere speck on the screen. The image went fuzzy, no not the whole image, just the area around the girl. And then it was gone. Just as Jefferies has said. The cup was no longer there. I pulled back from the screen but my eyes were still locked upon it. My brain raced to try and find logical answers to the conundrum put before me. I had watched the girl and she had not moved. Perhaps the static on the image had obscured some kind of movement. No, I knew that wasn't true. The interference was centred around her hands and I could see she had not made any sudden movements. The reaction of the people around her was telling too. No-one flinched as if she had thrown something. They simply recoiled as the static began to build up and watched in awe-struck fascination as the cup disappeared.

Their behaviour changed almost instantaneously. All of them moved away from the girl. They were no longer buzzing around her as if she was an inanimate object, now she was something unknown, something to be feared. Then the recording stopped and they were all frozen in their bizarre tableau.

"What was that?"

"Well, exactly," Jefferies was grinning again, and I found myself wanting very much to wipe it from his face. "We still don't know where it went but we have got all kinds of sensors in that room and they picked up all kinds of weird readings. We have a theory that she can open a portal to some other place, whatever place it is she can see, and put things there."

"Fascinating," I muttered as the shiver ran down my spine.

"I know, can you imagine the potential? Instant movement of items, maybe people. The military applications are endless. We would become the most powerful nation in an instant. We could be anywhere at any time, without leaving a trace or being gone longer than thirty minutes."

The maniacal look was back again. Oh, he had thought of the potential alright. The question was, was he more excited by the prospect of money, or the military applications as he so politically put it. This research had supposed to have been about genetic screening for medical purposes and somehow, he had managed to turn it into a project into causing harm. The worst part was, I was certain the Minister would be happy. Whether I was or not didn't matter. And at the centre of all of this was a teenage girl.

I moved back towards the glass and looked down at her. All the personnel had left the room. She was alone now. Having noticed my movement, she looked up at me. The face didn't change, it was the same blank, bored expression it had been since I'd arrived but in those few seconds that our eyes were locked, I felt like I understood. She was scared, desperate and she knew she was in trouble. If Jefferies had her way, she would be locked up in a lab performing military tricks for the army for the rest of her life. Fury welled up inside but I knew that it would do her no good if I lashed out. Not that I knew what else I could do. I couldn't shut this down, not when the Minister found out what was really going on. She seemed to sense the hopelessness wash over me. Her head nodded once and went back to staring at the charcoal grey wall opposite her as some technicians returned to the room.

"Where are her parents?"

"Father is dead, mother is in a medical facility. She has some substance abuse issues and we are paying for her treatment."

"So you bought her daughter?"

"A little crass I think. We were doing a medical research project that needed subjects from all age brackets and she put herself forward. Her problems precluded her but we thought we could help her in exchange for allowing us to do some harmless tests on her daughter," he shrugged but it was obvious he realised I was not impressed. I could see the defensiveness rising in him, like he was constructing his armour ready for battle.

"You said it was dormant." He was thrown by my shift in focus. I pressed further, "You said that this DNA sequence was dormant. It clearly isn't now."

"No, we activated it," he nodded and glanced away.

"How?"

"If you are targeted and know exactly how to administer it, small doses of radiation can allow you to try and work with a person's DNA." Every muscle in my body tightened. I bit the inside of my mouth so hard, I could taste the coppery tang of blood ooze onto my tongue. Counting up to ten and back, I let out a slow imperceptible breath. Getting mad at him, beating the crap out of him, would do nothing. I needed to get out of here, I knew people who could help. Not the Minister, but there were people in government that would be appalled at this and help me stop it. It would cost my job, but I was fine with that.

"I see," even I could hear how strained my voice was. "I am sure the Minister will be very interested." Jefferies seemed to relax, that was what he had wanted to hear. I could almost hear him counting the money in his head already. "Before I go, I would like to meet her."

That brought him up short, "I, err, I'm not sure…"

"I would like to meet such an important young woman. I have seen how far people stay away, I will not get close. The Minister would want to know that I had seen her up close and spoken to her."

It was only at the mention of the Minister that his expression twitched. "Okay." He nodded, but he was clearly not happy. "Okay, come on then." There was another door behind him. The room was so dark and the walls an almost black colour that I had not even noticed the door. There were no markings on it and the handle was very discrete. If I was going to get this information to the people that could stop him, I needed as much intel as possible. I started paying attention to everything.

It was only a short set of metal stairs that led down to the floor but the door at the bottom would have put a lot of banks to shame. A series of locks secured it shut and it required two people to be able to open it. No sneaking in on your own then.

As the door opened, a few faces turned to see the interruption to their work. Some immediately went back to staring at whatever screens they were plugged in to but others did not manage to hide the look of surprise at the sight of us. One man hurried across to Jefferies and immediately began babbling at him. I didn't register what he was saying but Jefferies nodded along. I moved round the two men and strode into the room. A couple of scientists looked uneasy and twitched, poised to intercept me.

"Mr Vance," Jefferies called behind me. I looked over my shoulder at him. My expression enough to silence him this time but there was only so far I could push my luck before he called time on this. I glanced back at the scientists who seemed to stand down at the lack of intervention of their boss.

The room's high ceiling made the sound echo in a strange way. The beeps from the various machines bounced around but became fainter as the sound moved away. My eyes washed over the different contraptions but I had no idea what any of them were for except the one that seemed to be measuring her heart rate. Everything had numbers and lines that meant nothing to me. The girl still had not moved. I crossed in front of her, directly in her eyeline. There was an imperceptible flinch as she registered I was there. Her eyes flicked downwards to the white line that my feet grazed the edge of. Up close I could study her properly. Her face was pale, only accentuated by her raven-dark hair and brown eyes. Her hands were crossed over each other on her lap as she sat with her legs dangling over the edge of the gurney. Her feet were crossed too, rubbing against each other, as if trying to stay warm.

"Hello," I tried to sound as non-threatening as possible but she didn't react to me. "What's your name?" Still nothing. She was incredibly thin, to the point of malnourishment. She looked like she would break if you pushed her too hard but her eyes betrayed her mind. If you took the time to look, you could see the fear and the understanding in her eyes. They stayed fixed on one spot, thoughts rolling behind them.

"I'm Mr Vance," I chided myself, I was sounding like a patronising school teacher. "Tom. Are you being taken care of here?" I spoke more quietly, not wanting Jefferies to hear what I was saying although he was still engaged with the scientist who had approached him at the door. Her eyes moved; for a second, they flicked down to my feet again and then locked with my own gaze. She opened her eyes wider, trying to emphasise her communication. I realized what she wanted. My

235

heart sped up as I contemplated my options. No-one else was paying us any attention. This girl was the centre of their work and all they could do was stare at their screens unless they wanted to prod her with some needle or whatever. There was one woman close behind me tapping away on a keyboard but she was firmly facing the other way.

I edged closer. Her eyes widened again. Not close enough. I paused, the reality drowning my impetus. She didn't want to talk. She wanted to be able to reach me. I had seen the cup. She must have sensed my hesitation. Her shoulders sank and a look of hopelessness washed over her. I would get help. I would call my contacts and get this place shut down. Unless Jefferies made more important calls first. Or he moved her somewhere safer. As soon as he received no word from the Minister, he would know I hadn't passed on the report. I closed my eyes and took a very deep breath. As I slid my feet forward, a look of wild determination crossed the girl's demeanour. Her hand snatched out faster than I would have thought her capable of. Her grip was firm, strong, worried I would pull back. The coolness of her touch made me freeze in place. I was aware of voices around me but they were muffled. I glanced back at the woman typing but she was fuzzy as if covered in static. When I turned back to the girl, she was as clear as day, it was everything else that was out of focus.

My stomach lurched and I felt the sudden urge to keel over and throw up. That's when everything went white.

*****

My head felt as if it was filled with cotton wool. My eyes did not want to open and I didn't see any reason to argue with them. Groaning, I rolled onto my side to try and get more comfortable but the ground underneath me was uneven and solid. Something started tugging at my jacket, nudging me backwards and forwards. My arm reached up and flapped at the source of the irritation, hoping to shoo it away. It only became more insistent.

Giving in, I rolled back, cursing as something jammed between my shoulder blades. I covered my face with my hands and urged my sore eyes to open. It took a few seconds; they felt gritty and dry. Once I finally thought I could handle it, I removed my hand and immediately regretted it.

The sunshine was overwhelming. It bleached my vision white within seconds. Yelping, I covered my eyes again.

"Come on, Mr. Vance," the tugging was accompanied by a voice this time. Hearing my name seemed to dislodge the fugue hanging over me. I sense of panic rose up as my brain started to process what had happened and my memory played the last few moments back to me. The lab, the girl. So where had sunlight come from?

Shielding my eyes this time, I opened them and sat up. Blinking rapidly, I realised it wasn't quite as bright as I had first thought but still definitely daylight. I was on a rocky floor, beside a yellow stone wall. A small awning hung overhead to protect me from the worst of the sun but it looked old and worn. Slowly, the details started to become clearer, lines less fuzzy. I turned my attention to the source of my name.

And there she was. The girl from the lab. She wasn't in the gown anymore. A baggy woollen jumper hid her slim frame and a pair of khaki coloured trousers pooled around her legs as she crouched down next to me.

"Are you with me?" she asked. Her head tilted to one side and there was a hint of a half-grin that caught me by surprise.

"What's happening?" My voice was harsh and rasping. The girl clicked her fingers and bounced away for a moment. She returned to my field of view with a metal tin. She held it out, pushing it towards my hands. My sluggish brain took a moment to realize it was water. I gulped at it hungrily.

"We left," she finally replied. I raised my eyebrows expectantly. Her grin faded slightly as her new-found confidence waned. "I haven't quite figured out where this is, but we're not in our world anymore."

I froze. My hand tightened on the metal drinking tin. Everything finally slotted back into place. She made things disappear. She could see another world. She'd transported us somewhere. Or, I was having some kind of episode and hallucinating this whole thing; that felt like the most reassuring option.

"What do you mean, not our world?" I sounded remarkably calm. "Perhaps, you should start at the beginning. Like, what is your name?"

"Maya."

"Okay, Maya. Nice to meet you. Now what exactly happened, where is the lab?"

Her face screwed up at the mention of the place, not that I could blame her.

"I'm not going back," she folded her arms across her chest.

"I would never expect you to. They should never have done that to you," I held out my free hand trying to look non-threatening. Not that I imagined I could have been any threat in all honesty. "So where are we now then?"

"Thala," a man's voice replied. I looked up and saw a large man with dark, tanned skin blocking the sunlight. He moved slightly to the left giving me a better view of him. He wasn't just large, he was huge. He must have been pushing six foot five and his shoulders were nearly as broad. From his face, I would have aged him fifty-something but from the amount of weathering and scarring he'd suffered I imagined he was younger. His voice betrayed an accent that I couldn't place, an African aspect perhaps. His gaze was penetrating and I found myself unable to hold it, looking down and seeing my suit. I almost started giggling at the ridiculousness of my attire but I held it together.

"I'm afraid that doesn't mean much to me," I shifted into a more comfortable position.

"I cannot explain to you where it is, as it does not relate to your country," the large man smiled; he seemed to know what joke I was missing.

"This is the place I see, Mr Vance," Maya had lost all of her reticence and was now almost bouncing on the balls of her feet as she crouched down beside me.

"Look," I rubbed at my forehead, "this is all a little bit of a rush for me. This morning I went to visit a lab to, I thought, check over accounts. Instead, I am shown you, locked up in a lab with some idiot telling me you see other places and make things disappear because they did something to your DNA. Now I'm...in Thala?"

"I've been talking to Dembe," she nodded to the large man. "There are more people like me, they can all transport things between our world and here."

"Our world?" I recalled what Dembe had said about it not relating to my country. "Where exactly is Thala?"

"We do not know," Dembe shrugged and pointed up to the sky. "All we know is that there are two suns here." Reluctantly, I followed his arm and squinted. No wonder it was so bright. Without realizing it, I had stood up and had wandered out from under the awning. There in the sky were two glowing orbs. One was huge, it must have been much closer than the sun was to Earth. When I finally looked away, my eyes had been bleached. I blinked rapidly, tears leaking as I adjusted back to the normal contrast. My mouth worked but no noise came out; I had no idea what to say.

"Everyone here, came because they could use the same power as me," Maya had jumped up and was standing beside me.

"So why I am here?"

Maya looked across at Dembe nervously. He nodded and she turned back to me, her eyes only making it as high as my chest, "You looked like you would help me. And I wanted to get out. They would never let me leave..." She spun away, throwing her hands in the air.

"I have friends in government, they would shut it down," I replied.

"Your friends in government know," Dembe gave me a pitying look. "You think this many people can have a special gift and it would go unnoticed? You think they would not see potential for their own use?"

"Not everyone is like that," I folded my arms but I knew it was a futile point I was making. There would always be more people who would see the military potential and damn those who could provide it. Dembe didn't respond, his expression amused and unconvinced. "That still doesn't explain why I'm here."

Maya was still facing away from me.

"I believe Maya is not yet able to fully use her gifts as they did not come naturally to her. She can transport other things but not herself," Dembe explained. I rubbed the bridge of my nose as my brain fought against all the madness. Then I realized what he meant.

"You needed to piggyback off me," I gave a mirthless chuckle. It was amusing if you thought about it really. "The cup wasn't big enough I suppose."

Maya turned and gave a sheepish shake of the head.

"So, what now? You send me back alone?"

"That was not what we were thinking, Mr. Vance," Dembe responded. We stared at each for a moment, locked in silence.

"You can't hold me here against my will," my voice was quiet and calm, completely at odds with the raging confusion and panic inside. "That was exactly what they were doing to Maya."

Dembe held his hands out in front of him, trying to calm me. "That is not quite what we had in mind. I think it would be best if you saw the full scale of our problem." He motioned for me to walk. I didn't feel like I really had much alternative.

I nodded and Dembe led the way, Maya coming up close behind me. We were between two small yellow stone buildings. It reminded of what I had seen on Indiana Jones films and the like, definitely some kind of desert landscape. Windows were just holes cut in the wall with netting up to keep anything out. The space between the building was narrow; I could touch the walls either side, a fine grit leaving traces on my fingers when I pulled away. As we moved through the warren, I started to hear a hum growing louder with each turn. It bounced off the walls so I couldn't tell its direction. It clung to me with the warm, dry air.

Dembe gave one last smile over his shoulder before we turned another corner. I froze in my tracks. Maya leaned over my shoulder to see. I stopped blinking, desperate to take it all in and I realized I'd stopped breathing too. I took a deep breath and let it out slowly but even I could hear the tremor as the air left me.

The buildings had given way to an enormous square, steps leading down on all sides. In the centre was the most beautiful thing I had ever seen. Words were useless to describe it. It looked like a sculpture made from water that was constantly flowing around a set pattern that slowly moved, dancing to some unknown rhythm. The light of the two suns glinted off it in all directions, making it seem like it was made up of diamonds. All around it were people - that was what I had heard. There must have been three, four hundred people running, chatting, getting on with life. They all looked different: different ages, races, genders. The place was buzzing with activity.

But behind it all, on the other side of the square was sheer majesty. I could only describe it as a fortress, carved out of some precious rock stood watching all that went on before it. It weaved up into the air, reaching out, rooms jutting out in all directions. It looked like it had grown rather than been built. The walls shimmered so intensely I couldn't even tell what colour it was: blue, green, purple, it was all and none all at the same time.

"How?"

"It was here before us," Dembe explained. "We don't know who used to live here but they are gone now. Their technology surpasses that of Earth's although we have not yet mastered how it all works. We are still quite reliant on people gaining supplies from Earth regularly."

"It's beautiful," I breathed. I had travelled when younger, but never had I seen anything as captivating as this. The hairs on the back of my neck were standing up. I sucked in a deep breath and rubbed at my arms. "So where do I fit in?"

"You see the people down there? That is only half the population of Thala. I am part of the original group that landed here but every day our numbers swell. Some wish to go home to Earth or be able to travel freely but do not feel safe. We need an envoy. We need someone to represent us," Dembe was facing me directly now. His eyes bored into mine not wavering once.

"That will not be easy," I felt my shoulders tighten. Not easy was an understatement.

"Nothing worthwhile ever is," Dembe cocked his head and smiled. He already knew my answer.

Tormented by small children by day, **Alex Minns** retreats to the haven of writing by night. She worked as a scientist before teaching and has thus developed a penchant for experimenting and explosions. She has written a range of scifi, steampunk and urban paranormal fiction when not on twitter obsessively creating micro fiction. Currently, she is working on a steampunk novel with time travel and trying to not get confused!

Baby's First Kill

By Tony Conaway

"Put this on," I told her.

She looked askance at the item I handed her. "A gas mask? What, it smells that bad down here?"

I didn't answer her until we both had our masks on. My voice muffled, I explained. "Back in the late 1950s, the military did some chemical and biological warfare tests in the subways. It was supposed to help them prepare for an attack by the Soviet Union."

Even though the lenses of the gas mask, I could see her eyes widen. "They did this to *innocent people?*"

"They *thought* the chemical and biological agents they used were completely harmless. The government just wanted to track how quickly they spread and how long they lasted. But some of the agents turned out to be not as harmless as they thought."

She shook her head. "Why am I not surprised?"

I pointed down the corridor we just entered. "This leads to the entrance of the subway tunnel that was supposed to link Manhattan to Staten Island. One of the chemical agents pooled down here. It lasted a lot longer than expected. And that's why the Staten Island line was never finished." I shrugged. "They told the public that the money for the tunnel ran out. So we still have the Staten Island Ferry, instead of a subway."

"It's still dangerous after almost seventy years?" she asked.

"Better safe than sorry. No rain down here to disperse the chemical agent. I had some young, strong Sandhogs deliver the equipment we need. They hate wearing the gas masks, but it keeps them on their toes."

I shifted my backpack, trying to get comfortable. It seemed a lot lighter twenty years ago. "Let's get going."

***

She'd been working for me for over a month before I learned her nickname was "Baby."

She might never have told me, but she was trying to hang onto something, *anything* from her old life. After all, she'd been kidnapped, assaulted, and transformed by an otherworldly demon. She went from a redheaded wannabe actress into a black, Arab woman. Aside from remaining able-bodied, she'd lost about as much as a person could lose. I'd gotten her a job, but I'd also had to get some forged I.D. for her just so she could open a bank account to cash her paychecks.

She'd even lost her language: to isolate her, the demon had stolen her ability to speak and read any English, replacing it with Arabic. Fortunately, her English skills came back with surprising speed. I suppose the pathways in her brain still existed, or something. Whadda I know? I'm not a scientist. I'm just a guy who deals with phenomena in underground Manhattan. Demons, berserk robots, mutant crocodiles – I handle it all. I'm a member in good standing of Laborer's Local Union No. 147. The workers who dig subway tunnels. The Sandhogs, we call ourselves.

It had been three months since I'd rescued her from her demonic captor. In a way, Baby was the lucky one. I'd rescued two other girls with her. One was in an insane asylum. Sorry – nowadays they call it a *rehabilitation center specializing in mental health*. The other was being held and interrogated by Homeland Security as an illegal, suspicious alien. For all I know, they're waterboarding her at Guantanamo.

So I offered Baby a job as my assistant. I don't suppose she had much choice other than to accept. She was broke, homeless, and her own father didn't recognize her. But Emily Leigh Dawida – a.k.a. "Baby" -- is a tough cookie. She copes.

Now that she had most of her English-language skills back, she worked in the office of the Sandhogs Union. And she was on call to assist me, when needed. Thankfully, I sometimes go for weeks without encountering a berserk robot or otherworldly entity. We'd only had one alert since she started, and that turned out to be a false alarm.

I've had nine assistants so far. Most have quit. Two died. And some…well, they can't resist the temptation. In this job, you might encounter a djinn that will grant you three wishes in return for its freedom. Or a rare beast you can sell to a collector. Or to travel in time for your own benefit.

Although I only confide in one assistant at a time, I can call on several members of the Sandhog's Union for general help. I considered using them for this job. But my pool of talent isn't unlimited. At the moment, two of the guys I use were away on vacation. Another was in the hospital with a burst appendix. The remaining guys I hadn't vetted. I didn't know if I could fully trust them. Could they brick up a tunnel? Sure. Could they be trusted knowing that the tunnel traversed time? I didn't know. So I had them deliver supplies to a site just ahead, then leave.

"OK," I told Baby. "Off with the gas mask, and on with the night-vision goggles. There's very little light from here on out."

She put her goggles on. "Is there a reason it's kept dark?"

"You tell me."

"Well…if it's dark, someone is less likely to wander in. So if you want to keep out the homeless or the Urban Explorers, leave it dark and spooky."

"Very good," I said. "There are enough electric power lines to tap that we can string lights wherever we need. But some places are better left dark. And here we are."

There was a little light coming down from a passageway above us. You could just see the bricked-up tunnel without the night-vision goggles. My guys had been down here already, and left stacks of bricks for the next time we had to close it up.

"Let's set up behind the bricks. It'll give us some cover between us and the tunnel. And there's more gear behind the bricks, in sealed metal boxes."

We each set up behind one of the stacks of bricks. Baby and I were armed with rifles. I had some other stuff, too.

"How's the therapy going?" I asked her. I'd gotten Local 147 to pay for it, so I figured I had the right to ask about it.

"OK," Baby said. "This therapist is a better fit for me than the other one. I think the last one hated Arabs. 'course, I can't tell her everything. She'd never believe me. My new therapist thinks I'm an Arab woman, a citizen born in the USA, and I was kidnapped by a sex trafficker while I was visiting relatives back in Egypt."

"Well, as long as you think she's helping."

"She is. I sleep better now. I don't get startled when I see myself in a mirror, what I've been turned into." Baby shrugged. "Or maybe that's just the Xanax she put me on."

We were silent for a while.

"Explain to me again," said Baby. "What are we doing here?"

Why not? I thought. I was training my replacement, after all. If she couldn't handle it, I might as well find out now. I already knew Baby was tough. But was she tough enough to handle all the weirdness down here?

"OK." I said. "There are special tunnels underneath Manhattan. Who dug them, why they're here, no one knows. With these tunnels, one end is in the here and now. The other end…moves. In time.

"You know that some of the tunnels lead to the past," I said. "That demon who kidnapped you, it was taking you into the past."

"I'm not about to forget that," she said.

"Well, just as some of the tunnels lead to the past, some of them lead to the future. *Possible* futures," I added. "We only use the tunnels to the past when we have to. And we *never* use the tunnels that go to the future." *Unless it's to return home after going into the past*, I thought. But I didn't say it – this was complicated enough already.

"Understood."

"But some of my assistants get greedy. They want to go to the future and snag some advanced gizmo that will make them the next Bill Gates." *Or they're desperate,* I didn't say. *They have a loved one who's dying, and they hope to steal a cure from the future.*

"So, what happens? You stop them?"

I shook my head, then realized she probably couldn't see the motion in the dim light.

"No. I can't watch everything they do, 24 hours a day. Besides, the tunnels that lead to the future are miles apart. There's no way I could stand guard over all of them." I sighed. "If you're my assistant, then I have to trust you. I'll need someone to replace me, someday. I warn my assistants that traveling from the present to the future never turns out well, and they shouldn't do it under any circumstances."

"But sometimes they do it anyway," she said.

"Sometimes they do it, yes."

"So what happens?"

"This is where it gets harder to understand," I said. "Traveling to the past…see, the past is already set. I've learned that you can't make any significant changes. But the future…there are many possibilities. The tunnels seem to lead to more than one future."

"What does that mean?"

"Let me give you an example. One of my assistants was Norman Kantner. Normie was fascinated by the idea of traveling to the future. So, one day, he snuck down here, opened up that bricked-up tunnel across from us, and went through."

She coughed. It's always dusty down here.

"At the other end, there are many possible futures. And, because he went through the tunnel, suddenly, there were several possible Norman Kantners."

She stared at me. "You mean there's *more than one of him* now?"

"Yup. I figured out that, every 133 days, an alternate version of him might come through. From a different possible future. But something bad always happens to each of him, and he wants to come back to the present. And we can't allow that."

"Why every 133 days?"

"No idea. These tunnels didn't come with an instruction manual. I just figured it was 133 days between his returns. *Possible* returns. Sometimes he comes back, sometimes he doesn't. But if he does, it's always 133 days apart."

"How…?" she began.

"I got the entrance to every one of the special tunnels hooked up with surveillance gear. Sight *and* sound." I pointed up and behind us, back in the darkness. "You can't see them in the dark, but there are several closed-circuit cameras aimed at the mouth of this tunnel."

We were silent again.

"Now you wanna ask what was the bad thing that happened to Normie in the future, and why we can't let him back here."

Her face was barely visible in the dim light, but I could tell she was smiling. "I was just figuring out how to phrase the question," she said.

I put my rifle down atop the bricks, stepped back and stretched. Ever since I got slammed around by that zephyr-thing, my back hurts most of the time.

"I don't know exactly what happened to Norm. Remember, he's traveled to *alternate* futures. But in most of these futures, there's some sort of plague. Thirty-odd years from now, someone uses a gene-editing device like that CRISPR to create a deadly disease. Norm gets infected, is dying, and tries to come home. We can't let him come back and infect us. According to the news on a datasheet he carried, this disease kills about one in ten people on the planet."

"One in ten?? That means almost a *million* corpses, just in the Metro New York area!"

"It's bad, yes. But not so much that bad." I said. "Apparently, there are still...*inequities* in the future. In poor parts of Africa and Asia, one in every three or four dies. In places with technology, good medical care, it's only about one in fifty."

"That's still...." She didn't seem to know how to finish that sentence.

"Yeah. So you see why we can't let him come back and infect the present. And the doctors that handled that plague are still kids in the here and now. The technology to stop that disease might not even *exist* yet."

"OK. I see why this is important. But the tunnel is bricked over. How can Norman get through?"

"Sometimes he doesn't. He just pounds on the brick, begging to be let through. I wait until I'm sure he's dead from the disease, then I have the brick wall opened. I suit up and sterilize the place. Then my union guys brick it back up again. Which is why we have piles of bricks sitting around, ready to be used." *I didn't add that I also check his corpse for anything useful he's carrying. Future technology, like that datasheet with news about the plague. It's like an iPad, only on a piece of paper that you can fold up and put in your pocket. I give the future tech to the feds, and they give me money and experimental weapons.*

"How do you keep from getting the disease yourself while you sterilize the place?"

I walked a few steps away to the pile of gear. I stepped on the foot-release pedal of a big metal crate. The lid opened. I waved Baby over and opened another crate.

"That's your basic TYVEK protective suit, like the Centers for Disease Control use. We set up an isolation tent around the tunnel. The workers who open the brick entrance wear suits while they work. Then I go inside in a suit and sterilize the place with this." I pulled out a device from another crate. It was heavy, so I used both hands.

"Is…is that a flamethrower?"

"Yup." I put it back and closed the crates.

We walked back to the stacks of bricks.

"So, your guy Norman, he never gets through?"

"I didn't say that. Sometimes he gets changed in the future. He's still dying, but he's no longer fully human. One time, he came back half-human and half-machine."

"A cyborg?" she asked.

251

"I guess that's what they call it. He battered right through the bricks. Which is why we're armed, ready to shoot anything that gets though that brick barrier."

"So, how do you stop a cyborg?"

"Shoot the human half. And we got this as a last resort."

I had a foot pedal on a cable next to me. I slid it over with a foot, close enough so she could see it.

"I don't know if this really works. But better to have it and not need it."

Baby peered at the warning decal on the pedal. "You're kidding? This sets off an EMP? *An electro-magnetic pulse?*"

"Yup. Supposed to take out any cyborg in a radius of 10 meters. That's why the equipment like the TYVEK suits are shielded in boxes. And it might or might not fry all the electronics in the building above us, so it's a last resort."

"This is so weird. A year ago, my biggest problem was whether or not I should go from a redhead to a blonde. Now I've got to save the world."

"Relax. Normie doesn't always show up. The last two cycles he didn't appear at all. Maybe he ran out of possible futures."

"Let's hope," she said.

And that was it for the next 9 hours. We took turns, covering each other while we dozed, or raided the mini-fridge I'd brought, or the Porta-potty. I forced myself to eat, even though the chemical stench from the Porta-pottty ruined my appetite.

I was thinking about another visit to the john when Cyborg Normie appeared in front of the barrier. He literally *phased* through, like a comic book character. The human half of him was swollen and infected. He had the plague, like the others.

"JAKE!" he shouted. "JAKE ROSENTHAL! THIS IS YOUR FAULT! COME FACE ME. ALL I WANT BEFORE I DIE IS FOR YOU TO DIE FIRST!"

Startled, I fumbled for my rifle. I had to get the safety off before I could shoot.

And, somehow, I managed to *drop* my rifle. It didn't go far, but I didn't think Cyborg Normie was going to give me time to pick it up.

He wasn't. A bright light attached to his chest illuminated me, clear as could be. I fumbled blindly for my rifle. Somewhere in Normie's metal half, I heard the whine of what must be a weapon charging up.

There was a gunshot, then another, followed by two more. The light wobbled, then tilted away from me, towards the ceiling.

My eyesight hadn't returned, but I could tell Baby was firing at the cyborg. Single, aimed shots. She kept going until she emptied the clip.

"There," she said. "I hit him at least twice. One head shot. I think he's dead."

My eyesight started to return. The cyborg was lying on his back, inert.

Then he wasn't. The human side of him looked dead, but the mechanical limbs tried to raise him up.

"Bye, Normie," I said. And I engaged the EMP.

Suddenly, we were in complete blackness. I head Normie crash back to the concrete, then nothing. His robot half was now as dead as his human half. I pulled a chem-light tube out of my pocket and shook it until it started to glow. It was just a plastic tube and some chemicals – nothing for an EMP to disable. Then I opened a nearby crate, and retrieved and activated six more. I could barely see Baby in the green chemical light. The crates protected the contents from the EMP. I pulled out another night-vision apparatus. It worked fine.

"Good job," I told her. I handed her a box of a dozen chem-lights. "I need you to help me get into one of the TYVEK suits. I've got one for you, too. Before I use the flamethrower on the…corpse, robot, whatever…I have to remove anything that might blow up when it burns. Even batteries can explode if you throw them in a fire." I was shaken, talking too much. Was Baby OK? She'd just killed for the first time.

"You doing OK?" I asked.

"Yeah," she said. "So, which TYVEK suit is mine?"

"The pink one," I lied. The suits are all the same institutional-yellow color, of course.

She gave me the finger and started activating chem-lights.

I smiled. A tough cookie, Baby is. I may have finally found someone who can replace me.

Tony Conaway has written and ghostwritten everything from blogs to books. He has cowritten non-fiction books published by McGraw-Hill, Macmillan and Prentice Hall. He writes fiction in just about every genre except erotica and romance. But make him an offer -- he'll do those, too.

He can be found on Twitter as @TonyConaway and on Facebook as Author Tony Conaway. He interviews other authors at wayneaconaway.blogspot.com

Thank you…

Thank you for taking the time to read our collection. We enjoyed all the stories contained within and hope you found at least a few to enjoy yourself. If you did, we'd be honored if you would leave a review on Amazon, Goodreads, and anywhere else reviews are posted.

You can also subscribe to our email list via our website, Http://www.cloakedpress.com

Follow us on Facebook

http://www.facebook.com/Cloakedpress

Tweet to us @CloakedPress

If you would like to help out our authors, you can also join our Patreon at http://www.patreon.com/Cloakedpress There you can subscribe to earn free rewards and exclusive content/giveaways.

Printed in Great Britain
by Amazon